Never
Too Real

Never Too Real

Carmen Rita

KENSINGTON BOOKS
www.kensingtonbooks.com

KENSINGTON BOOKS are published by

Kensington Publishing Corp.
119 West 40th Street
New York, NY 10018

All Kensington titles, imprints, and distributed lines are available at special quantity discounts for bulk purchases for sales promotion, premiums, fund-raising, educational, or institutional use.

Special book excerpts or customized printings can also be created to fit specific needs. For details, write or phone the office of the Kensington Sales Manager: Kensington Publishing Corp., 119 West 40th Street, New York, NY 10018. Attn. Sales Department. Phone: 1-800-221-2647.

Kensington and the K logo Reg. U.S. Pat. & TM Off.

eISBN-13: 978-1-4967-0131-2
eISBN-10: 1-4967-0131-3
First Kensington Electronic Edition: June 2016

ISBN-13: 978-1-4967-0130-5
ISBN-10: 1-4967-0130-5
First Kensington Trade Paperback Printing: June 2016

10 9 8 7 6 5 4 3 2 1

Printed in the United States of America

For all the women who came before me,
especially Guadalupe and Ana,
and the magical one who follows me,
my Bianca Luz

Chapter 1

Never forget how far you've come.

This was Catalina Rosa Rivera's mantra, one she whispered to herself for the hundredth time as she made her way through the behind-the-scenes maze on the set of her television show. The stomp of her faux-lizard heels echoed against the walls of particle board surrounding her, an embrace of corners and wiring. Catalina's pace was more brisk and the grip on her blue-card notes tighter today. She was ready. At least she looked ready, war paint and all. Just an hour earlier the show's makeup artist, sensing bad juju, gave her extra body armor with a full strip of fake lashes, crimson lips, and hair sprayed into architecture.

Turning the bend into the hot spotlight on her desk, Cat, as she was known to her national viewing audience, ran fingers across her teeth to remove any stray lipstick. As she came into view of the show's staff and her guests, she instinctively replaced her clomping elephant gait with a more appropriate, professional stride.

The one-hour show was mapped out, no big changes in format or topic. But the tension on set was viscous. Usually self-assured, Cat's hands began to tremble in a combination of anxiety and relief. As her wide, dark eyes shifted from commanding her hands to be still to looking up at her set with the broad-smiling mask of a professional national television host, she was now 100 percent sure that the end of her time as the captain of this TV news ship was on the horizon. Despite solid ratings, the signs were stark—the shakiness of the economy, the migration of eyeballs from TV to the Web, the loss of nearly half the usual advertising revenue. All business reasons, money reasons. And she had heard and seen the buzz around the halls and blogs, the mass layoffs and cancellations at other networks.

It's just a matter of time. And it's not my fault . . . Right?

Painfully, the strongest confirmation of her cancellation instincts was personal. The once-enthusiastic head of her department had stopped returning her calls, or picking them up at all. And just two days ago, she had received the most passive-aggressive form of communication of all, a sin of omission. Cat was left off the invitation to a regular staff meeting, changed from its usual time without her knowledge. She was *always* in her staff meetings. She was not only the host of the show, but the co-creator. Nail in coffin.

Stab me in the front, people. I can take it. I prefer it.

"Hey, baaaybays!" She greeted her set crew as if all were well.

These were guys you'd see at the local pub, biker tees, baseball caps, and, for the most part, warm smiles. Only one didn't smile. The steady-cam guy. A burly, military-cut, late-thirties, bearded blond, he erased his grin in response to Cat's. All had been well with the whole on-set team of sound and camera crew, and there was a solid teasing camaraderie among a bunch of fairly macho males and Cat's big-sister persona. That was until the new steady-cam guy arrived. At first, he folded in nicely. Then he made an amateur mistake—he took Cat's kindness and joviality during commercial breaks for weakness. He began to talk over her and disregard her need for quiet when time got tight—this was a live show, where one second could mean the camera catching an errant gesture or expression that could mar a career. Or, she'd just be thrown off and mess up. Cat may not have been the boss behind the scenes, but damn well she was the boss on the set. It was her face, her name, her career on the line. She needed some deference, some respect. After gently asking the new guy to cool it a few times on set, and receiving no compliance in return, Cat had turned to his boss, her director. Since he spoke to the yapper, all Cat got from behind the steady-cam that trailed her every move was a steely glare.

Fuck him.

"Hey, girl . . . Sup," the rest of the crew replied with a bit less enthusiasm these days.

Hip-hop thumped through the speakers at Cat's request. It helped her gear up just before going live. Out of respect for her usually non-urban guests, it was usually the clean, radio version, but sometimes words leaked through that jarred James Taylor–trained ears.

"I'm young, bitches . . ." Jay-Z's voice threw out over the speakers.

"Ayyy yay yay, guys! Shhhhhhh . . ." Cat's blue-manicured hand gestured her sound team to turn the music down as she shimmied onto her stool, skirt tight, bottom round. She aligned her Spanxed navel up to the ragged snip of black duct tape stuck to the glass desk's edge, marking her spot. The rap faded quickly.

"We're gonna scare our guests . . ." She threw a diplomatic, soothing smile toward her anxious desk companions, her head swinging back to the script notes set down swiftly in front of her by an intern seconds before. "Thanks, hon—can you snag me an extra water, too, please? I'm parched." Cat could usually make it through a show on one network-logoed mug of water, but tonight her mouth was as dry as a bag of saltines. *I wish this was tequila.* She smacked her lips quietly thinking of the sour, strong, mind-numbing taste she'd rather have in her mouth.

The show's guests shifted; Cat watched them out of the corner of her eye. For every show she noted like an interrogator which one seemed eager or excited, which was potentially hostile, and which was just shitting his pants because it was his first time on live television. She knew their bios, but they were all newbies to her set. Bringing in fresh talent after so long seemed also ominous, rather than bringing in her regular superstars or potential new hosts. Maybe they were trying to kill some ratings so they could blame Cat for the show's demise. Or, maybe they just didn't give a crap anymore and they were saving their energy for what's next.

I'll go with option two.

Cat winked at her floor crew, ignoring the steady cam. She then turned to her three suited, very pale, and very male guests sitting to her left. Knowing that jittery guests don't make the best guests, Cat considered it her job as host of this fiesta of folly to put everyone at ease.

"Sorry about the music, guys. Gotta go with the PG version, right?"

"Yeah, I'm more of a James Taylor kind of guy myself," said the rosacea-faced fund manager directly to her right, as he tightened his tie.

Cat narrowed her eyes and took a moment to discern if he was being antagonistic and condescending or was simply an uncomfortable Boomer.

Boomer.

"I think I've heard of him," she responded, within her sweet grin a teenager's eye roll at a dorky father.

The men and crew smiled while Mr. Red Face blushed further, charmed. Cat was charismatic and beautiful, powerful weapons in her day-to-day battles, particularly in the finance industry she covered, where an attractive woman's presence had the power to throw men off their game. Her black hair glistened in the robust lights, its glossiness brushing her shoulders and her skin just bronze enough to make clear her non–Anglo-Saxon heritage. As news television dictated, she was "dressed as a crayon," encased in a cerulean blue dress assigned with the job of making her "pop" on screen, while also making her gender clear.

Now, it was time to make some TV.

In rare form, Cat barreled through the first half of the show. Not one to reveal what was behind her eyes, her anger at all that was going unspoken between her higher-ups and their host had a way of focusing Cat, giving her a buzz—it was fuel. Anger and self-righteousness had always been something for her to run on. The pattern was set when her drunk, absentee father left her and her mother broke and on their own when she was six. She'd show him. She'd show them. Cat knew her bosses were watching—thousands were watching. She channeled ire into spunk.

"I'm sorry, what?" Cat asked sharply during a commercial break.

She was speaking into the air, not to her guests. Cat received feedback from the control room directly into her ear, plus notes on upcoming segments. Her producers and director watched her through the cameras facing her, as the audience did, but from the control room on another floor. In many ways, hosting a show was like driving a fast, expensive car. There were pricy parts and pieces, and all had to work smoothly. But in the end, the host worked the clutch, gearing up, gearing down.

Cat worked hard to focus, to package up the ugly feelings caught in her throat, to not let them see. As no one on the set with her, including her guests, could hear what she was hearing in her earpiece when the control room was speaking to her, it appeared to newbies as if she was just lost in thought, silent during the break. So, she was often interrupted.

"Cat, so, are you really Spanish?" It was the Red Boomer again, directly to Cat's left, whispering to her. She drew a deep breath and straightened her back as she remembered that this one had flown himself in his own plane from Salt Lake City to be on the show.

Mr. Carbon Footprint, James Taylor–listening, old man . . . I'll give you a Utah pass on this one.

Without moving her eyes from her script, Cat responded coolly, albeit politely. " 'Spanish?' Do you mean, am I Hispanic?" She offered up a side-eye.

He nodded. "Yeah."

She nodded back, now looking at him head-on. "Yes, Bob. I'm Hispanic. Not Spanish."

Even though she answered his question, his expression became confused.

"Wow. You're so smart!"

I can't even . . .

Cat's executive producer came into her ear and teased her about the ad-libbed outro to the last segment, a ditty she made up about the LIBOR, the most boring yet important interest rate in town.

She busted his chops back through her mic, then ran through some time cues with him. "Yup . . . okay . . . sure." She was grateful he was such a good guy.

"Hey, guys?" She decided to take advantage of her guests yabbering among themselves to talk directly to her control room team and riff off the un-PC item they'd just heard. "Um, so, is Rich really a Canadian?" Cat envisioned the room chuckling. "Rich, seriously. I mean, I heard the rumors, but I had no idea!" She gestured to the plug in her ear. "Like, there's a Canadian in my ear . . . and he's so smart!"

Rich opened her ear feed so she could hear the laughter wrapped in relief from behind the scenes in the control room. This "Are you Spanish/Hispanic?" comment was the second one that week alone, and it made everyone uncomfortable. Cat was proudly her brown self and for the most part, her staff was young and savvy and her Canadian head was, well, Canadian. He knew what was up. Her first year they made it a mock drinking game. Every time a guest (usually male, usually white, over forty) asked her to confirm or not "what" she was, Cat would look into camera one, her main communiqué to her team in the control room, point, and say, "Drink!" The guest doing the asking had no idea why she was responding that way. Unfortunately, it happened so often, the joke got old, so Cat found new ways to play off of it. To remove the sting.

Twelve minutes and twenty-one seconds later, the show was done. Cat shimmied off her stool, attempting to keep her mummy-band dress in one piece. Curvy girls and high stools: a challenge.

"Bye, guys. Thanks for coming. You were great." The host gave an adept smile to each guest, made solid eye contact, and shook their hands with an authoritative grip, even one for Mr. Utah. Cat thought each time she encountered someone like him, maybe she'd opened some minds today, solved some problems. Maybe.

"Hey, Cat . . ." Rich, her head producer, was back in her earpiece.

Cat sighed. "Whassup?"

A female sound engineer worked to unhook Cat's mic from inside her dress without flashing anyone, turning her into a brief contortionist.

Rich's pause in response lasted a beat too long. "You . . . uh, you gotta head up to Heather's office. Now."

"Oh, hi. Hi. Come in, come in. Sit down." Heather Kraven, the head of the division, Cat's top boss who didn't answer her calls anymore, was in hyper mode, squawking like a caged macaw. Her boho blouse sleeves fluttered with her arms like wilted, feeble wings. Cat noted the usual presence of a pink Pepto bottle on her desk. Heather had built a hit show for the network five years earlier and had tried and failed ever since to recreate that same magic. She took out all her impotence on the staff, particularly the on-air talent.

"Hi." Cat seated herself, keeping Heather in the corner of her eye as the producer passed behind her to close the door. Cat imagined she caught a whiff of sulfur and sickness behind the musk oil.

"Well, so . . ." Heather sat hunched forward across her desktop, clasping her aged hands punctuated with short, unpolished, chewed nails. She forced a Cheshire smile but offered no eye contact, her skin lacking maintenance and revealing too many late nights, long days, and bad food choices. "We really wanted to tell you before it hit the *Post* in the morning . . ."

"The *New York Post*?" Cat tendered a false grin, her eyes thinned in suspicion.

"Well . . ."

In Heather's two-second pause, Cat quickly summed up her hunches: *She's already leaked whatever she's about to tell me to the* Post. *Jesus Christ.* Cat sucked her teeth, raised her brows.

"Yah?" she prompted.

Heather, a normally intense, in-your-face boss, couldn't meet her eyes. "We've had to cancel the show." She put her thumb to her mouth, taking her nail between her front teeth, making a sucking sound as she then pulled it away.

Yuck.

"Really?" Cat continued to grin, this time bizarrely, honestly. A bubbly feeling brewed inside of her; she felt her forehead relaxing for the first time in, well, a long time. It was a sensation Cat would have to work out, because it was surprising her.

She locked her eyes on Heather, moving away from the pleasant feelings inside, toward sealing the deal of the business. "But wait, didn't you say just a couple of months ago that I saved your contract—your job?" Heather pursed her lips like a politician—*I can neither confirm nor deny . . .* Cat continued. "You were thanking me for that. And we beat Joe's show twice a week." A blowhard who resembled a hobbit, Joe was the "star" Heather took credit for having created years earlier. He'd taken a hit in the ratings lately—but then again, everyone had, as

TV continued to bleed revenue like a lanced sow. "So how's this happening?" Cat asked.

Heather nodded, mulling her response, still not looking Cat in the eye. She absentmindedly rubbed her stomach and glanced at the constant bottle of pink elixir in front of her. Looked like she needed some.

"We took a big chance on you, and we gave you a lot of time. And it was good! We did good!" Heather's arms fluttered again.

She looks like a crow about to steal my lunch.

"So, then . . . what was it?" Cat aimed her focus on leaving the office with answers and she was determined not to allow even a glimpse of feisty stereotype into the room.

"Listen, we probably overestimated what kind of audience you could bring." Heather shrugged.

"What do you mean?"

"Y'know, the numbers were there and we really had hoped for a new—more—demographic . . ." This reveal turned Heather into a babbling faucet. "And the whole, y'know, AltaVision thing was something we really needed." AltaVision was the network's Spanish-language partner and one of the only spots where business growth was happening.

"AltaVision? Listen, I never once said I would go on TV speaking Spanish. You didn't even bring it up in negotiations."

"Well, y'know, we tried, we tried with the show. But, well, it's in the paper tomorrow so . . ." Heather was done. She threw up her hands in surrender.

The abrupt end caught up to Cat. Maybe four minutes had passed since she'd sat down. "Wait—so that's it? We're dark? That show—the one we just taped—was my last one?"

Cat could not believe her eyes as she watched the once-fawning Heather, the Heather who'd wanted to hang out and gossip about who's-dating-who or who would slap Cat's back with joy about their ratings, instead end their relationship by standing up and stepping forward from behind her desk, toward the door. Cat was being ushered out.

Business is business.

"I'm afraid so. It's done," Heather said coldly as she lumbered behind Cat and opened the office door. Heather's two research minions stood waiting on the other side. Armed with new reports, surely, on what people wanted to see next, or whom.

Wow. Great choreography, Cat thought.

These two were also Cat's enthusiastic allies only months ago, but now the two small men mumbled hellos and couldn't meet her eyes. She was tempted to turn back toward the office and yell with pointed finger at Heather, to remind her how recently she had been the one crying gratefully to Cat as the show's numbers had saved her job. But that was then. This was now. And now, as humiliated and steamed as Cat was, she was all too curious about the feeling of joy ruffling her feathers inside, beckoning her to come closer and away from these people.

Numbly, Cat walked back to her desk, back straight. As the only brown girl in her private school growing up, the scholarship girl, she had learned how to silo herself in, to protect herself with a psychic bubble. And she was not going to let this be a walk of shame. In her head, she fell onto another mantra that helped her when she was ostracized as a kid: "Fuck 'em."

It took fifteen years post-college for Cat to scale her way up from intern to local news producer to, with little on-air experience, host of a national cable news show on screens big and small, five days a week. With this network she'd also packed in hundreds of supporting appearances on its highest-rated national morning show, the local news outlet, online post-show shows, blogs, vlogs, and evenings hosting philanthropic events—a thousand smiles delivered, one after another. She'd been featured in dozens of magazines and even had an Ivy League degree. Internally, as she walked with concentration, Cat recited her accomplishments, the lines in her bio, one with each stride. Reviewing all she'd come through, all she'd accomplished functioned like a vaccine. It stopped her from feeling small. From letting her circumstances determine her self-worth.

But as Cat got to the back elevator, stepping in, rather than taking the main staircase in view of the whole newsroom, other thoughts began to seep in, dark thoughts. She was alone. She'd had no other life. No child. No spouse. No siblings. Just a suffocating, overbearing mother. So focused on accomplishing, building herself and her career, she hadn't slept in years—hadn't gotten laid in at least two. What had she done? What was she going to do? What was next?

Though Cat knew it was only an excuse, Heather said that the cancellation of her show had depended on one thing: Cat hadn't brought in the hoped-for Hispanic demographic. Sure, Cat wished she were fully bilingual, but an absent father and a mother obsessed with her daughter being as "American" as possible, aka Anglo, white—add that to a New England education and the odds had been stacked against her. But no Latina whom Cat knew in the business was fully bilingual either. Which meant that you were either AltaVision material or SBC network material. The network had assumed that Cat, a gesticulating second-generation Mexican-American, would appear on their sibling network in Spanish. They hadn't even mentioned it to her agent two years previous when they'd plucked her from her brief correspondent gig at a rival network. What, did they think she'd crossed the border yesterday? Stereotyping was just too easy for these people. This mistake had been costly for everyone.

Cat's English-only policy came through the first week of taping when she was asked to appear on AltaVision to promote her new show.

"I don't speak Spanish on air."

"What do you meeeeean you don't speak Spanish on air?"

Heather had wailed, grabbing at her parched hair as she paced her office.

"But—but you're Hispanic!" From the couch along one wall of Heather's office, the muscled, miniature research director croaked.

"And?" Cat replied with a smile, doing her best to make light of what she realized was a lose-lose situation. "We don't all speak Spanish that well, you know. More than half of us don't. I was born here, just like you." She turned to the bald research director with an Italian last name. "Can you speak Italian?" He averted his eyes. She continued. "I can talk to relatives and give people directions on the subway, but I'm certainly not going on TV with it."

The room went silent. One side was panicking at their mistake. The other, recalling many mistakes along the way, including being forced to take eight years of French in school.

Approaching her pod of cubicles, after what felt like a long walk through the desert, Cat found her staff quiet. She realized that they were probably all out of work, too—or, hopefully, just reassigned. She wouldn't be. She was now an embarrassment to the network. The Great Brown Hope who failed them. She kept her head down, maintaining face.

Rich, the Canadian, popped up by her side as she dropped into her chair, the cubicle walls shielding her from sight. "Cat, I'm so sorry."

Without looking up, Cat replied, "I'm sorry, too."

She hustled phone chargers into her bag and grabbed a favorite coffee mug. Behind her hung a poster made of a national full-page ad created for the show, Cat's face and body taking up two-thirds of the space, her arms folded for authority. Heather said that poster was to go up in Times Square. Well, that wasn't happening. The image already felt nostalgic. "I gotta go. Can we talk later?" Cat needed to clear her head. She wasn't close to breaking down, she was just roiling inside, still baffled by the murmuring of glee vibrating in her gut. She couldn't meet his eyes.

"Yeah, yeah, sure . . ." He sidestepped her gently. "Just call me, okay?" Rich was legitimately concerned for Cat, but he also had to deal with the rest of their staff, and his own future.

"Yup, I'll call ya." Cat, shifting a packed bag onto her shoulders, put out her hand for a shake.

Rich took it and sighed.

One more walk down the halls. At least for today.

She'd come back for everything else, her clothes, her handwritten notes from grateful guests. Cat still had time on her contract, and they'd surely find a way to make their money off of her once the fog cleared. She'd be back in some capacity, she hoped. But as Cat strolled out, lighter this time, not one person looked up—she was an instant nobody. Folks who always had time to throw out a "Hey, C!" her way kept their heads down, watching her out of the sides of their eyes. Protective bubble in place, all Cat could think was, *Everyone knew but me.*

Chapter 2

"No POTUS today? Not even FLOTUS?" The deep voice belonged to a tall, slim woman with a Leonardo DiCaprio haircut circa *Basketball Diaries,* standing ardently dapper in a custom-fitted, designer pantsuit. Magdalena Sofia Carolina Reveron de Soto not only cut a sharp, gender-bending figure in the room—contrasting with the handful of women around her who glistened in colorful dresses and jewelry—she was the only blue-eyed blonde, male or female, in a sea of brown and black faces.

Magda, as she preferred, was mingling among the bustle of handpicked business-owning insiders jammed into the concrete meeting room in the Executive Building of the White House. The president's head of minority investment, a *dulce de leche* thirty-something who matched Magda in height, gave her a macho backslap in greeting. "Sorry, girl. Ghanaian president was here and the meeting took too long."

Magda leaned back at his "girl" but patted his arm with affection. She needed him on her side for some pending deals. "African-American president pushes blacks and Latinos off the sched for an African president . . . Ha! Funny. How've you been, man?" As she asked, Magda scanned the room, everyone on break between the day's sessions, looking for opportunities. Always lookin'.

"Y'know, good. All good. And how about this thing, right?" He swept his hand across the chamber in which, rumor had it, Thomas Jefferson preferred to hold his summer meetings thanks to the room's concrete coolness. "We cannot go wrong with the people in this room."

The White House's chief technology officer, communications director, and chef had just left the stage. Gathered for the full day, among rows of red velvet chairs, were fifty well-groomed bodies, nearly all of color. One-third of the room was female—black, Latina, and a smattering of Asian. The men were the same mix, including a stately turbaned Sikh. And then there was Magda.

Magda's appearance was a natural calling card in the room. She was a sunny-haired, butch, self-made multimillionaire lesbian with an enviable effect: She glowed with money, success, and charisma. Groomed by her Miami-based Venezuelan family to be a beauty queen, Magda was instead the irresistibly handsome king of her domain. Her face model-like, with makeup and a dress she would have slain the straight male half of the room. But that would be wearing a costume. Magda had much more swagger sans feminine packaging because she presented herself as herself. Besides, she was a devoted lady-killer.

"Magda! Hey, guuurl. Have you met Dev yet?" Kristina Jo, her face framed with a lion's mane of curly, ebony Caribbean hair, her pantsuit fighting her curves, was the chattiest master-connector presidential appointee in D.C. Hustle skills honed in the Bronx, Kristina spent the next several minutes swinging her friend and ally, Magda, around, showing her off to the room.

Nearly everyone present knew Magda's name, if not the face of the richest, independent, minority venture capitalist in the United States, possibly the world. She purposefully had no press, all the knowledge mostly built word of mouth. Having been in the closet until college, Magda was in the habit of conducting business close to the vest—all business. Everyone was thrilled to be introduced to Magda, from the African head of Facebook global, the Latina officer at Twitter . . . she'd make their follow-up lists at a ninety percent rate. The other ten percent would miss a gravy train. Magda had made much of her money early on, wrangling wise, front-end moves in social media and green energy. Her mind raced at a quantum rate and she preferred to operate without waste—every minute had a reason, every hour something to be done.

"Kristina, hon, I've got to check this e-mail." Magda squinted at her cell. "What's with the lack of service down here? It's like a bunker in eighteen fifty. Shit."

Kristina's face dropped, but relit quickly. "Okay, listen, just ooooone small favor. The White House press corps is interviewing folks here on the event. Can you *por favor* do one in Spanish, too? There's one other person in this room who speaks—"

"Fine, fine. But it's gotta be real quick, all right?" *Man,* Magda thought, *this girl is so good she's got even me doing press. Be careful.*

The stage bustled with handheld audio sticks, phones set on "mic," and one guy with a video camera.

"Here's our guy!" Kristina waved Magda through and set her up directly in front of the young, Euro-styled videographer.

"Okay . . . Magdalena?"

Magda gave him a look that set his back straight. There were many ways in which she was absolutely untraditional, but when it came to addressing someone, someone older and accomplished, she'd never shake what her mama taught her.

He corrected himself. "*Señora Soto.* Can you tell us why this meeting of minority small business leaders is so important?"

Magda switched into "on" mode, a function of years of pageant training. She also had the rare ability to fuse conviction and concision. The few within earshot hushed to listen, then stifled the urge to applaud when she was done.

Magda's Spanish wasn't perfect, but it was authoritative. The greatest gift her parents had given her was neither her swimmer's body nor her gorgeous face, computer-like brain, or work ethic, but the superpower of being multilingual. Multilingual meant global. And global meant powerful. Global meant money.

"*Muchisimas gracias, Señora Soto.* So happy you could be here and help us!"

Magda nodded a good-bye and looked around to note where everyone else was headed. Like cattle to feed, most were moving toward the door that opened on lunch. Magda's stomach commanded her to follow.

"Excuse me, Ms. Soto?" called a dulcet voice.

"Yessss." With polite exasperation, Magda turned around, then looked a bit downward, toward the much smaller person speaking to her.

"Hi, I'm Paloma Sala."

It was the fortieth hand of the day offered in greeting. Magda took it while she also drew in the woman before her with her eyes. Beautiful skin. Umber. *Her mouth could be in a toothpaste ad.* This had to be the most attractive woman here, well, to her taste—and she was in a red dress. Magda's groin awoke, silencing her hungry stomach.

"Paloma." She rolled the name in her mouth. "That's my *tía*'s name."

A quiet three seconds moved like glue as their hands remained together as Magda took Paloma in and Paloma lay in her gaze, hypnotized by her striking figure and noted power.

"Hey, kids! You've met." It was Kristina. "Paloma, this is Magda. Magda, Paloma."

"Yeah, hon, we just got that done." Magda snickered gently while continuing to gaze into Paloma's full, blushed face.

Kristina caught on as Paloma looked away, suddenly a bit shy. "Good! Okay, so . . . Paloma runs an amaaazing education firm that specializes in financial curriculum for schools."

This mention of her work, her passion, woke Paloma up

and she chimed in. "Yes, and we're doing great so far. But we're always in need of more funding, so . . ."

Magda let go of her hand and snapped back into business mode. "Listen, I've gotta nab the CTO during this break, but are you in town for the night?" she asked her new acquaintance in the fitted red dress.

Kristina put on a knowing smile as she watched the two women.

"*Yes*." Paloma nearly jumped on Magda, most likely excited about the source of "funding" she was about to spend time with, mildly unaware of Magda's possible intentions. "I'm staying just a few blocks down. Here's my card—feel free to text me. And can I have yours?"

"Sure." Magda handed it over like something precious. "Just keep it close, okay?"

"Absolutely. See you soon." Paloma bowed slightly and made her way to the door with her fellow lingering networkers.

Kristina followed Magda's covetous gaze. "Maaagdaaa . . ." Her head tilted in a here-you-go-again.

"She wants to talk. So, we'll talk!" *We'll do a lot of talking,* Magda thought as she ran her fingers through the front flop of her blond do.

"Shit, girl . . . *coño*. Listen, she's straight. Coming out of a bad marriage—husband cheated, yada yada—so the last thing she needs is for you to screw her over."

"Sounds like what she needs is some lovin', ya heard?" Magda threw on her urban-vanilla persona when she could, for fun. She was no crasser than her closest straight female friends. Shoot, only Cat held it all too tight in—she was nearly a novitiate, and mostly because she was a workaholic. Luz could catcall a man like nobody's business and Gabi, damn. Gabi had been one of Magda's first post-closet conquests but now was simply a dear friend who knew her all too well. And shit, that girl could talk about pleasuring men in graphic detail, without a stutter. Not that Magda ever wanted to hear about that.

"Ugh." Kristina knew her warnings fell on deaf ears. Magda, just like many of the men in the room, thought with what was between her legs. She savored her plan to text Paloma later, wrapped her arm around her friend, and led her to the door. "C'mon. Let's eat."

Chapter 3

"Now . . . do me a favor—be nice!" commanded a sunny-faced woman—bronzed, crowned with black curls, wearing red lipstick, a flowing dress, and Spanish shawl. Boho chic.

"I'm always nice," Magda responded in a flat, tongue-in-cheek tone. She and her former girlfriend, Gabi, a Puerto Rican, Ivy League–educated psychotherapist, were finding their seats in a large event room, decorated tastefully but unremarkably in fund-raising-dinner style. An unoffensive flower arrangement sat in the middle, glasses and utensils outnumbered anything else in the room, and circles of tables were surrounded by gold-painted bamboo chairs.

It was six years ago at Magda's front of center table for her largest philanthropic effort, the Sol Fund, directed toward environmentally friendly urban planning. Gabi was also Magda's former partner of two years and was just starting up her media persona, landing multiple TV guest spots and named in influential media outlets as an expert in her field. But her time with Magda came after living her life never having dated a woman, or even entertaining the idea that it was a possibility. Her traditional background had no room for it. But after a bad breakup with another long-term boyfriend, Magda had swept in a few years ago and rescued her mind, won her heart, and loved her body in a way she'd never experienced. Yet, after one too many nights spent trying to talk sense into a drunk, one-a.m.-just-getting-home-Magda, smelling of other women's perfume, Gabi had to leave. But she never left Magda as a friend. Gabi's love for her and understanding of the self-destructive pain that was her propane kept her around, but platonically. Besides, Gabi was a problem-solver, a therapist extraordinaire. She wasn't going to let this "problem" get away from her until she was fixed.

"Watch that belly," said Magda as Gabi squeezed her wide hips onto her seat, the bump of her pregnant stomach barely noticeable as it brushed the edge of the table.

"*Ay*, I'm fine." Gabi swatted Magda's concern away.

A mass of fellow dinner-goers milled around them, everyone looking for table numbers, sparkling in gowns, jewelry jangling, judging whom they wanted to commit to making small talk with for the next two hours.

"Why'd you have to go and have his baby?" Magda whined playfully. "Why not my baby?"

"Mags . . . Stop it." Gabi raised her hand to stop the flow of sass coming from her ex. "I'm happy, okay? You know I want this baby more than anything . . ." As she trailed off, Magda raised an eyebrow at her in defiance. Gabi took in air, ready to chastise her jealous former lover, but was interrupted, catching the eye line of one of her guests, an up-and-coming television producer.

"Hey, *chica!* Come, come!" Gabi's face radiated welcome like an electric stovetop.

"Hi!" Her guest, Cat, was on "low" compared to Gabi's "high." She was nervous. This was her first big fund-raising dinner and was a bit intimidated by what she'd read up on Magda, a publicly gay woman, who was nearly a tycoon. Cat was amazed, even more so once she shook her hand and felt just how captivating she was.

"*Un placer.*" Magda gave Cat a nudge of a smile while her eyes told Cat that she liked what she saw. Gabi elbowed Magda.

Cat rambled a bit in reply. "Thank you so much, Magda, for having me—and Gabi. I've never really been to one of these things, ya know, because of course the network doesn't pay for much and then when they do, it's like I'm just not there yet, ya know?"

Gabi waved off Cat's nervousness while acknowledging her feelings of vulnerability. Magda had gotten up to talk with another board member, which gave Gabi the chance to assure Cat as she sat down. "Sweetie, this is just the start of many! So . . . help us out here and make this not a dull night, yes?" Cat smiled. She wasn't yet the stomping, strong woman who commanded a network show. She seemed smaller, was smaller, in her own head. Her hair wasn't perfectly blow-dried and ironed flat. Her makeup was obviously done all too gently by her own hand, and her dress was as nondescript and "blend-me-in" as possible. She was not yet ready to be seen. But Gabi saw her—saw the fireball of intelligence and drive under all the politeness and nerves.

"*Ay, mujeres,* what the fuck!" A stunning blue-eyed, African-American woman with a nearly shaved head of pale gold approached the table, feigning exasperation. "I've been looking for you everywhere!"

"*Ay, belleza,* Mami-Luz, come here!" Gabi enthused. She embraced Luz as her friend bent down to give her a full-lipped kiss on the cheek.

"Don't get up, don't get up," the woman said in Gabi's ear as she looked down at Gabi's growing belly. "So, does everybody know?" she whispered.

"Oh, yeah, yes, all good." Gabi nodded, with her eyes closing in acknowledgment. She patted her own belly while her friend squeezed her hand on her shoulder.

They paused for a moment, then Gabi introduced Cat to Luz, who then greeted Magda as they all sat down.

"Yo, mama, thank you so much for letting me tag along— you know I'm going to get the company to give big next year. They *need* to buy a table."

"That would be great, Lu. Thanks." Magda smiled. Luz was a longtime friend and grad-school buddy of Gabi, a rising powerhouse in advertising. A stunner visually, the super-cool buzzcut, the velvet brown skin and light eyes, but she was too tall and model-like for Magda's taste. Not enough to hold. Besides, Luz was another supreme alpha, like Magda. She loved alphas, but only as friends. Besides, Luz was married to a Silicon-Valley Chinese-American from Queens who was grinding his life away at his start-up for God-knows-what chance he'd strike it rich. Might as well be mining for gold. Then again, Luz was no idiot. Magda just didn't like the odds. She preferred to play it square in business. Just not in life. But that didn't stop both Luz and Chris from pitching her to invest in his business.

It was nearing time for the opening speaker and Magda's table was now filled by three of her staff members: a young, brunette intern with the flowing locks of youth and the angled shoulders of a salad diet; an Adonis thirty-something vice president, with ebony skin and Colgate-white teeth; and the hipster accounting guy, coiffed, full beard, checked shirt, contrasting slim tie and all.

"Ladies and gentlemen! If you could all please take your seats—the program will soon begin." The voice of God, as events folks call it, boomed over the speakers. Half of the attendees, still standing, shuffled to their seats as conversations wound down, hugs were given, cards exchanged.

"Are you saying anything tonight?" Gabi asked Magda as she sat down at the head of her table, closest to the stage, smiling, mouthing hellos around the table.

"Nah, don't wanna." Gabi noted Magda's tequila-laced breath. She didn't remember seeing her drink more than one, but she already sensed she was on to number three at a minimum. Gabi knew better than to berate Magda or tell her to cool it. That would just result in a scene. A clear cause and effect. And, as the server filled Magda's wineglass, she took it from under her pour so quickly, Gabi was amazed nothing spilled. It was like a magic act. With no magic.

"So, Cat, how's the show going, hon?" Gabi turned her attention to her newest friend.

Cat rolled her eyes and sighed. "The host is just such a bitch—I'm sorry, please keep this just between you and me, okay?" Cat's professional façade slipped for a moment.

"No, no, listen, nothing's going anywhere."

Cat sighed. "Thank you . . ."

She ran through the wild stories of behind-the-scenes shenanigans on her show—a national show to boot. Cat's host was a longtime TV vet and that stance was a double-edged sword. She had the tenure to make demands, and the older, loyal viewership to make her feel secure enough to berate her staff and blow smoke every which way possible. She also had the shoulder of the network boss, another *viejo* as Cat called him, an old man. And he loved blondes. But, as Gabi pointed out to Cat, old and blonde wasn't the future—it was the usual. And pressure from younger or migrating viewers meant that it would be only a matter of time.

"Why don't *you* do it?" Gabi whispered to Cat in between speakers and clapping.

"Do what? Go on air?" Cat's eyes saucered.

Gabi answered her stunned response with, "Yeeees! Well, why not?"

Cat couldn't speak. *Why didn't I ever think of that?*

"You sooooo have a face for TV—look at you! Big eyes, strong features . . ."

"But I have brown skin, though, Gab!"

"Even better, no?! It's about freakin' time that that was a plus . . . ! It's time." Gabi punctuated her message, pushing her pointed finger into the table with a light thump.

They both looked to the stage and clapped as the room did. They were lost as to why the room was applauding, but they were there to support Magda and her cause. Their presence, and a small donation, were more than the eighty percent.

Magda had gone quiet. Gabi noted that she seemed to be focusing on the podium, but she watched as her eyes glazed over, in and out of being present, another glass of wine gone, something turning in her mind. *Oh, please, Mags, make it through this.*

"Hey, Mags, sup!" The program broke for some music, giving Luz's husband, Chris, a chance to pull up behind Magda's blond head and striped Italian suit jacket to say hello.

"Hey, man, sup, how you doin'?" Magda slowly, with concentration, began functioning again. She looked pleasantly at the handsome, Asian-featured man.

Luz threw an air-kiss his way as he winked back.

"Good, good." He kneeled next to her so she wouldn't have to get up. He sensed that rising might be an effort for her right now. "We are just plugging away and I managed to get CasaWorks to nab a table here—"

"That is so cool, man, thanks." Magda was genuine. After business updates were made, Chris wasn't one to squander time.

"And you know, a lot of this couldn't happen without you—" he said.

"Oh, man, well, ya know—"

"No, no, really—without your initial investment, which

gave us such a halo effect by the way, I dunno if we would have gotten over that hump."

"My pleasure, man, my pleasure." Magda shook his hand, nearly blushing, as he rose to swing around the table to his wife, Luz. Points scored by Chris for gratitude.

"Wow—wait, I didn't know you backed Chris's company!?" Gabi leaned over.

"Yeah, well, ya know." Magda shrugged.

"I thought you didn't feel too hot about the whole deal—too risky . . ."

"Listen," Magda slurred slightly, "I'm not a complete monster. She's our friend." She gestured over at Luz, her husband leaning over her, adoring. Adoring. How Magda wished for something so real.

"In the end, I back the person. I backed Chris, not necessarily the concept. He's a solid guy. Knows his shit. Works like a mutha." Magda slugged down her last drop of red wine.

Gabi smiled at Magda's fierce loyalty. She backed people. Though she was messed up when it came to lovers and romance, she was the most loyal friend and ally one could ask for.

Magda patted Gabi's thigh. "Be right back."

"Where ya goin'?"

"Three o'clock."

Gabi looked where Magda's hungry eyes had landed, at three o'clock. "Oh, Magda. Wait." Too late. All Gabi saw was the strong, broad back and tapered neck of her friend heading toward a '50s pinup of a young woman, dark and curvy in a strapless, mermaid-style dress. This wasn't going to be good.

"Oh, Gab-eeeee!"

Gabi was rattled by a voice so shrill it cut through the buzzing around them and even Cat, Luz, and Magda's office trio broke their conversations to locate the source.

It was a robust, short, olive-skinned woman, a keg-on-legs, as Magda would say, hair done at the salon down the street from her apartment, the makeup of someone in insurance, applied, but dull and unskilled. She offered a broad smile but gave off an aura of acid. Vitriol. Falseness. Gabi's right hand went instinctively to her belly, protecting it.

"Oooooh, are you pregnant?!" the woman asked much too loudly.

What kind of question . . .

Fifty percent more quickly and politely, Gabi responded, "Um, yes." She nodded, wanting to wring this woman's neck.

"How fantastic! Congratulations to you two!" She leaned down for a hug, which Gabi kept from full contact. "So where's Bert?"

I hate this woman and her rude-ass questions.

"Well, he's at the restaurant. Where he's the chef. Because it's dinner." Gabi paused between each statement, hoping her passive-aggressiveness registered.

"Oh! Yes, of course, silly me—"

You got that right.

The mood at the table finally sunk into the skin of the interloper. Everyone's eyes were on her, like a phalanx of guards around Gabi, making sure she went no further. She'd gone far enough.

"Okay, well, bye, see you later and I'll look for you on my TV in the mornings!"

"Who the heck was that?" Cat leaned in as Gabi drank water, tempted by her wineglass.

"Oh, just a woman who sits on another board with me. I gotta just live with her."

"God, she's rude."

"Yup."

The voice boomed again, instructing folks to take their seats for the final awards of the evening. Gabi was bumped in her chair, still on edge, as she tended to get when exposed to a person like that—an emotional vampire. Her symbiotic tendencies were great for therapy, but harder to deal with off hours. Or, maybe it was the hormones. It was Magda who had bumped into her, too drunk to hide it well anymore.

"Hey, *mujer,* gotta go. Cover for me, m'kay?" Magda ran her hand up the back of Gabi's neck into her curls. Gabi hoped no one had seen her do it.

"Yeah," Gabi mumbled back as Magda did her best to sneak out, all five foot ten of her blond, suited self. This had happened countless times.

"Hey, is she gonna be okay?" Luz, watching the exchange, walked over.

"Yeah."

Luz sighed as she kneeled down to Gabi's side, ready to help if it was needed.

"You know, do you mind . . . I don't feel so well. I think I gotta go, too," Gabi said.

"Sure, sure, can I help?" Luz offered.

"No, no, I'm good," Gabi whispered, just as another award of the evening was announced. She waved a silent good-bye to all, threw smiles, and mouthed thank-you's to all at the table as she made her way out.

She made her way down the once-crowded red carpet, clutching her shawl about her. The doors to the hallway were wide open and the air made Gabi feel a bit better. It wasn't all Magda's fault, why she'd suddenly felt woozy. There was a tug of sadness as her pregnancy progressed. Her husband of only a year was still working on solidifying his rank as a top chef in the city, which meant he wasn't around much. There was always an event, and then press, and crises. She felt a bit alone. But she knew she'd work it out. She always did.

Trying to pull the shawl in place over her growing-into-a-C-cup breasts, Gabi's eyes caught sight of Magda standing in profile at the valet drop-off point with the beautiful woman she had left the table for. It didn't look good. She was extending her taut, toned arm, pointing at Magda's face, accusing. Magda's body language was a mix of pleading and defending. She'd rock back and forth between the two with what seemed like ease.

Then abruptly, all eyes and ears around, including Magda's, were shocked as the woman's meticulously manicured hand shot straight for Magda's pale pink cheek with a slap. Then silence. Without another word, the slapper then turned and walked into a black car with impeccable timing. Magda stood stock-still for a beat, as slowly her right hand made it to her burning right cheek. The world started moving again as Magda turned her back to Gabi's gaze, her eyes following the car.

"Well, what hurts more, your cheek or your pride?" Gabi asked.

Magda didn't turn to Gabi's voice coming from just behind her right shoulder.

"Ah, fuck it," Magda murmured as she looked after the departing car.

Normally, Gabi would take Magda's arm in hers, lead her to a taxi, and take her home, make sure she was all right. But tonight, Gabi had a baby in her belly. Someone else to think about. She just wasn't up for it this time.

A yellow cab pulled up and Gabi opened the door for herself while her friend, her once lover, stood in the same spot, like taxidermy.

"Take care of yourself, okay?" Gabi asked Magda as she hopped into the cab, not waiting for an answer, as she left Magda with the doorman who had probably witnessed worse in his day. A handsome and still-fit gray-haired man, he walked gently up to Magda.

"Women, huh?" he asked her, as if man-to-man.

"Yeah," Magda answered, narrowing her eyes.

"There's a great spot just around the corner for late-night drinks if you need one—seems like you could use one." He pointed just past the line of waiting cabs and black cars.

"Yeah, thanks," Magda said as she started walking. Having stood so heavily in one spot for so long, her feet ached a bit going into motion. "I could use a few."

Chapter 4

"Oh, I just love you, guuurl!" came a pleasant squeal from the book-signing line.

One of Gabi's fervent fans handed her his book to sign. She noted that her queue was satisfyingly long, leading out to the escalator and down to the entrance of the store next door. Lots of frustrated, married moms here in Battery Park City, she noted. Frazzled, spin-class ladies cordoned off from the rest of the world by the West Side Highway, living in sanitized high-rise rentals, rushing from overcrowded schools to unsustainable careers, praying to avoid another Hurricane Sandy. After all, just one more year until they—or their husbands—were getting that raise or that next baby that would move them uptown, or out of Manhattan altogether.

"Can you make it out to Stefano?" The fan pointed at the title page. This was certainly not a BPC housewife, but he was fab. He rolled his eyes as he rambled: "So, the whole reason I got this book is because I was Googling *Golden Girls* to look for this specific episode to watch with my girl, Nitika, and this book popped up—*You Are Golden*—as I was typing and I was, like: What. The. Fuck? But then I started reading and I was, like, I love this lady, love!"

He was tall, she'd give him that much, with almond-butter skin and a waist like hers at twelve years old, wrapped in skinny jeans. Gabi chuckled at Stefano's rambling, noting the impatience of the folks behind him. There were too few moments of amusement in her life, a life where she listened, then fixed, people's problems, letting their issues fill her head rather than pay attention to her own.

"Ha! That's too funny—but let's be clear, I'm years from *that* club of girls." She winked. He smiled back, happy she reflected back his reference.

Gabi placed his freshly signed book to her far right, gently leading him to the side. "Now, don't stop now—read my other books!" she called out, pointing at him like a teasing schoolteacher. Gabi broke her furrowed brow into a bright smile. "Ciao, Estefano! Mmwah, mmwah." She blew him kisses, which he happily blew back.

The next fan in line was two feet shorter and two feet wider than the previous.

"Oh, hello!" Gabi continued to give everyone in line for her the same genuine smile and wide-eyed attention. She adjusted her Anthropologie on-sale sweater between guests. She did well, financially and professionally—but for this city, well was never enough. And she was now the main breadwinner. No slacking when you have to bring home nearly all the bacon—which means no buying things that aren't on sale.

Gabi Gomez Gold, Ph.D., continued to greet and sign, greet and sign, doling out snippets of advice each time. Twenty down, how many more to go? She never asked and did not keep track. She greeted each new person like the first person in line. After forty-five minutes, though, Gabi was waning and sensed—hoped—the end was near. She allowed herself to ask the staff person nearest to her, through the side of her mouth, "Rachel. How are we doing?"

"Great!" replied the bookstore staffer rhythmically passing out Gabi's books. "Do you need water?"

"I'm good. Thanks . . . Oh, hi!" On to the next. She was a machine. "And how do you spell that?"

"Ms. Gold?" the next reader asked. "I mean, Dr. Gold?"

"It's just Gabi, hon." The woman was an awkward sort—squat, pale, long unwashed hair, ancient glasses. Physical intake be damned, Gabi spotted a Mensa brain behind those eyes, most likely clouded by Asperger's. She peered in.

"So . . . um, Gabi . . . I've been going through such a hard time, taking care of my mother and all. She's got Alzheimer's. And I was laid off. So, money's tight."

"Ooh . . . I'm sorry." Gabi's face showed genuine concern. She laid her hand closer to her visitor's, resting on the table.

"Well, so, you really helped me not feel so guilty about not being with my mother twenty-four/seven—like, one time, I snuck out to see a movie. So, like you say, I'm taking care of me. Putting the oxygen mask on myself first so I'm in a position to help others."

"Mmm hmm. Good. Good." Gabi patted her hand, smiled, and patiently let her finish.

"So, just wanna say, thank you so much." She didn't look Gabi in the eye, instead focusing on the flat, false eyes pictured on the back cover photo on the book.

"Listen—what's your name, hon?"

"Um, Sara."

"Sara, what you're doing is sometimes the hardest job of all: becoming a parent to your own parent, okay? Shifting roles in a family is never easy, but for most of us, it's normal. So, stay with it, and keep taking care of *you* so you can help her." Gabi waited for a nod from Sara, that her words had sunk in. "E-mail me if you need a pep talk, okay? Go right through my Web site and click 'Contact Me.'" Sara—no 'h'—smiled brightly with only the lower half of her face before shuffling off, hugging her autographed book.

As a psychotherapist, Gabi's policies were to always use someone's name, and to say it often to acknowledge that he or she was being heard. Another modus operandi of Dr. Gold's was to make herself available to any and all people as much as possible. E-mails were answered within twenty-four hours, forty-eight if she was on the road. As her sales climbed and her press mentions accrued, it was becoming hard to keep up. But that's what interns were for, right?

"Gabi." Her public relations gal, a demure hipster rocking an obligatory topknot and owl glasses, crouched beside her, whispering. "Your phone. It's 'X.'"

"Oh shit—I mean, shoot!" Gabi raised her index finger. "One second . . . Rachel, I'll be right back." She started to rise from her chair, eliciting a few panicked looks from those who remained in line. "Don't worry!" Gabi assured folks. "I'll be right back—two minutes!" Gabi held up two fingers, patience and peace.

The PR gal stepped in to assure folks that the amazing, lovely "Dr. G" would return promptly. "No worries!" she sang in her Aussie accent. Folks in line buzzed.

Gabi slipped behind the nearest bookcase to the back wall, pulling off a large, glitzy clip-on earring, like Mrs. Robinson taking a call in the hotel lobby before heading up to her rendezvous with the young Benjamin Braddock. Oh, how Gabi missed having time for her movies. At five years old she'd watched weekly movies, old and new, as a way to bond with her sullen, distant father, appropriating mannerisms and styles of the characters she admired. But always careful not to internalize their angst. She had her own. No need for more.

"X"—the latest in a line of her most unstable, needy clients— was a call she was pressed to take. "X" was a suicidal, forty-something, female executive who was bipolar, single, and had just been dumped by another married man full of empty promises.

"Bonnie, I'm here." One finger went into Gabi's left ear to block out the bookstore chatter. She heard the telltale snort of a crying jag.

"I just can't take it, Gabi! He sends me this text and I just can't take it! It hurts too much. It huuuuurts!" The sound was not unlike that of Gabi's five-year-old having a tantrum. This woman was eight times as old.

"Okay. Okay. Listen, do you feel like you're going to do something to hurt yourself or anyone else?"

Gabi heard a snort before the answer. "Um, no. I dunno."

"Bonnie. I mean it, Bonnie. Are you—" Gabi strained to hear for any other sounds or clues that would signal that Bonnie was doing something else besides talking and crying.

"No, no, I won't, I won't . . . I just really need to talk to you right now." Gabi heard tissues rustling.

"Tell you what. I'm going to have Dr. Wong call you in the next twenty minutes. She'll ask you a few questions and figure out if we need to change your dosage—that will help you have a clear enough head to implement some more exercises, okay?" Gabi could hear her client's breathing shallow down and her crying drop from boil to simmer.

"Okay." Almost a whisper, but of relief, not despair.

"Okay?" Gabi pressed for better affirmation.

"Yes. Yeah. Okay." There was a sniff. "Thank you, Gabi. Thank you."

"You got it. Text me if you don't hear from her in exactly twenty minutes, okay? Watch the clock. And remember, it's not about him, it's about you—take care of you!"

Grow a spine.

"*Holaaa!* I'm back!" Gabi waved as she made a grand entrance back to the author's desk, sitting beside a five-foot-tall mockup of her book cover. She clipped her earring back on, jangling her bracelets along the way. Some people were all about jackets. Gabi had her jewelry, showcasing her love for Caribbean priestesses with their rows of bangles and flouncy white dresses.

The fans were pleasantly surprised at how Gabi returned quickly, as promised; glowing smiles again lit up the line. Gabi resumed grinning herself, followed by asking how to spell each name. She accompanied this by doling out two-sentence advice nuggets and tidbits of en-couragement that she knew could lift people for days. She had some sort of power, she surmised, a gift. It was as if she had an internal generator that could throw off light and warmth. When Gabi looked at you, she saw you. Gabi was convinced she had been born with too much love to give, so releasing it little by little to so many people decreased the pressure inside her, her own pressure. The pressure of a need to give, to help. So if you didn't need fixing, didn't need helping, your time in Gabi's world could be cut short.

She felt the cell phone in her pocket buzz.

"Oh shit . . . Again!" Gabi hissed.

"Everything okay?" asked Ms. Topknot.

Gabi pulled her glowing and buzzing phone out of sight, to just under the table. "Oh no . . ." she said.

"Do you need another break?"

"Nope! Nope. Not going anywhere," Gabi proclaimed loud enough for all to hear. "Just one sec. A little baby-sitter guidance is needed." Parents in line chuckled knowingly. Gabi typed both frantically and deliberately, her nerves and big thumbs preventing the even more rapid clip she preferred. It was her husband. She saw that he'd called her already, twice, hung up, and then sent texts.

> *He's being hateful. Come home now.*
> *OK, wrapping at store, will skip dinner.*

"June, I'm going to have to go right after this," Gabi got out before her next greeting: "Hi, hon! Who is this for?"

"But . . . what about the dinner?" June had her hand to her chest, just under her buttoned-to-the-throat collar. She had sexy-librarian-living-in-Bushwick down pat.

"Can't do. Family emergency—gotta head right home." Gabi kept on greeting, signing, advising. "Can you call JC and fill her in?"

Gabi couldn't look June in the eye. She, her agent, and her editor had planned to celebrate making the *New York Times* nonfiction top three. But family first, right? Gotta fix family first.

Chapter 5

"Whew . . ." A burly junior staffer set a box of bottles on the concrete floor of the funky, open office. "Well, they didn't have enough cava for the order, so they threw in some prosecco," he sighed.

"Ugh. Let me see." Luz Tucker Lee, fussy but fair, ran her pale gelled nails along the label. "Pffft. At least it's cold. Run three up front and the rest to the back, okay? Let's get poppin'!" She raised her voice and twirled her hands in the air above her curly faux-hawk. The interns, her assistant, and Luz were prepping for a party starting in fifteen minutes.

"Luz! Woman, you did it." Stella was her only colleague who was a true equal, and her only confidant in the firm—a blazing ad sales and marketing firm that, due to some blue-chip client turnarounds, had become the hottest in the country. The women hugged.

"Nah, nah, *we* did it," Luz said to Stella, then added in a whisper, "and what a fuckin' relief." Warm and supportive, Luz was known as a cipher of a colleague and boss, some would say, a tough bitch. But after fifteen years of scaling the ranks with Stella, Luz trusted her enough to expose small dents in her armor, admitting relief.

The women's embrace was a visual yin-yang. Luz's skin glowed a golden dark in contrast to her outfit, funky white

Alexander Wang jeans and asymmetrical top, while Stella, a good Southern gal gone city, accessorized her long blond blow-out and freckled skin with the urban go-to uniform of black skinnies and black top. The seemingly genetic, racial opposites shared one feature: their eyes. They both peered through lenses the color of tropical waters. "The Blues," interns would call them out of earshot. "The Blues are stepping out." "Do you have deck for The Blues?" "The Blues are on their way."

"I hear ya, girl," Stella responded to Luz's feeling of hard-won comfort. "Damn right."

Luz moved her hands from their embrace to sit them on top of Stella's shoulders. "Okay, Chiquita banana. Let's get this party started right."

Stella gave Luz's cheek a friendly smooch and glided off to rally the stragglers. The interns—paid, per Luz's insistence—were efficient. Glasses were out. Napkins, chips. Bottles started to pop. Luz gently directed the buzz as she shifted focus from directing the scene to receiving accolades, the person of honor. Luz had achieved what few in the biz, let alone a black woman, had done: She'd turned around a stodgy multibillion-dollar company—once led by a sunburnt, spoiled heir who was asked to step aside—into a cool place again, turning up the heat with a rush of new clients, following a winning lead, each bigger than the last.

Luz greeted colleagues as they made their way to the tables lined with champagne glasses. Meanwhile in her head she ran a tape: *I wonder what time he's bringing the kids. Hope Mom and Dad take a cab—his vision ain't so good at night. . . .* Her internal sound track of concern was cut short by someone moving into her line of sight. As the figure came into focus, her body tensed.

"So, lemme guess . . . next, a profile in *Vogue*?" A pale woman in unimaginative professional wear, ashy blond-brown hair in a ubiquitous blow-out, green eyes, and a sly smile said this in a voice that to Luz's ears was lemon-sour.

"Hmm." Luz smiled only with her lips. "Oh, Graciela, you're so funny," she replied, just as sour.

"Well, it's just a matter of time, right? I mean, a Blatina turns around a blue chip . . . The headline writes itself." Graciela cocked her head, still carrying a smirk.

Why did villains always do that cocked-head, flighty-hand thing? Luz wondered. Gesticulating in a "Check it, plebs—I'm so witty, and fab, and just bad . . . bad, bad." *Nah, it just looks like you're flinging tissues, twat.*

"Yes, well, what's important is that we rock—the company—and *that's* the headline." Luz underlined her words with her finger. Catfighting and corporate culture shenanigans were not Luz's style. But damn it if Graciela wasn't out of central casting. The depressing part was that Luz had always liked villains. But this one, not so much. Graciela was a fellow Latina, but of the pigment-free, unsullied European-descent variety. The "G," as Luz called Graciela out of earshot, didn't call her a "Blatina"—a black Latina—as a compliment. She'd recently stolen a huge Mexican client from under her, emphasizing that after all, Luz's Spanish wasn't as good as hers and please, "She's not Latina, she's black!" Luz was never interested in a who-is-more-authentic contest and if the client wanted to kowtow to G's racism and ignorance, well, she wasn't going to stop her or them. Success is the best revenge. And here, this was Luz's success party. Without another look, Luz turned her back to Graciela, leaving her pouting, and headed toward the door.

"Oh, look who's here!" Her arms reached out and the glow returned to her face.

"*Nena! Ay,* we are so proud of you." Luz's mother, Altagracia Tucker, known as Alta, was a slight woman with expressive layers of jewelry, always a splash of bright lipstick, and a tendency to over-enunciate. She shared Luz's skin tone, her long, generously featured face topped by a shock of close-cut gray curls, and the expressive warmth of a Dominican family.

"*Ay*, Ma, this is so good. So good." Luz held her mother tight. There was little baggage between them. Her mother had always been supportive and loving and Luz always aimed to please her. She was Luz's biggest support in life and biggest fan.

Luz's father was rarely far behind.

"Pops!" She went in for a hug 'n' smooch with her handsome, slim, and dapper African-American father. "So glad you guys are here."

"*Donde estan mi* grandchildren?"

"*Ay, Mami,* any minute. Pa, help yourself to the bar, have some bubbly."

"Oh boy, bubbles!" Roger's delivery was tart and dry, a legacy of boarding school and summers at Martha's Vineyard; a lifestyle unmistakably noted by his polo shirt, khaki trousers, tortoiseshell glasses, and neatly trimmed salt-and-pepper goatee. "As long as I don't have to drink microbrews, hon. I met my annual hipster fancy beer quota at your last party." He patted her on the back. Roger was in his late sixties, but he prided himself on always being in the know, naturally, and younger adults gravitated toward him, drawn in to his professorial air.

Luz laughed. She always laughed at her dad. He was a beacon that kept her on course, a dependable New England lighthouse that never failed her, her brother, or their mother.

"Okay. Move it along, amigos." Luz chided her parents. "You're holding up the line."

Luz's mother gave her face one last proud pat as she strolled by. A dozen more guests had streamed into the office to celebrate. Luz was pleased by all the support.

"*Mami!*" Two brown angels ran with open arms through the door, followed by a wobbling afro'd toddler in overalls.

"My babies!" Luz never hid her enthusiasm for her three Benetton-beauties, as she called them, twin seven-year-old girls and a boy. The girls, Nina, short for Cristina, and 'Fina, short for Josefina, sported afro-poufs at different spots on their heads (mostly to help teachers tell them apart). Her two-year-old son's eyes, Benny, short for Benecio, were balsamic pools. Nina, 'Fina, and Benny. With those she loved, Luz had a compulsion to shrink everyone's name to a length nearly as brief as her own.

"Oh, *mi amor*." She greeted her husband, Christopher Charles Lee, with a quick, heartfelt kiss on the lips. She couldn't love this man more. The only competition between them was who read more often to the kids before bed. "Chris, look at this madness!" Luz directed his gaze around the room while little Benny clung to her legs, shy, and her daughters stood awkwardly but excitedly by her side, staring at potentially sweet snacks, while most of the room took in the striking sight of the multi-culti, multicolored Tucker Lee family.

"So, who's this party for again?" Like her father, Luz's husband, Chris, loved to tease her. She'd hit the jackpot with this Chino from Cali. Owning and selling a couple of start-ups for several millions, one bigger than the next, had made settling down, helping with the kids, much easier. Besides, he cherished being the Asian-American fun-guy in this emotive black, brown, loving family.

"Seriously, though. You did it, sweetie." He whispered conspiratorially in her ear: "Who's *la reina* now, yo!"

The twins headed to the snack table, tugging along their brother, who was in danger of taking the whole thing down with a yank of the tablecloth. Luz made sure the interns were watching.

"Umm-hmm," Luz murmured as she still held her husband. "Where did I get you again, hottie?"

"At the mall . . ." Chris playfully took a handful of Luz's flesh right below her waist.

"*Not* made in China!" Luz and Chris had fun with their shared ability to culture-jest. It was one of their deepest connections, as both had spent much of their lives working and socializing with people who would mindlessly blurt slurs in their presence, followed by the excuse of "But you seem white to me!"—thinking it a compliment to be just one of the majority.

Luz turned toward the door. "Aww, check it out, there he is." A tall, classic-looking black man in a suit entered solo, turning more heads than Luz's. "Ma brothah, whassup?"

"Hey, sis. Congrats." They hugged. Luz's younger brother by five years, Tomas Franco Tucker was devoted to his big sister. They had grown up torturing each other, but when there was a Tucker Lee family gathering, he was there—this time particularly, as Luz had just helped him through a nasty divorce. "Looks good, looks good up in heya." He assessed as he gave a good look around the faces, and bodies, in the room. "Got any cuties for me?"

Luz gave him some side-eye. She hoped he was joking.

"Seriously, I've got a gala coming up and need a date!" he pleaded.

"I'll fix ya up with someone good. Meanwhile, grab a drink, *hermano*. And stay away from the interns. Or I will slay you."

Chapter 6

The door to the hired car hadn't even shut before tears began to fall down Cat's face.

Usually one for peppy small talk, instead she hoped the driver noticed her crumpling into the tight back seat, trying to hide from the demands of the world, her feet throbbing, head spinning. Cat dabbed at her cheeks with the sides of her fingers, just under her sunglasses. She caught the driver checking in on her in the rearview mirror, but she was well past the point of being able to care, as she usually would. She couldn't keep up with the flow as her tears carved salt paths through the thick makeup still on her cheeks. She unearthed two tissues in her purse and started dabbing gently. *Can't let people in my building see me like this,* she told herself. *I should call my agent.* Instead, she called someone who was, if anything, more influential.

"Ma?" she croaked.

"Oh, hi, dahling. How are juuuuu?" Cat's mother's voice was a Spanish-accented singsong via Mexico. It was a striver's voice, seeking to sound blue blood even when she was servicing customers at the cheap buffet and steak joint where she used to wait tables.

"Ma, I've been canceled." Cat hiccupped back a sob.

"Whaaaaa? Wha' do ju mean, canceled?"

"My show!" Cat caught the driver looking into the rearview mirror. *Calm down, girl.*

"*Ay Dios mio!* Wha' do ju mean?" Her mother's voice turned shrill and whiney.

"Ma. The show is gone. I'm done." Cat pulled herself inward and made herself small. Parents create buttons. And then they push.

"*Ay,* no. Wha' happened? Did ju say som'ting bad?!" For a moment, Dolores Ana Rosa Rivera dialed her tone down a notch—not only out of concern for her daughter, but also out of a need to get a rise out of her. Cat bristled at her puppetry—too many years of it, she was all too aware. But what she needed right now was love and understanding, not a codependent dance. The desire to talk to her mother disappeared as quickly as the original urge to call had appeared.

"No, no, Ma. It was nothing."

"Well, it canno' be no'ting! Wha' did ju do?"

What did I do, Cat thought. *It's gotta be what did I do.*

She moved to playing defense. "It was ratings . . . or something. The ratings." She blew her nose, loudly.

"Did ju call jor agent? Doesn' he haf somet'ing to say? Maybe ju can take a pay cut." Did this woman ever take a moment?

Cat couldn't believe her ears. "Ma! You don't go back to work and ask for a pay cut after you've been fired!" Shit. The dance began.

"Well, why no'? If it's about money, den save dem money!"

"Ma, you have no idea how this all works. You just don't do that!" Her mother's insistence on giving her professional advice rankled Cat to no end.

"Listen, I'm no' es-stupid! Jor no' de only one who knows t'ings, ju know!"

Dolores's education had stopped at fifteen when she came

to the States from D. F., Mexico City, and went straight to work in a factory. She'd never even held a desk job, instead waiting tables for years to help put her daughter, her only child, through school. Cat had turned out to be a great investment. Her daughter was on TV. She was famous.

"Ma, I gotta go. I need to call my agent."

There was no arguing with delusion. In classic hopeful-immigrant fashion, Dolores had poured everything into Cat. But she also had developed a toxic habit of living through her, as if the cord had never been cut, as if Cat pulled her as well along through life. It was exhausting.

"Well, we need to talk about wha' ju're goin' to do! Dey jus' canno' do dat to ju."

"Yes, they can, Mom. Oh, here—here's my agent. Gotta go. I'll call you later."

Cat hung up. Any guilt from lying about another call dissipated immediately. Dolores was probably calling her own sister right now to complain about what a horrible, selfish daughter Cat was for hanging up on her. And a mother who had sacrificed so much—she was the reason her daughter was a star, no?

Back home, Gabi's bags jostled and bumped as she searched for her house keys. Her heart was already pumping in anticipation of what was behind this door number one. She couldn't hear anything but the television through the fireproof apartment door, and the quiet made her more anxious than yelling and crying would. *Silence is the worst,* Gabi thought. She was the oldest of a gaggle of kids from Spanish Harlem, and as painful as it was to hear her mother and father screaming at each other, everyone there knew that the quiet was much more insidious.

"Hellooo?" Gabi called out tentatively as she entered a dark foyer, wanting—needing—to see her son's face. Only the television screen illuminated the apartment, along with a sliver of light from her son's bedroom. Gabi's insides dropped in both disappointment and relief at the sight of her husband splayed on the couch watching a show, one arm up, one leg up, taking up as much space as physically possible. She hated this position. It reminded her of an orangutan. But comatose also meant that maybe the drama was over, or, could at least be avoided one more night. She stared at him for a beat as his eyes never left the screen. *How did we get here?*

"Guurl, you're finally here!" Gabi's publicist friend, Nitika Solani, sang out to her, waving her hands above the mass of heads between them.

Gabi waved back and squinted as she concentrated on making her way through the gaggle of partiers, their drinks seemingly all too ready to spill on her. Gabi's hair was a bit less tamed, her eyes a bit less sunken. It was six years earlier, and she had managed to get dragged away from another early night to bed after a long day in residency at a psychiatric ward for teens by her graduate school friend who took a different path of "mental" practice: publicity.

"Listen, chica, this guy all right, this chef is just beyond. Gorgeous, Jewish!—I mean, hello, amirite?—and his food is to die."

Gabi smiled, but rolled her eyes at her friend's attempt to get her excited for another man. The only way this one differed was that Nitika had been working with him for months as her client and they both were on very good terms. Gabi didn't hear any diva behavior from him, either, something Nitika loved to dish—or bitch—about with Gabi.

Nitika pulled Gabi's arm with one hand and grabbed a drink from a server's tray with another, handing it to Gabi, all while they made their way to the chef's station. Gabi and Nitika were equally attractive and equally brown. Though Nitika's brown came from Mumbai, originally, via California. But Gabi in that moment was feeling subpar as the income difference between public relations and psychology became clearer. Nitika donned the latest clothes and looked slick, her blow-out and color screaming expensive. Gabi tried to tell herself that her sale items and more grungy Brooklyn look was just that, her own look, and fit perfectly into her world. She couldn't resist, though, taking note of the gut feeling that she wanted what Nitika had: success.

"Okay, my dear, here he is, hottest chef on the planet right now, Bert Gold!" She introduced him as a publicist would, with flair. Gabi couldn't see who Nitika was gesturing to. She only saw the back of someone, bending down, scrambling behind the massive wooden cutting table, chef coat on, a denim-like texture, very much worked in. It seemed he was doing some sort of display cooking with his sous-chefs or assistants standing around him, arranging bite-sized tastes that were going around the room with servers. The attendees were munching rapidly whatever came off the table with many *mmmms* and *wows* coming from all sides. "Um, Bert. I've got someone you have to meet." Nitika, this time, stating calmly with a bit of impatience.

"Yup, yup . . ." A muffled response came still from below the table. "Ah, okay, hi. Hi."

Well, he was handsome, Gabi would give him that. Sweaty a bit. That Mediterranean tendency toward growing hair nearly everywhere, but she liked that. He had a strong neck and Gabi strangely noticed that he had particularly small ears for his head. Funny.

"Hi. Gabi." She reached out her hand. He put out his elbow instead to bump hers. Gabi hesitated a second, then realized that as he was still cooking and serving, there'd be no hand shaking. They bumped elbows and both smiled politely.

"Bert, Gabi here is my dear friend from graduate school who does the good work, ya know, helps people. She's a psychologist."

Bert's eyes opened a bit wider, their small three-person scrum maintaining a mini-cone of stillness, if for but a moment. "Uh-oh!"

Gabi eye-rolled him. "Yeah, I get that a lot."

"Well, you don't want to start shrinking chefs because seriously, you'd be the one needing meds!"

Ha. Right. Gabi didn't find that funny. Childish humor. Nitika caught on. Feeling Gabi's frost, she turned professional. "Ooooh, kay. So, listen, I've got *New York* mag coming to you in five, you ready?" she asked Bert.

"Yup, yup, I'm good." He shook his head like a boxer going into a match. *Chefs are so physical,* Gabi thought none-too-happily as Nitika turned both the ladies away from the increasing madness of Bert's table performance. "Bye." We waved.

"Okay, so?" her friend asked.

"Eh." Gabi shrugged.

"Oh hon, we are never going to get you married! Don't you want to have kids?!"

"Yeah, of course! More than anything. It's just . . ." Gabi lost her mouth in her drink, some peachy-looking possible-margarita with a spicy kick.

Nitika sighed. "All right. Let's deposit you with some good folks and I'll head back to the super-fabulous man of the evening you want to have nothing to do with."

Two hours later, most of the crowd had dispersed and Gabi was surprised to find that she'd had a good time. Those peachy-spicy drinks helped, but Nitika had also made good on her introductions and the conversations she had and subsequent possible future-friendships were real. They were mostly females, or boyfriends of someone, but it felt pretty good to go out for once and connect. If Gabi didn't have her friends, she would simply work herself to the bone and hire a sperm donor. Dating was such a time suck.

"Can I get you another one of those?" She felt a tap on her shoulder.

"Oh! Oh hi," Gabi said to Bert, now sweatier than ever

but somehow also nearly tasty looking. Probably the drinks. "No, no thanks. I'm good. Probably should have stopped before this one."

Bert smiled and put his hands on his hips, stocky but still slim. "Well, hey, I'm really sorry I couldn't pay more attention to you ladies back there—it was kinda a madhouse."

"Yeah, I saw that." He was cute, but Gabi's small-talk abilities felt burnt out for the evening.

Bert seemed to feel her lack of interest. "I bet you think I'm a total ass for that 'shrink' comment, right?"

Gabi raised her eyebrows in partial agreement. "Well, maybe 'ass' is a bit harsh."

"Nah, nah, that's okay, I deserve it a bit. I get a little flustered when I'm nervous." Gabi nodded at him. "Ya know, I mean, this whole night, and stuff, but really I think you made me nervous!"

Oh geez, Gabi thought, *here we go.* She set her drink down. "Oh, I saw you tonight; you were doing pretty good."

"With the cooking? Oh yeah, that I just get into the groove, ya know . . ."

"No, I mean with the ladies—you were doing just fine." Gabi noticed out of the corner of her eye during the night how many women of all ages fawned over Bert, passed him numbers and cards, took photos, and even the men were kowtowing to him like cultists of cuisine to a guru.

Bert gulped at Gabi's straightforward swipe. "Well. Okay then. A ballbuster." He took off his bandanna, exposing the mop of wet dark brown curls underneath. Running his fingers through his mop, he raised his head to Gabi and went in for one more try. "Go out with me."

"Excuse me?" Gabi asked, surprised.

"Will you go out with me, maybe for coffee in the morning?"

"Can't do mornings. Work." Though Gabi noted his offer of a non-alcoholic meeting. Usually a sign of either someone who actually wants to get to know you, or someone who doesn't want to spend money on you. Seeing how well Bert was doing, Gabi was going to hedge her bets on option one.

"Okay, well, I don't go in until later on Mondays—can you do coffee at, like, five?" His eyes pleaded, and Gabi started feeling a tug coming from her insides. She noted the shape of his scruff, the lilt to his upper lip when he spoke, his strong brows. But mostly she noted his tenacity. She loved that quality in a person.

"Sure. Sounds good."

"Oh! Okay—great!" Bert visibly brightened. "I'm so looking forward to it, Gabi." He shook her hand this time.

"Nitika can get you my contact info," Gabi offered.

Bert nodded, winked at her, and walked away. She could have sworn she heard him humming.

After they dated for a while, Gabi asked Bert why he was interested in her in the first place, with all those women after him. He told her, "It was because you weren't impressed by me."

Years later, Gabi was even further from impressed.

"Hey" was all Gabi got out of him, her husband's eyes not breaking contact with the screen. She dropped her bags softly so as to not wake their son and mustered a polite and plaintive "Hey . . ." in return. But the moment her bags landed with a rustle and a clink, the little boy ran out of his bedroom, grabbing and squeezing tight his mother's legs in a save-me hug. He had been waiting up.

"Oof. Hi, baby," Gabi said gently.

"*Mamiiiii*," little Maximo wailed into his mother's side.

Snapping out of his TV trance, Bert sprang forward from the couch.

"What did I tell you? Stay in your room! Get in there, right now!" he scolded.

Tall, and scruffy as a Brooklyn-creative was required to be,

Bert Gold bore little evidence of his time as a star chef. When he'd met Gabi, he'd just snagged his slot in the Meatpacking's hottest nouveau-American restaurant by winning an episode of *King Cook,* an all-male cooking competition on SpikeTV. But bad management led to the closing of the restaurant, and the next restaurant that followed. Bert could cook but he could not lead people as he needed everyone to like him, and, had too-little fire in his belly. That tenacity that she once saw seemed to give way with each failure. It culminated in him describing himself to Gabi as a worker bee now, not a colonel. *I should have listened harder to that one.* Winning the cooking competition got him the accolades and fifteen minutes of fame he'd craved, but it thrust him into roles that he had no desire to play, particularly as his wife's star rose as his fell. For a few years now, Bert had found it all too easy to hang around his "home office" in a T-shirt and shorts, maintaining his supposed online presence, cooking for personal clients once in a while. Gabi earned plenty of money, after all, and she came preloaded from the womb with limitless energy and fortitude. When they'd met, Bert was at his peak. Gabi was doing well, but the fulfillment of her potential had only just begun, while his was in full swing. Now the tables had turned and Bert was outearned as well as overshadowed in the public eye. It was a recipe for resentment.

Flinching at the thrust of his father's pointed finger and sharp voice, the auburn-haired five-year-old held on to his mother and wailed louder. A little bit of drama in his feelings, but it all added to a whole lot of truth to Gabi.

She put out her palm and instinctively turned her body to protect her son from Bert's aggression. "Okay, that's enough," she told both of them. When Gabi was a teenager and had grown close to her mother's height, she would stand between her mother and her sisters and little brother, forbidding the bullying and the hitting that would come their way. The pain that she'd been first to experience. Gabi was very comfortable with this position: *You'll have to go through me first.*

"Don't talk to me like that! Don't order me around!" Bert yelled at Gabi.

"Just calm down, okay? Max's had enough for the night and you have had way too much to drink." Gabi worked to keep her voice as sedate but as unyielding as possible.

"Oh, fuck you, I have not." He waved her off and sat back down, eyes on the television, arms and legs again splayed.

Gabi saw red. He was obviously drunk and maybe even high. This was why she never went out anymore, unless it was related to her work. She didn't trust him to stay sober with Max.

"Are you kidding me? You're two whiskies in and it's a Tuesday, at home with your son so I can work to support you guys and you can sit on this couch!" As soon as it came out she realized that emasculating him wasn't going to solve any problems. But she was exhausted, filters not functioning.

"Oh, fuck that. You know, I'm sick and tired of your high-horse bullshit—"

Maximo was holding on to his mother's legs, tight.

"High horse! I wish I had a fucking horse, but noooo, I'm stuck in this apartment that reeks of liquor and pot and your . . . your . . . self-pity, and you can't see for one minute what you're doing to this family! You. Need. Help." Gabi kept her hands on her son, who was now quiet and shaking.

Bert set his glass down, grabbed the sides of his head, stood and bleated, "STOP trying to fix me, goddamnit!"

Maximo flinched his little body, echoing his mother's reaction. An angry drunk is a scary drunk, and a dangerous person. Gabi shut down, stunned by Bert's obviously pent-up vitriol. They froze in place as Bert grabbed his keys and wallet and stormed out the door. *Thank God.*

Gabi finally breathed in, and out, then whispered a hush-

hush as she shuffled her son back to his room, imagining that she was placing a psychic cloak of protection over her and her boy. Gabi was a sensible, rooted-in-science person, but she always felt that energy was energy—it was real and present. Her mother was into Santería and ghosts, priests' blessings and sage burnings. And Gabi had had childhood visions and strange dreams, which made her feel at times like a closet *bruja*. One foot in the world of social science. The other, in a very messy, yet potent place.

Max had been too often at the receiving end of Bert's alcohol-fueled rages since the child could talk—and talk back. But this year in particular. This was a very bad year. Gabi bent down and held her strong-willed son, half Puerto Rican (which meant Spanish, African, a smidge of Taino), half Jewish, whispering to him, "It's okay, *mi amor*. It's okay. *Mami* loves you. *Te amo mucho*." Rocking and rubbing his back, envisioning her ardor radiating from her chest, into Max, trying to bring their breaths into sync. She took his cherubic face into her hands. "*M'ijo*, let *Mami* wash your face before you go back to bed, okay? It'll feel so so good."

Sniffles. "Okay, *Mami*."

One of the few, but treasured, memories Gabi had of her temperamental, depressed mother was of her taking a warm washcloth and gently wiping the salt trails from Gabi's teary, young face. She could never remember why she had been crying, and how many times, but she did remember that in this display of affection from her mother she felt loved, even if only for that moment.

Bracelets jangling, Gabi directed Maximo into the bathroom. The washcloth was warm, just so, and the boy closed his eyes as the cloth approached his face, ready for its healing blessings. Gabi gently swiped Max's flushed face, with a soft, melodic "Shhh . . . shhh . . ."

"*Mami*, why do you have to leave me with him?"

"Shhh . . . shhh . . ." Swipe, rub. More warm water, squeeze.

"*Querido*, sometimes *Mami* has to work long days." She took her son's cheeks into her hands and locked eyes with him. "I don't like being away from you, but sometimes I have to, *amor*. I have to work so we can have this home and you can have your nice things, okay?" She wasn't telling the whole truth because there was a part of Gabi that loved to work hard. She was as ambitious as she could be, always wanting more than what had been expected of her female, brown, 'Rican self. But now Gabi was supporting the family financially. And the way Bert was spiraling downward, she wouldn't be surprised if he never worked again. And if she was truthful with herself, she wondered if subconsciously she didn't work so much and focus on Max all in defiance of him and what he'd become; maybe she did it even in disgust.

One of Gabi's nicknames as a kid was Weeble-Wobble, because life might make her wobble, but nothing could keep her down. Coming from nothing meant she had the equipment to handle nearly anything. And she'd seen how the other half lived. From sixth grade, Gabi was shipped off to boarding school in New Hampshire on a scholarship, the only curly haired, brown-skinned girl in her class, with too much polyester in her wardrobe and not nearly enough polo shirts with animal crests. There was no fitting in for Gabi, but by her second year she was running for student government, breaking records as a class fundraiser, and mingling across cliques. She disdained the rich girls who had made fun of her clothes and her name, but befriended them anyway. She knew what she had to do to survive and, more importantly, to get ahead. Fake it 'til you make it. Just be sure to take names and notes along the way.

But because her husband hadn't done the same, had failed to rise up and meet his own challenges, Gabi knew she thought less of him. She had so much compassion for others, strangers even, but had little for the father of her child. Disdain was displacing desire. It seeped into her veins like poison. She knew she was also part of the problem.

"Okay, *mi amor*, let's get your 'pee-yammas' on." Gabi liked to slip on her mother's accent when she was doing the mothering. Her son found it funny and comforting.

"*Mami*," Max gulped, "can you please sleep with me?"

"*Ay*, hon, I can't sleep with you all night. Look at how small your bed is! You barely fit in it anymore, my big boy!"

She managed to coax a proud smile out of Max.

"How about this: I'll tuck you in, sit next to you, and whisper a story to you until you fall asleep."

"Oh, yes. Yes!" Maximo led his mother out of the bathroom and climbed into his too-tight toddler bed. It creaked.

With the TV still humming from beyond the door, Gabi told Max a tale of a handsome space explorer and his trusty alien pet who escaped together from a dark planet, only to find a new home in the Milky Way with shooting stars and bubble gum, happiness and fun for all.

Gabi's head dropped sleepily next to Max's. She dozed off, too, thinking, *Space Man . . . take us with you.*

At this four-star franchise hotel bar, no one would know who Magda was. The Jefferson or the Four Seasons, five-star all the way, was definitely a risk, but here she was grateful to be incognito. Anyway, it was just a business drink.

You're lying. You want your hands on her, and in her, so bad.

"Magda Reveron?"

Talking to her was a thirty-something techie bro in a tie. *Great.*

"Adam Herzog, FastForward. I saw you speak at the Angel conference a month ago."

Magda reluctantly released the grip on her sweating tumbler of tequila to shake hands and exchange cool pleasantries with the gent. She gave him a nod.

"So, my firm is working on a new MOOC model. Can I ask for your info to shoot you an invite for a preview?"

"Sure, sure." She handed him the fattest card he'd have in his wallet for years. Magda knew that her stationery pick was a bit *American Psycho,* but she enjoyed folks' surprise at the old-school touch.

"Great, thanks. And here's mine." He gave her his card, holding it at each corner with two hands. Nice attempt at charm, Magda thought, but she spoke little, nodding again instead.

The man kept trying. "Actually, I'm waiting for a friend who's running late. Mind if I join you for a bit?" he asked.

"You know, I'm waiting for someone as well," Magda said as she protectively placed her hand on the stool she was straddling between her legs. "But definitely follow up with me later, okay?" The brush-off, bookended with a promise of tomorrow, was a good way out.

"Oh, sure. Thanks." Adam blustered a bit, thwarted. "Great to meet you. Have a great night."

Magda's hand fell back to where it was meant to be for now, around her glass. She toasted herself with relief as the ice jangled, reminding her of pretty girls' bracelets.

As she drained the glass, Magda kept Adam in her side view. She noticed that his buddy had shown up. They sat down in the lounge, two tables out—well within range, unfortunately. She'd keep an eye on him all night. She didn't like anyone knowing her business.

"I see I've got some catching up to do." Paloma had arrived from behind. As she turned, Magda drew in the red dress, still on from their first meeting, the control garment Magda suspected was underneath (a telltale lack of rolls on her curvy frame), and the slight frizz to Paloma's blown-out bob. This was a grown-ass woman. All realness and rough, frazzled. Magda's favorite, usually problematic, blend.

They cheek-pecked, Magda's hand on Paloma's back. Feeling for the yield of her flesh, her bra, warmth.

"You a tequila fan?" Magda signaled the bartender like a pro.

Paloma smiled and pulled in a breath that made her round chest rise. "Absolutely. I'll do a clean margarita, on the rocks with salt."

"Perfect." Paloma's use of "clean" made Magda's mouth wet. The lady in red knew her way around a bar.

Paloma scrunched her handbag into the space between the stool and foot rail. "Thanks for meeting me here. I hope it's not too out of your way?"

"Not at all. I'm just down the street. Sit, sit." Magda patted the bar stool between them. "Or would you rather sit in the lounge?"

"I think we may be too late for that." Paloma pointed to the now-filled seating area.

No matter; bar stools were sexier to Magda anyway. Their temporary feeling, their precariousness, the bustle of the bartender. Some creative people liked to do their business in coffee shops. Magda liked bars.

The ladies developed a quick chemistry and the drinks flowed. Magda punctuated her speech with the hand gestures and arm flailing of a traditional Latin. But her legs were apart like a man's, occupying as much room as possible on either side of Paloma, enveloping her in a precursory, mildly possessive embrace.

An hour in, Paloma was on her second margarita and Magda had lost count after four gimlets. It was time to shift from business talk to personal. Magda knew she had a tendency to come on strong and that she could lose on this one, but it was an itch that needed scratching.

"I hope you don't mind, but Kristina mentioned you're separated?"

Sucking her teeth, Paloma slowly bobbed her head. "Yeah."

"Are you okay? I mean, is it okay?" Magda wanted to

confirm her hunch that she was dealing with an adult, not an immature, clingy maniac.

Paloma's verbal floodgates opened just enough to reveal the basics of the story—that she'd been wronged—and they closed well before "psycho." Magda smiled. She wanted to slip in one more little nudge. First, she snuck a glance around the room. Shit—Tech Boy was still there. His gaggle was up to three bros, no ties, one T-shirt. But she was relieved as they were all tipsy and knee-slapping, not looking Magda's way.

She liked hearing Paloma talk. She had an interesting background. And like Magda, Paloma was the oldest of several daughters in a big Latin family. *Dios,* she just had to have her, naked and soft.

"*Palomita,* you okay?" It was almost midnight, nearly five hours after Paloma sat down. They'd blasted through the evening without a moment's silence, but the lack of a full meal plus too much drink had snuck up on the smaller of the two and was starting to take a toll. Paloma had slipped a bit as she tried to climb back onto the bar stool after a bathroom break.

"Oh, shoot. It's so late . . ."

Magda flicked her wrist for the check and mouthed *La cuenta* to the barkeep.

"Wow, it *is* late." Magda added a big tip and signed her tab quickly.

"*Ay,* thank you soooo much," Paloma slurred as she watched the bartender pick up his payment from Magda. "Sooooo much for everything."

"What floor are you on? I'll take you up. You're a little tipsy there . . ." Magda held on to Paloma's elbow, supporting her as she dropped from the bar stool.

"Really? Oh, you don't have to . . ." Paloma rustled in her purse for her keycard. Her brush-off was less than halfhearted.

Inside the elevator, Paloma went from giggles to a buzzy, happy quiet. Magda savored the anticipation hanging over them like a crystal chandelier. She was still holding Paloma's arm and Paloma was allowing it, leaning on it. The doors opened and jounced.

"I think I'm this way." Paloma pointed. The ladies ambled in silence down the hall. It looked a bit like a ceremony of some sort, down an aisle of transformation or, in Paloma's case, indoctrination. As she inserted the key at her door, Magda stood just behind, her suit jacket grazing the back of the red dress. Magda breathed in the scent of Paloma's hair, ran her left hand up her arm, placing her free hand on her waist. They both breathed in deeply. The key wasn't working.

"Here. Let me." As Magda reached for the key from behind—*click*—the door's green light offered them both not only entry, but permission.

The women moved into the room together, slowly. As she closed the door, Magda slid around to the front of Paloma, looked down in the fluorescent light of the foyer, and cupped her heart-shaped face in her hands.

"*Tan bella,*" Magda whispered, then bent down to take Paloma's mouth to hers. Years of pent-up, end-of-marriage pressure were set free in Paloma, and her gut-hungry response surprised Magda, setting her appetite alight. Within minutes they were naked and tangled on the white sheets of the bed, clothes thrown aside, having done their job for the day. Paloma let Magda take her. She was thrilled to be ravaged, maybe even more so by a woman. They explored each other for hours, dozing off for a few minutes before the other prompted more with a touch or a nibble.

Just before sunrise, a groggy Magda made her way naked to the bathroom, looking first for her phone. The night-light in the foyer made odd shapes on her lean, muscled belly. Funny, she didn't remember plugging in her phone, but there it was. Not remembering nights happened more often than Magda liked to admit. As she popped her head out of the bathroom to see her sleeping companion, Paloma's curved, naked back like an hourglass on its side, Magda noted, well, this one had to be good.

Shit. Back to her cell. She had a conference call in two hours. She ran the tap cold and threw the water on her face and ran wet hands through her hair. She'd take a shower back at her own hotel room.

Grabbing her clothes and dressing, Magda didn't want to wake Paloma up. She was lovely, and it had been a blast, but really, it was time for business.

Chapter 7

"*Niños*—don't run so fast! You'll trip on the rugs!" Luz's kids had barely made it through the front door, whipping off their little shoes and throwing them into the entryway bin, before they ran like little drunks down the hall, screaming with pleasure as they bumped into walls and each other.

"Yeah, well, they're hopped up on the crack that is chocolate-chip pancakes." Chris placed his stylish loafers neatly on a shoe stand reserved for the adults.

Luz made a face. "I feel the opposite with all that food. I'm sugar-crashing, even after three coffees."

"Wanna go lie down? You're on vacation for two weeks! And a well-deserved one, I might add."

The large colonial house on Martha's Vineyard had been in Luz's father's family for generations. Surrounded by so much wood and history, there was a magical effect on Luz, like a quasi-spiritual vortex she'd been told existed in the deserts of Arizona. She hadn't felt that kind of peace when she'd sneak out with Gabi or Cat every other year for a couple days of hiking, spa visits, and juicing. Luz enjoyed herself on those trips, but it was more the solace of friendly love, not necessarily a spiritual experience. This place, though, felt like a womb to her. A great-grandmother's womb. Fiercely safe and warm.

And Luz had hit the jackpot with her husband. Not too

many kind, loving, rich, sane men in the tech world. But Luz's husband had had growing up what she had: a fairly normal immigrant upbringing. First-generation money. Granted, Luz had lucked out in a lotto way when her Dominican mother, whose formal education had stopped at fifteen, married her black-legacy father. Her mother's dear friend, who lived down the hall from her near the Columbia University campus, had introduced her to a brilliant, well-raised African-American student she had been taking a class with. It was instant love and decades later, Luz still saw the warmth in their eyes. But her mother never let Luz forget the luck of her birth. She often brought Luz and her younger brother back to the old neighborhood when they were kids to stay with her grandparents with their plastic-covered rococo furniture to spend time with her cousins. Cousins who were fed a daily diet of fried plantains and cartoon television. Luz's home was salad, PBS, and the news.

"I'll take care of dinner tonight then?" Luz asked.

"Sure, hon." Chris gave her forehead a smooch. "Okay, kids—I hear ya, but I don't see ya. I'm coming!" They loved when he played tickle monster. Thankfully, their screams of joy would be confined to the finished basement, with Luz oblivious to the melee, two floors up on her bed.

As she was climbing the creaky stairs to the second level, the hall lined with photos of her various strains of flesh and blood, all kinds in shade and decade, the landline phone rang its charming, retro ring.

"Hon? Can you get that, please?" she called out, still between the floor she had left and the floor she needed to reach to take that much-needed nap. She hesitated as the phone stopped ringing and after a moment her husband called from out of sight downstairs. "It's your brother, Luz!"

My brother . . . on the landline? "What's he want? I'm tired!"

"He says it's urgent," Chris called back. Now both of them back at the bottom of the main staircase, Chris held the receiver with one hand and blocked the phone's mouthpiece with the other. "He sounds upset—you should take this." His round, dark eyes communicated concern.

"Okay. I'm gonna take it upstairs." Luz swallowed.

Luz had cared for her brother as if she'd birthed him herself. She was only five years older, but since he was a baby she had been like a second mama to him. Her little brown brother, who now towered over her, had been the best *Navidad* present a little girl could ask for—a sweet, happy baby who rarely cried.

"Hey, man . . ." she said into the phone as she heard the *click* that signaled that Chris had hung up his end of the line. "Everything okay?"

"I've been trying to get you on your cell." Tomas's voice was strained.

"I'm unplugging, ya know? Vacation . . . Whassup?"

"Luz, you need to come back to the city. But, I can't tell you why over the phone."

"What do you mean you can't tell me why over the phone? Is Mom okay? Is Dad?" Her heart began thumping and her hand reflexively went to her chest.

"No, nooo! They're just fine."

"Are *you* okay?" Luz asked, worst-case scenarios running through her head.

Tomas had been crushed by the breakup of his brief marriage. He interpreted the divorce as failure, and their family did not do failure well, if at all. Luz had been there for him but worried many nights just how late he'd be out; how much he'd drink; that he'd get pulled in by cops who only saw a tall black man, not an Ivy-educated sweetheart. The fact that he'd gone this far in life and had only one run-in with the po-po gave Luz little relief. She assumed that the day would come when the odds stacked against him would take him down, if only briefly. It was just the cloud that hung over a man with black skin—no matter how many diplomas he racked up.

"No, no, I'm fine. Listen, I just need you to get back to the city. I know you just got there, and I know you're taking a couple weeks off . . ."

"C'mon, what is this?" Luz just had to know what was going on. There had never been a time when her brother wasn't completely open with her. They were confidants. And family was family. "I can't just leave Chris and the kids and say—what? That 'something's up'?"

"I just . . . Please, it's just important. We have to talk in person." He was pleading now. Strongly, though—not whining, just firmly entreating. The tone of his voice gave Luz some assurance that whatever he was holding on to, he at least felt in charge somehow. She sighed. She took a full minute to think.

"All right, let me figure this out. You need me today or tomorrow?" Luz was intrigued, but damn if she hadn't wanted a quiet night with her own family. Maybe even some lovin' with her man once the kids were down. Something about how cool it could get at night here, the kids far down the hall, a lock on the door, all made Luz look forward to snuggling naked.

"Can you get back by tonight?"

"Let me see, okay? Worst case, I'll leave first thing in the morning."

After hanging up the phone, Luz paused again. She had a feeling that she'd remember this moment for the rest of her life. There was going to be a before-the-call and an after-the-call. A "B.C." and "A.C." She didn't know if this shift would be good or bad. She just knew that life would be different. And wherever she was headed, a carriage filled with family would be coming with her.

Luz had to prepare herself first, though. Mentally. And she had to make sure her family was set with provisions, that they were safe and feeling cared for by *Papi,* before she set out to do whatever it was she needed to do. *I'll leave first thing in the morning,* she decided.

She caught her reflection in a mirror at the top of the stairs. Two deep frown lines marked her brow. *I don't remember those,* she noted. They were just like her mother's. Ma had once been tempted to Botox them away but feared the possible side effects; besides, Luz's father had said over-my-dead-body. But her mother had earned those crevices above her nose. She'd had a hard life before meeting Luz's father. She'd lived five times more lives than Luz ever would. Those lines made sense.

Now, seeing them on herself, Luz thought: *Is it my turn, now? My time to earn those lines?*

"Can I have a glass of cab, please?" Cat leaned into the bar, fairly empty at five in the afternoon. Finding herself suddenly with too much time on her hands, no show to go to, no makeup room to run to, Cat had worked diligently to avoid being at a bar, any bar, at 5:00 p.m., but this was an essential exception. She was meeting up with the girls for some much-needed *hermana* support. The early hour had been Gabi's request. Gabi wasn't currently going out at night unless it was directly tied to her business. She'd said her little one was having trouble and she had to pick him up from daycare by 7:00 p.m., at the latest. Cat wondered if that was the whole story. Gabi was more than capable of handling things, but she'd been harder to reach than usual. It wasn't like her.

Ah. Cat took her first generous sip of wine. *That's so good,* thought Cat. *I could do this every day. But I won't. Have to make sure I don't.* She was secretly pleased in that moment that her friends tended to operate on Latin Time when they met: L.T. Working in broadcast had trained Cat to live her life by the clock. Late was never a good thing, and even though she knew her posse was always half an hour late, she couldn't break herself of her on-time habits. And now she was grateful to be alone, calming down a bit more with each pull of drink from her glass.

"Oh, hey!" A tipsy, red-faced commuter in a suit and open tie called out to Cat from his bar table two yards away. He sat with a middle-aged blonde who, rather than being a fellow red face, was stone-faced. Cat saw him out of the corner of her eye and hesitated, sensing him as an "NF," a not friendly. She couldn't ignore him, though, lest he turn cranky and raise his volume. She looked at the bartender to make sure he was paying attention to this. He returned Cat's look and gave her a nod: *I got you, sister.* Cat turned only her head toward the voice.

"Yes?" Though she tried to give folks the benefit of the doubt, she'd had her share of stalker-crazies in the past, so her body was tight in apprehension.

"Hey, aren't you that girl with that show?"

Oh no. He was a worse person than she'd thought. She should have been late, just this once.

"Yeah, I am . . . that girl with that show," Cat replied, her tone between possibly friendly and don't-mess-with-me, smiling without her eyes.

The bartender kept his eye on the tipsy guy while the rest of his body went about the business of cleaning and prepping the bar.

"Yeah, good show. Good show." The man raised his glass. His companion stayed quiet.

"Thanks." Cat turned her head back to the bar, gave him a small glass raise in return, and took another sip of wine, checking her phone with her other hand. Body language for "we're done here."

It could be pleasant to be recognized, but it didn't always turn out so well. Her first red flag was this guy's happy-hour crimson face. The second and third flag were his shoes (ugly, but functional, trading-floor shoes) and his hair (ashy blond, tamped down with too much product). Cat recognized that he was likely not someone who lived in the city, around brown people, or liked things brown people liked, like immigration.

"Ya know, do me a favor and tell that Joe guy with the other show that he's an asshole." The drunk paused to swallow. "He lost me a ton of money."

Cat didn't respond but instead gave him a nod just like the bartender had given her: *I hear ya, brother.* She then thanked the stars for sending in a large group to sit down between them—just in time, preventing *Dios* knows what. *Geez, where are my friends?* Cat wondered.

"You want another one?" The bartender gave her a feel-for-you face.

"No, no, thanks. I'm good." Cat craved another glass but knew she'd have to pace herself. It could be a long evening and she was much too thirsty and on edge.

"Hey, *chica*." Magda had snuck in behind Cat and now leaned in for a cheek-kiss hello.

"Thank God you're here. Freakin' douchebag over there was giving me shit." Cat gestured with her head. At the same time she also noted with envy how Magda never had bags with her. It seemed so freeing. No baggage.

"The fat fuck. Want me to tell him off?" At nearly six feet, with a rich chip on her freckled shoulder, Magda feared no one.

"No, no. Just . . . Anyway, how are you?" No television talk for Cat. Moving on.

"How are *you* doing? You okay?"

There was no getting away from talking about her show cancellation yet. Each of Cat's friends had to check in and make sure their girl was going to be all right.

"Ya know, life goes on," Cat said, rather unconvincingly. "I'll figure it out."

"You'll do more than that. You're a brown girl, for Pete's sake! We're in demand, *chica*." Magda's drink arrived quickly and she promptly sucked down half of it in one swig, ice clinking.

Cat had filled in the gang via group text on the night of her last show. Her substitute set of sisters had pinged her back all night, back and forth, until they were assured Cat had exhausted any rage or despair that could move her to do anything that would bite her in the ass later.

"Sorry, gals, I'm here!" Gabi shuffled in, loaded with bags, Cat noted. Including a handbag big enough for Mary Poppins—though stylish as all heck—plus what Gabi called her subway bag, a tote with extra shoes, books, magazines, water bottle, snacks, and whatever else she needed to get through the day. Cat felt exhausted just looking at it all. She loved Gabi, but anytime she felt torn and depressed about her lack of a husband and children, Gabi would bluster in loaded down, scrambling with her bags. It was a reality check.

"Okay, where are we?" Gabi embraced her friends as they made room for her at the bar. "Oh, and wine list please!" She waved to the bartender eagerly.

"*Ay, Catalina-mía,* how are you feeling?" Gabi patted Cat's well-coiffed hand and bored in with her eyes of truth. Gabi could see through souls. She wouldn't tell you that she could, or what she saw, but she always knew what was really going on behind your words. There was no sense in hiding anything. Though sometimes, she would reject or ignore what she saw. She knew she did that many times in her marriage.

"I'm . . . I'm okay." Cat's eyes welled up as she reached for her near-empty glass. The bartender brought her another, plus a water, as he took Gabi's drink order. *He must recognize me, too,* Cat thought. *That's the only time I get special service.*

"So, where's your mind at? What's your agent got cookin'?" Gabi the Fixer.

"A few things, some pilots. But I can't work for another six months—contract ban." Cat paused. She'd never stopped working since she was at least twelve years old. This was a new way of living, life in a foreign land.

"But you're getting paid, right?" Money-balls Magda. "'Til your deal ends?"

"Oh, sure. *Gracias a Dios*. And I have a couple of speeches coming up, so . . . that's something."

"You have got to know that this is really the beginning of new things, new opportunity, right?" Gabi nudged.

"Gabs, I know that, but right now it just sucks."

"Of course it sucks . . ." Magda chimed in. Sunniness not her strong point.

The women were quiet for a moment. Gabi's tendency to move quickly and forge ahead was inspirational but at times it came off as too instructional, so she stepped back a bit. Magda wasn't onboard to let Cat mourn either. She knew how cutthroat the media business had become and she knew the power of timing, of keeping yourself always in the game.

"Look," Magda said, "you've got one more day to feel sorry for yourself. And then you need to realize that you cannot take this personally. You are great at what you do. People love you. Some sucky execs don't. But the streets are littered with on-air folks laid off in the past five years whose faces will never meet the gaze of a studio camera again. One day they're in your kitchen every morning, the next day, they're out. Right?"

"Yeah, I mean, Karla was great in the mornings and I can't even get a hold of her now." Cat held back a tear. "I think she's done . . . And she was great."

"Hon, you've got something, though, that others don't—a niche, right?" Gabi had built herself up from a small client base, from her first book, to guest spots on TV, and then eventually a thriving speaking and consulting business. She knew branding and she knew niche. Cat had to admit that.

"Yeah, but, and here's the thing, I hate doing it. If I have to talk about a fucking loser company again . . ." Cat's eyes stared at a knot of wood on the bar. She knew she was dropping a bomb on her friends. Cat herself hadn't known this for sure until she articulated it—that she was worn out when it came to her main topic. As the words left her mouth, she felt there was no turning back. And it felt good, if very frightening.

"Cat!" Gabi said. "Really? You hate covering business?"

Cat nodded, her eyes down in a bit of shame.

"Okay, well, that requires more thought," Magda said as she chewed ice. She was on her second drink and it was barely six o'clock. "Have you told your agent yet?"

"No, I mean, I've hinted . . . I suppose I have to."

"Have to? Listen, *chica,* if this is your happiness, head that way. But make sure you're not just angry. This would be a big move, no?" Gabi took a levelheaded stance, then paused for Cat's nod that she'd heard her. "Look, your bills are getting paid. Give yourself some time to figure out what's next before you make a big jump."

Cat knew what she *didn't* want to do, but she didn't know what she wanted. She felt rudderless. And she could never swim that well. Cat had been the personification of purpose ever since grade school. But, without purpose, what was next? If she didn't figure it out soon, she'd fall off the grid.

"Hey, you—don't forget to talk to Joe!" the red-faced interloper halfheartedly called out to Cat on his way out of the bar, pointing.

"Yeah," Cat responded. His blond companion looked over, eye daggers ready. Cat followed with a soft but snarky, "I'll do that." Taking a slug of water, she watched his back as the door closed behind him. *Well,* she thought, *at least Joe still has a show.*

Chapter 8

Magda's oxblood designer loafers were propped on her desk, soles barely scuffed. As she reclined in her office chair, closed her eyes, and massaged her temples, she thought, *Can I go one night without drinking? Just one.*

The door was closed, Magda's office quiet. The loudest thing was the vanilla air spritzer, a few *pfft-pfft*s to smoke out any lingering scents emanating off her from the night before. Magda didn't like the quiet, didn't like sitting, but she had little choice as her hangover was holding her hostage. Of course, there always was her favorite cure. The bottle stood at the ready in the bottom drawer of her desk, and a coffee mug rested next to her keyboard. When tempted, she'd tell herself, *No, not at work.* Okay, maybe. But not until 5:00 p.m.

It was well before five.

Magda was jostled by her cell phone's ping, alerting her to a voice mail. She couldn't bear to look, refusing to acknowledge the Siren song of the notification, grumbling instead at herself inside for forgetting to change her settings. Thirty seconds later, there was a knock at her door. The leader of this multimillion-dollar business straightened herself up, opened her eyes for the first time in several minutes, and popped a breath mint.

"Come in," she croaked. "Oh, hey, guys."

Magda loved her team. As the five young staffers entered,

each offered a "Hey," "Hi," or "*Buenas,*" then sat in whatever chair was available, some on the floor. Though a sincere financial leader in venture capital, Magda's firm was aligned more quasi with the casual hipness of west coast tech style—hoodies, kicks, and jeans—rather than the Brooks Brothers and Tory Burches of Wall Street. But unlike the typical west coast venture capital firm, which was lily white and completely male, Magda's was led by a gay Latina with a colorful, gender-balanced staff. Diversity was her competitive advantage. Plus, she had a chip on her shoulder about straight white males like her father. They've ruled for too long, she thought. Our turn.

"Troops! What's up?"

Her vice president, Ricardo Huang, a thirty-something curly-haired brown Jamaican brothah with a Chinese grandfather, began rattling off updates on their to-do list as some took notes quietly and others listened carefully, ready to chime in. Magda was a fun boss, a fair boss, but she demanded the best of them, just as she did of herself, at least professionally. Today, though, she struggled to focus. Magda's thoughts kept wandering to her mother. It had been a month since her last visit and she was due for a drop-by soon. A tug of curiosity pulled as Magda remembered that she'd seemed different when they spoke yesterday, off. Magda couldn't put her finger on it. She had sounded weak—tired. And how skinny she was lately. What was going on? Was she stressed? Was her dad having (another) affair? What—

"Magda?"

"Yeah?" She straightened.

The only other blonde in the office stood at the door: her South African assistant, Lyra. "Um, it's your dad?"

"My dad?"

"On the phone." Lyra scrunched up her round, pink face. Magda checked her cell on top of her desk to see if he had tried her there. The voice mail was from another firm. No call or text from family. Weird.

"Tell him I'm in a meeting and I'll ring him back."

The room was full of wide, quiet eyes. Once she came out of the closet, living and identifying openly as a gay woman, Magda's father had considered her essentially dead. There was no screaming row. It happened quickly and quietly, the way she suspected her father would get rid of anyone he wanted to get rid of.

"Sorry, Magda, but he says it's urgent."

Three months after her college graduation, Magda (still addressed as the more proper "Magdalena" by her family) came home to Miami following a mind-expanding backpacking tour of Europe—the usual wealthy-kid-finding-herself rite of passage. Unlike her compatriots from college, however, Magda went abroad not only to drink and sleep her way through Italy, France, and Spain, but to put enough miles between herself and her family so she could listen to herself, *be* herself. That meant a sultry affair with an older, wealthy, married Spanish woman who loved young ladies without shame. It also meant shedding femininity like old skin. Magda molted away her skirts, lipstick, and long hair. No more pretending to be what she wasn't. Magda was gorgeous, but from now on she'd be her kind of gorgeous, which meant jeans and T-shirts with designer sneakers or loafers, and custom suits tailored to accent her figure in a more boyish way. And a floppy-front, under-buzz haircut that made her look like the lead singer of an eighties synth-pop band. Her signature move became flinging that blond flop of hair back, like Elvis, sending many women, straight and gay, into a swoon.

After the trip, sauced and savored, Magda showed up at her childhood home in the middle of a Wednesday morning, looking much less a prodigal daughter than a son. Her siblings were off to college themselves or hanging out with friends before the start of the high school year. When Magda showed up unannounced, she could see through the windows only her mother was home, busying herself around the garden, household staff puttering on the sidelines, all busy. Magda had her hands full with bags, so rather than drop them and go for her key, she rang the front doorbell instead. The sun sat on the back of Magda's neck, exposed by her new haircut, and it felt good, liberating and new. She'd missed the hot, tanning sun and humidity of home, but not long hair. The door swung open.

"*Ay!* Magdalena?!"

Magda's eyes struggled to adjust to the house's dark interior to see who answered.

"Oh, *hola,* Miranda!" Magda noted the open jaw and drained pallor on the housekeeper's shocked face, but she just smiled and walked right in, straight through her stupor.

"*Holaaa . . .*" Miranda managed to mumble. She was struggling to close the door and release the handle. This dear woman, whose own daughter the family had put through college as if she were one of their own, wasn't surprised that Magda was gay. She'd walked in on Magda kissing a female friend when she was a teenager, and probably knew her inclinations even before then. Miranda didn't need a diploma to know the truths of the people she had seen nearly every day for the past thirty years of her life. The people whose drawers she had to tidy up and papers she would pile neatly. What shocked Miranda was Magda's physical transformation. She had hoped that as long as Magdalena remained feminine, the beauty queen, that no boats would rock, that there would be peace *en la casa.* She might even have done like Miranda's friend Elena did back home: She married *otro gay;* then they did what they had to do to have two children together but kept their true lives and loves as secret as possible.

But this. This look. Magda's hair gone, her makeup gone, dressed like that. Oh no. Miranda watched her ward walk down the hall, even her walk now different. More confident.

"Mama?" Magda called into the kitchen.

"*Ja, m'ija?*"

Magda plopped her bags onto the floor by the breakfast table and went into the refrigerator for something to drink. Her mother stomped the soil off her shoes and took off her gardening gloves as she entered the kitchen. In front of her was the backside of someone wearing a pair of hiking boots, partly covered by half-tucked cargo pants. The rest of the body of the person in her kitchen was behind the refrigerator door. She was confused.

"*Hola* . . . ?" Magda's mother said tentatively.

"Hi, Ma." Up from the fridge door popped the sheared blond head and makeup-free face of her beautiful daughter.

"*Ayyy!*" Still holding her very dirty gloves, Ma clutched at her chest as her eyes grew big.

"Hi." Magda was not interested in her mother's drama. She had rehearsed hard on how she was going to ignore it. She knew she'd have to be the one with feet on the ground. So, she gave her mother a "Wha?!" face, closed the fridge door, and turned to get a glass from the cabinet for her cold drink. Her mother still hadn't moved from her spot, nor even moved her face. Normally, she would have run to her and hugged and kissed her darling, gorgeous, pride-and-joy daughter Magdalena. She was her first and, as everyone knew, her most treasured.

"*M'ija* . . ." she managed to whisper. *My daughter.*

At least it wasn't a yell. Magda had prepared herself for some extremely negative reactions, some screaming and throwing things. But she had also hoped dearly that her mother wouldn't be anything other than sad but accepting. Isn't that what all gay kids want?

"Whatcha got back there, Ma?" Magda was determined to pretend all was well, and she gestured easily toward the garden and its blooms while she made her way to the breakfast table to sit. This table was the family conference center, the space where her mother held court and all the family enjoyed being Reveron de Sotos. Announcements, arguments, decisions, confessions, forgiveness: all happened at this table. But her mother was not going to talk about the peonies in the garden right now. Her beloved daughter was shorn. Send a child to Europe . . .

She sighed.

Magda picked up a magazine and drank a soda, as if absolutely nothing out of the ordinary was going on. So her mother sat down, too, next to her, still staring, mouth agape. Her dirty gardening gloves left a dark smudge of fertilizer on the white Saarinen table. She didn't speak.

"Well, the flowers look great," Magda offered.

Her mother still didn't speak.

"So . . . can Miranda make me something to eat? I'm starving." Magda spoke into what she was reading, her face toward the table. She was doing a worse job of hiding her growing discomfort in this moment.

Her child was now in need, so Magda's mother broke her silence, "Jes. *Sí,* sure. Miran—"

"*Sí, señora.*" Miranda was right outside the door, all too eager to hover around this conversation. "Magdalena, *mofongo, 'ta bien?*" Magda's favorite dish of salty, mashed plantains was usually best for hangovers, but right now, it'd taste like a hug.

"*Ay,* Miranda, *te amo!*" Magda smooched the fingers on her right hand and blew a kiss Miranda's way. Most families kept a bit more distance between themselves and their employees, but Miranda protected what she knew all these years and Magda loved her for that.

"Magdalena . . . *querida,* what is dees?" her mother asked her, more gently than she'd thought.

Magda turned the page of the paper, adding the crinkle of folding paper to the sound of sizzling food coming from the stove.

"Wha?" she asked her mom, shrugging.

"What do ju mean, wha?" *Mami*'s eyes looked fiery—and not with anger, but with fear.

"What are you talking about, *Mami?* I'm fine!"

"Why ju do dees? Dees?" She gestured toward Magda's makeup-free face, chopped hair, loose white T-shirt, buffed arms, and burly posture. Ma switched to English when she didn't want Miranda to understand too much. If she had taken the time to know Miranda better, she would have learned that her housekeeper understood English perfectly well. She just acted as if she didn't.

Magda sighed and put down the paper. Moving her mother's dirty gardening gloves to the side, she took her mother's hands into her own. "Mama, this is who I am."

Her mother's response was a deep swallow, a gulp, as her eyes welled up with tears.

"Ma?"

"Jes," Magda's mother whispered as she maintained her stare at her grown daughter who left their home one way only to return a completely other person, in her eyes.

"Things aren't going to be so bad." Magda squeezed her mother's shaky hands. "I can't live my life like someone else, you know that."

"Jor father, Magdalena . . ."

At the mention of the patriarch, Magda straightened up and pulled her hands away from her mother's.

"I can't live for him anymore, Ma!" Magda hissed. Her mother straightened her back, stiff, in response.

As the sweet odor of plantains and reheated pernil wafted from the stove, Miranda materialized behind her long-time *jefa* and slid a small box of tissues to her side before soundlessly moving back to the stove. Magda's mother slowly pulled a tissue out and wiped her eyes. She blew her nose loudly. Finally, she sobbed, "I don't know what he's going to do."

Magda's father was no more abusive or oppressive than any other macho, successful Latin father. But his wrath could still be a frightening thing.

Over the past several months, Magda had been so single-minded in her quest to live her life as she wanted that she hadn't thought much about how her mother would handle this. Magda knew she'd be disappointed. And she knew that her mother would have to manage her father's anger somehow. But she was pretty good at that.

"*Mami*. I'm sorry. This is not your fault, okay?"

"I know." She sniffed. "I jes don't know what to do."

"I'll take care of it, okay?"

Suddenly a lightbulb went off in her mother's head.

"*Ay, m'ija!* What about marriage and children? How can you have children?" She started to wail.

Magda had not seen this coming. This was the time before marriage was legal, even well before living with a partner of the same gender was considered normal. She leaned in again and gently pulled her mother's arm toward her.

"Mama, calm down! I can have kids, somehow, or maybe someone I'm with can have kids. But really, I'm way too young for that right now, okay?"

More wailing.

"Anyway, don't you have other kids who can get married and start families?"

"Is anyone else *un gay,* too?"

"No, Ma. No one else in this family is gay. I'm pretty sure," Magda assured.

"Okay." She stared into space now, sniffing and adding to her pile of wet tissues.

"It's going to be okay, *Mami.*" She patted her mother's jeweled hand. Those gloves protect and cover so much, Magda noted.

Miranda swung over Magda's place setting and laid down her plate. Magda dug in.

"Oh, Miranda, *tan rico!*"

"*Gracias,* Magdalena. *Disfrute.*"

As Magda moved her silverware swiftly from the plate to her mouth and back and forth, stifling her grumbling stomach, probably upset both from hunger and nerves, she looked at her mother.

"*Mami,* I'll talk to him, okay? I'll make sure things are all right."

"Okay, *m'ija.* I need to go lie down . . ." Her mother didn't make eye contact, just pulled away gently from the table in a daze.

But things weren't going to be okay. When *Papi* got home, Magda tried her usual, casual greeting as if nothing had happened; as if her father hadn't had a beauty-queen daughter—a tomboyish one, admittedly, but a glamorous one—for twenty-one years. Instead, this tall, blond, athletic-looking, gender-bending person in front of him.

Again, there was no yelling. No throwing things, no threats. He gave his first-born daughter a look like a long, slow sip from a cup, then climbed the stairs slowly toward his wife, bed-bound in shock. Magda felt the ice of his eyes behind her as she attempted to walk nonchalantly to the driveway to greet one of her siblings, meeting her before she got inside the house just in case things got heated. But that stare from him, that stare, screamed and yelled and glowered a thousand decibels. It was the loudest she'd ever hear him, for decades.

After going for a run on the local college track—sweat always cleared Magda's head—she showered, changed, and checked in with her mother. It was nearing evening and all in the home remained eerily quiet. It seemed dark and the humidity inside hung low and tight like a fog. Without even turning around in bed, her back to Magda, the mother told her daughter that her father was out and it was best if she packed her bags and left before he came home after having too much to drink, potentially exploding at the sight of her clean-scrubbed face with rage at her betrayal, which is how he saw it: betrayal. Magda was a fighter, but she didn't want to cause her mother more harm, more stress. She had known this might happen. She had hoped that it would not. She kissed her mother's hand before she left, both of them crying, her mother's hand still wet with wiped tears, and decided that it was best if she did do just that, leave. And as she raised herself up from her mother's bed, *Mami* asked her to make sure she locked the bedroom door behind her, just in case.

It was done. Magda was out. And it would be years before she'd ever see her father again. He came home after she had gone to bed, left then before she awoke, taking packed bags with him. He returned within a few days—once he knew Magda was gone. It then took a full year before Magda's mother had the fortitude to see her daughter in person, having to carve some lies to get out from under the watchful eye of her husband. Magda's choice created a house divided. Her siblings, all in their own youthful worlds of college and high school, fell to the side. They were hurt by the aftermath, living with an angry father and a quieted, meeker mother. They were too young to do anything but blame Magda, because to them, in those years, being gay seemed a choice. One maybe done by their much-stronger, more independent sister, selfishly. But only *Mami* remained on Magda's side. She knew the only choice Magda made was in changing how she looked, not who she was. The distress at home still had her a bundle of nerves, but she was also unable to tear herself away from her firstborn child, gay and all.

Chapter 9

"Oh! Sorry . . . sorry." Cat mumbled apologies as she bumped into a grumpy, burly man heading up the subway stairs. *I've gotta wake up.* It had been a while since Cat rode the subway during the day. It was cabs all day every day when she was hosting a daily television show. Not anymore. Cat had shifted into the eat-out-less, no-bottles-of-wine, no-shopping, hunker-down-on-every-dollar mode. Her bank balance was still healthy, and the checks continued rollin' in as her contract clock ticked down, but she knew the drill: It was feast to famine in this business. She knew the streets were littered with laid-off TV people. She had to be ready for famine. But she also needed to get her head on straight.

When not fully made up for the screen, Cat's face was still more colored in than the faces of most women she passed. But that wasn't just the habit and influence of her job. Cat was one of those women who didn't even walk to her mailbox in her apartment lobby without putting mascara on. For her, it was a Latin thing. Her mother was always put together perfectly, so Cat grew up with the lesson that "ju never know who ju gonna see—or who gonna see *ju!*" It went far back. In college she was even teased for wearing skirts with her collegiate sweatshirts instead of the more apropos sweatpants or jeans. And every day for years, sneakers were only for the gym. Whatever, she'd say to herself, it was true. She never knew who she was going to see. Or who was going to see her.

As she rose from underground like a manicured mole, Cat's face took in the sunlight for a moment before looking downward at her buzzing phone.

"Looks like the local folks want to see you." It was the voice of her increasingly frustrated agent. Young buck on the rise that he was, he couldn't understand why Cat was so particular about her next gig. Money was money and a job was a job, right? Not for his client, Cat.

"Local? C'mon, Guy. We're heading in that direction now?"

"We're heading in the direction of the interest, okay? It's what we've got—you want it or not?"

Cat stood on the street corner, tears welling in her eyes as strangers buzzed around her. She reached quickly for her sunglasses before answering.

"What is it?"

"A new, like, daily lifestyle thing that actually may roll out to the other affiliates if it works. Promising!" Few people made Cat cry out of frustration—and *Dios,* did she hate getting emotional, falling into the "hotheaded" stereotype—but this guy just did it to her, moved her mind into that space. He worked for her, yet he acted as if he was doing *her* a favor. At the start of their relationship, when she'd been the biggest talent on his books, it was all fawning and cupcake deliveries for great ratings numbers. But a couple of years later and here he was, repping a sportscaster who got more "likes" for her sky-high hemlines than Cat did for her reporting. Now he had decided that he was in charge and she was the needy one.

"When." Her voice was an icicle, hard and cold.

"I'll shoot you a note—look in your e-mail."

"Fine." She cut him off and swallowed her disappointment. She loved the folks at the local affiliate. And they loved her back. But everyone in the business knew that once you went from national to local, local was where you'd likely stay. Cat had met for lunch the previous week with a former network colleague of hers who had had twenty years as a national network man-of-color trailblazer—and now had little choice but to move his three kids and a very disappointed wife to Cleveland. But that was all there was for him on air: local.

"Shit, shit . . ." she hissed through gritted teeth. Just standing there talking, then thinking, she had lost nearly ten minutes—now she was going to be late meeting her mother for lunch. Now, Ma could be late for lunch, but you'd better not be late for Ma. Hell no. *My time ees valuable! Don' ju know how rude eet ees to be late? Didn' I raise you right, to be on time?* Yeah, Ma, Cat thought. *You raised me for a lot of things. Doesn't seem to be working out so well right now.*

Cat had waited tables alongside her mother from the last three years of high school through college. Every school break, every long weekend, Cat was back working those tables, while most of her college-mates were off to Jamaica to get their hair braided and lie in the sun, getting waited on by people like her. She so resented those girls and their cultural appropriation of braids and burnished, dark skin. They returned from school breaks like peacocks with new feathers, feathers that divided the haves from the have-nots. Cat, on the other hand, returned from breaks with sciatica from hauling dishes over twelve-hour shifts, relieved just to sit in a chair and study. School was her break. But working alongside her mother was a challenge Cat longed to forget, every day.

One summer, working with her mother proved particularly difficult. It was her last summer before graduation. By mid-July, Cat got the creeping sense that her mother was envious of her impending "escape" into the land of white-collar work after this final college year.

"I got a lucky penny!" Her mother held out the grungy coin, admiring it, before dropping it into her uniform apron.

Cat was busing the section next to her mother's, wiping spit-up baby bites and squished nibs of cheese.

"Where did you find it?"

"Dat table gave it to me." She pointed.

"What table?"

"Dat one." Her mother had pointed to an empty two-spot, already cleaned and set for the next couple. "But dey're gone."

"Ma . . ." How was Cat going to say this? "Ma, that's not lucky."

"Whatchu mean? O' course it is!" Ma was offended.

But the cat was out of the bag, so to speak. Now, as had happened many times before, the daughter was committed to educating her mother on the ways of the "gringos." Sometimes, Cat would just let things go. Let her mother think that "taking the bull by the horns" is an appropriate idiom in this moment. Let her think that making Cat wear an old-lady slip under her school uniform is okay. *I'll just take it off once I get to school. I pick my battles.* This time, however, Cat couldn't let it fly. She was fueled partially by the anger she felt at the couple who had insulted her service by leaving her a penny. The fuckers. Cat looked straight at her mother and propped her arm up on a railing separating booths.

She had said to her softly, so as not to embarrass her in front of the other women working, but firmly, "When someone leaves a penny as a tip it's because they didn't like your service. They're insulting you."

"Da's ridiculous! I know dees is luck and ju don' know whatchu're talking about!" her mother hissed, then stomped off to take a poll of the other servers. They might tell her the same, or maybe not. They saw Ma differently. They saw more where her insistence on luck came from—her need to believe it. Her need to believe that things were so wonderful that someone would wish luck upon her. Cat was too weighed down with feeling shame for her mother. Sensing that it was a racist incident, the gesture of bigots. After all, they were the only two brown folks in a ten-mile radius, at least.

Plus, in the "lucky penny" moment, all Cat could see was a stupidly proud woman who could never be wrong. Who barely had an education but presented herself to the world as if she were third in line to the throne. That was her role, though, as the American-born daughter—wasn't it? To be an antidote to her mother's immigrant insecurities? But what she didn't realize at the time was that the penny wasn't about her, about Cat. It was about her mother rationalizing a lack of money, of income. And why couldn't Cat allow this by-the-bootstraps woman one victory, even if it was a delusion?

The answer was because the world that Cat lived in was lonely. She was the first in the family to make it this far. And like a frightened child asking Mom to please turn on the bathroom light in the middle of the night, she wanted her mother to be with her there, in reality. Not in her fantasy land, her comfort castle. To instead be with her daughter in her difficult-to-navigate cross-cultural world. *Over here, Ma. I'm over here. Please be with me. Please be like me.*

Trying to assuage her mother's need to make sure her daughter would stay on top and on her telly, Cat suggested treating her to a fancy café uptown for lunch. She knew her mother just adored being seen with her daughter, and impressing her mother provided Cat with satisfaction in turn.

"Hey, Ma."

Her mother was standing at the host station, talking with an edgy, pocket-rocket beauty, all in black, brows raised in wonder at the mildly deluded, small woman in front of her.

"*Ay, m'ija,* I was telling dis young lady who ju are because she didn' recognize jor name." Dolores's hair was hair-sprayed just so; her lipstick, as always, was in place; her eyeshadow, as usual, was too metallic and colorful for her age. But the starch in her skirt and the neatness of her jacket balanced her overdone face.

Cat pshawed her embarrassment away, and the host shared a sympathetic smile.

"Not everybody watches the news, Ma. But wow, I'm hungry." She tried to corral her smaller mother with her arm, but didn't touch her warmly. Some would have noticed a subtle but telling lack of tenderness between the two. They cheek-kissed hello but did not fully embrace. Dolores emanated a mini-polar front that prevented anyone from coming too close. *Touching my mother gives me the willies,* Cat thought. *I don't hold her hand. It's cadaverous. I barely lean into her when we kiss.* It felt strange when Cat noticed this.

They were led to a table near the center of the room and Dolores made a show of speaking what Cat called her high-falutin' Spanish to the server helping them to their seats. *Seriously, Ma, we're not from Montevideo.*

"I canno' believe dat dis girl says to me dat she doesn' watch da TV!" She waved her hands in emphasis.

"Not too many young people read newspapers either." Cat picked up her menu. "That's just the new reality."

"Oh, hellooo ladies, my name is Ray. I'll be your server." Ray was a special breed of New York City waitstaff, a visual brand-match of his surroundings. Crisp and spit-shined, he was tight in all the right places, with just the jaunty pompadour and suspenders that said to Cat: Nope, not for your consumption, hon.

"Oooh! You're . . . *Cat.*" His lashed gray eyes shimmered in recognition.

"That's me. Hi!" Out of the corner of her eye, Cat swore she could see her mother grow two inches in height.

"Hon, I loved your show!"

Ma was still beaming. Cat was blushing.

"It was that white-haired diva, right?"

"Uhhh . . . ?" Cat was stumped.

"He took your place, hon! But know this: *no one* can take your place, Catalina!"

"Oh! Um, yeah." Cat tried to smooth over the shock she was feeling. *What?* she thought. He *took my time slot?* She had purposefully not been paying attention. Hadn't even looked at blogs or social media in at least twenty-four hours. A record.

"Listen, let me bring you lovely ladies some waters and then I'll take your order, okay?" Ray singsonged himself away.

"*M'ija,* who es he talking about?" Her mother had leaned over to whisper but made sure to maintain her haughty smile.

Cat snapped out of her stupor. She had been letting the news seep in.

"Wait, Ma. Let me check something." She pulled out her phone and headed straight to the media gossip blog. And there it was: *New Show for Grant Burge.* The son of a prominent society family and fully out of the closet, Grant had been a favorite guest on Cat's show, and though she had always sensed his ambition, he was so friendly to her that she waved off any possibility of betrayal. Was it betrayal to replace the host of the show that you started on? Probably not, but that didn't stop Cat from feeling deceived. He had to have known for a while. Yet he never mentioned it, though they had met for coffee just two weeks before. The nerve.

"So. What happen'?"

"Grant Burge got my time slot."

"Who's he?"

"The white-haired guy who used to come on my show."

Ma sucked her teeth in response. After her usual dramatic pause, she asked, "Isn' he a gay?"

Cat's eyes rolled like a teenager's. "Yeah, Ma, he's gay." Her jaw started tightening. *Here we go again,* she thought.

"Ju know I don' haf any problem *con los gays.* But, I don' see how dey could give him a show—jor show!"

"Yeah, well. He's connected . . . and talented."

"So wha' he connected!" Ma was getting loud and her bejeweled hands were starting to fly around. "Dis ees America an' it don' matter who jor parents are—ees da work and da education!"

Cat's eyes were stuck to the table. If she looked at her mother she felt she'd cry. A duo of sweating glasses of ice water were laid down, along with accompanying glasses of white wine.

"These are on me, okay, ladies? It can't be all work and no play! Now what would you like?" Ray smiled.

Cat felt brightened at the alcohol, but because she was with her mother, she was also embarrassed. She could see that there was little or no ill-will from shiny server-man Ray—he was just a bit tone deaf in this moment, not feeling the deep chill from the elder Rivera. Her mother requested the flounder in a snooty tone and Cat just muttered, "Thanks. That's so nice. Same, please."

Ray walked away briskly. Just out of his earshot, Cat's mother started back up again. "What ees dis? Why did he give us wine—for lunch?"

"Ma, he's just being nice. Probably saw us talking, and with the show and all . . ." Cat pulled the wineglass closer and breathed deeply into what she liked to call her happy juice.

"No, dees is not right. Does he feel sorry for ju? We need to talk to de manager." Her judgmental left brow rose, while her nails clicked on the table.

"Ma!" Cat sat upright. "It's just wine!"

"Listen . . . I know how dis goes and how dees people are. And it is bery bery insulting to meeeee."

"To me." *Of course.*

When Cat would do impressions of her mother for her friends, her favorite part to enact was that stance: chest out and up, neck rolling, finger wagging, drawing out vowels. She barely needed to exaggerate to get folks rolling in laughter. But in this moment, Cat was far from laughter. *My Lord, everything with this woman, everything is a fight.*

"It's not insulting to me, Ma . . . Here." Cat reached across the table and took her mother's wineglass, making a big show out of pouring it into her own, which was already only a quarter full. "I'll drink it. I'll take it." Eyes from the other tables glanced their way.

"Das disgusting." Dolores crumpled the napkin in her lap and dropped it on the plate just as their lunch entrées arrived. She stared at her daughter, eyes full of vitriol. "Okay den, ju drink and ju eat . . . since it es all about ju."

Another server had approached, balancing their flounders, just standing by, frozen in confusion, as Dolores raised herself up. And as curious parties watched, Cat's mother stomped off. She stalked out the door and Cat thought, *At least she didn't yell at the manager.*

"I'm sorry, did you want both of these?" the server inquired in a hushed tone.

"Just one's fine. And a dessert menu." Cat offered a sour smile as her double glass of wine beckoned. *Oh yes, my friend. It's you, me, buttery flounder, and some chocolate. Don't know when I'll be back here again.* She raised her glass to the people at the table on her left, who were still staring.

"*Salud!*" she said, then took a generous swig from the top. *Salud.*

Sun rays blessed Cat's hands and face as she busied herself around the apartment, getting ready to walk out the door. She was on a last-minute call with her agent before heading to tape another test show. If this worked, it would most likely blow past the usual protocol and the pilot phase, going into production right away. It was exactly what Cat was looking for: a basic talk show format à la *The View*, where she'd been a regular guest. Every network was seeking to recreate that former gold mine, though daytime TV in general was bleeding out across the board. Fewer people were watching television. All Cat cared about was landing an outlet that didn't ask her to cover the business beat. It bored her to tears, and she had so much more to offer.

Earpiece in and cell in her pocket, Cat paced and talked. "Okay, so she likes my nerdy thing," she said to her agent. "But are we sure about who else is going to be there?"

"You can expect maybe some other folks thrown in, but really, just be yourself—they love you already!" Guy was younger than she was, a Persian "Shah of Sunset" smooth-talker. *I like what he's saying to me,* Cat thought, *but compliments are not guidance. I need more info going into this—it's such a big deal. Damn it, I need someone with more experience.*

"Okay, running to a cab." She grabbed her keys. "I'll ring you as soon as it's done." She barely registered his "Great. Let me know."

Cat rushed out the door, heart pumping, scenarios running through her head. She made it to the studio in record time. Early was good.

A cute, barely-out-of-college intern greeted her at security. They made small talk as they walked down dusky hallways to small offices turned into mini-lounges, green rooms. The intern's headset squawked as she gestured to Cat to enter a room with a number taped to the door. "Make yourself comfortable. There's someone with you here—she must be in the restroom. Can I get you anything?" The intern held her clipboard tight.

"I'm good. Thanks." Cat noted an empty chair and clothes draped over a mini couch. Mini water bottles, energy bars, and snacks were piled neatly in the corner of a desk.

"Oh, Cat!" A lithe brunette with cascading locks, false lashes, and a scorching blue dress warmly greeted her.

"Oh, my gosh. Hi, Lisa!" They gave each other a hug. *Thank God this is who I'm stuck with today,* Cat thought. Lisa had been a contributor to Cat's network—and a very friendly one at that. Rare in this line of work, particularly for women. Unfortunately, she wasn't particularly talented. At least not as talented as Cat. But she was thinner. And taller. And younger. *Ay.*

A noisy group approached them from down the hall. A familiar-looking silver-haired man passed through with suitcases, followed by a woman who left both Cat's and Lisa's jaws wide open. It was the most famous reality-show mom ever. Amy had a haircut with its own following and a farm's worth of children due to fertility treatments. She had been on the cover of every tabloid for at least six months and had the highest ratings at her network. *Holy shit,* Cat thought.

"Oh my gawd. *She's* here?" Lisa was on the same wavelength.

"This is crazy." The producers had given Cat's agent the impression that it would be her and maybe four other women trying out today, but surely this meant that they'd brought out the big guns. Ms. Reality Show was just the tip of the iceberg.

"Lisa, come with me." The intern was calling Lisa to the set.

Cat was confused. How was this working? How many women were here? Her stomach roiled. This was completely unknown territory for her—a quasi-celebrity talk show with a bunch of tabloid folks. Had she ever felt so unsteady? She had to find out more.

Risking the intern missing her call—if they needed her, they'd find her—Cat made her way down the hallway. Through one open door she saw another woman, Sandy Fox, a comedian who had been a tabloid fixture in the '80s and early '90s. Cat was impressed and hoped she would be teamed up with her.

"Hi," Cat said politely. Sandy said hello, smiling in return, and Cat was sincerely tempted to stop and chat, but she reminded herself she was on an intel mission so she had to move on. Next door to Sandy was the wife of the best-known black director in Hollywood. *Dios,* she was beautiful. And tall! Cat gave another friendly "Hi." She got a wave.

NEVER TOO REAL / 93

Another intern stopped her tour of the hallway.

"Oh, Cat." She looked at her clipboard. "We'll need you for the next round. So if you could follow me, we'll get you a touch-up."

"Sure." Cat passed more potential hosts along the way—many of them familiar, but none as big as Reality Amy.

Her thoughts raced: *How do I act? If Amy is here, they can't be expecting me to act smart. But Matt told me to be myself. Well, "myself" is smart. The executive producer told him she loved how smart I am—that I reminded her of Charlie Rose, who she worked with years ago. And Sandy's a smart comedian. Lisa's very pretty, I get that. I'm the Latin flava' with a few extra pounds. But I'm just not sure who to be here to get me the gig. You do you. Me do me.*

All the prep talk was now out the window. The confidence Cat had felt before she walked into the building was gone. As a makeup brush fluttered across her lids and her hair was run through a curling iron in an extra tight, makeshift makeup room, Cat was experiencing a feeling she hadn't encountered in a while. She was feeling small, very small. She made superficial gab with the hair and makeup crew, as she always did. But inwardly, she was babbling above a pool of self-doubt. *Oh shit, what am I doing here? What am I going to do?*

"Cat?"

A producer with a headset, battery packs hanging off her thick leather belt, had popped her head into the room. *She looks like someone reporting from a war zone.*

"That's me." One more look in the mirror. It was Cat, but it wasn't Cat. Professional hands made a big difference in the business. But for Cat it wasn't just makeup versus no makeup. As a preteen, she had thick glasses, braces, and unruly mounds of "Indio" hair that required cans of spray and a crusted-over curling iron to tame. She knew there had to be some beauty trapped inside, though, as her mother was gifted with a screen Siren face. So once the braces were off, the contact lenses were in, and hair products caught up with her needs, Cat turned into the swan her imagination had wished and foretold. Now, years later, she was back to seeing mostly that nerdy, chubby twelve-year-old when she looked in the mirror—especially at times like these. Did she really want to be on a talk show with people she held in absolutely no esteem? Tabloid divas? And if not, why didn't she just walk out?

Because you never say no in television.

Cat and the producer walked rapidly through halls strewn with wires. When they finally reached the set, it was bright and elaborate, as if the show was going into production that day.

The executive producer who had compared Cat to Charlie Rose sat in the audience seats, in the near-dark, along with several other producers in a row. *If this were a soliloquy, I'd nail it,* Cat thought. It was the last shot of confidence she would allow herself.

"Hi, Cat! Great to see you," she heard from the seats. Cat smiled and waved, managing not to teeter too much in her faux-alligator, lilac platform heels. An inner rock 'n' roll gal, Cat allowed herself the small rebellion of funky shoes in the cookie-cutter world of television news, where Crayola colors were preferred and sheath dresses that showcased your boobs and ass were on high rotation.

"Cat, you're over here, to her left." The stage manager pointed to her to sit down.

"Great. Hi. I'm Cat." She shook hands as she passed the two other women who were on her panel. Reality-show mom was nowhere in sight. *Should I feel relieved?* Cat wondered. She was looking for comfort where she could find it.

A blond comedian sat to Cat's far left—no one huge, but recognizable. Cat gave her an internal "Feh." There was a former college-kid reality-show brunette who'd aged out into broadcasting. So perky and cute. And thin. *She'll get this,* Cat thought. And to Cat's right, an armchair psychologist, middle-aged but also fairly perky. Again, not a huge name.

When mics were under bra straps and behind behinds, one of the producers in the darkness spoke up.

"Cat, why don't you start on the topic of men and women and their arguments about who does more at home when both work."

The moment she opened her mouth, Cat knew she was going to fuck it up. She did. Afterward all she could remember was babbling on about clinical studies and gender roles and even Neanderthals—pronouncing the "th" with a hard "t." They had told her to be herself, that it was who these folks wanted to see, right? Her smart self? But the presence of these new people, so different from the original crew her agent heard about, meant the show's focus had changed in the past twenty-four hours. It had gone from smart women kvetching to an on-air version of *In Touch* magazine. Cat was fucked. Or so she thought.

"Okay," one of the voices from the dark said to everyone eventually. "Thanks."

The stage manager stepped forward.

"You and you, come with me." The blond comedian and the psychologist were pulled off stage. They hadn't done much better in response to Cat's initial topic intro. But neither had Cat nor her perky panel-mate, who remained in their seats. Cat was surprised but tried to play it cool, clamping her jaw shut to keep it from opening up in surprise.

Wow, she thought. *I'm still here. One more chance. Okay, woman. Rally!*

Awkward silence followed as Cat's two co-panelists were led away. It felt like Ultimate Fighting—yet the bruising was on egos only. Cat tried to regroup, her eyes darting to each movement on the set for clues as to how she'd done and who was coming to join her next.

Dun-dun-dunnn . . . Cat heard in her head. *It's her.*

Reality-show-mom Amy had entered stage left. She refused to make eye contact or greet anyone except the producers sitting in the dark, and she was scowling. *Shit,* Cat thought. *She's not going to be fun at all.*

As if this weren't enough, just behind Amy lumbered another middle-American celeb of sorts. Round, silver-haired Gloria Keene was a celebrity chef from the Deep South. Known for her love of butter, she was big beyond her waist size.

"Ooo-eeeee! Look at those shoes!" Gloria sounded so close to an actual pig farmer that Cat's ears couldn't stand it. Fuck all these surprises. It was too much. Freakin' chaos up in here. How the grand-fuck-oh-la had she ended up on this stage with these people?

"Cat always rocks some major shoes," remarked a producer in the audience.

"And they're actually comfortable," Cat said in an effort to stand her ground and just be, well, nice. But shit if she didn't sound like a whisper. Like Alice after saying okay to "Eat me," Cat felt herself shrinking. No longer did she feel five foot four (five eight in her heels), the glamorous TV personality with a serious bio and men leering at her online. The American Dream personified. She wasn't even the coke-bottle-glasses-wearing, big-haired, metal-mouth girl she'd once been. Cat felt invisible.

Her black friends spoke of often experiencing the same dynamic. How some people make you feel invisible. That they own the space they take up in this world with entitlement and privilege, and they're happy to remind you how much space *you* should be taking up. Less. Much, much less. Let me remind you, Cat. Let me remind you of your place, now, ya hear?

"Are you serious? Y'all can't be serious, those heels!" Gloria—puffy face, poufy shirt, cotton candy hair, and blue eyeshadow—

stood above her, pointing at Cat's shoes. Meanwhile, she hadn't greeted Cat yet, didn't even say hello, and hadn't even looked her in the eye. It's as if Cat didn't even exist.

Southern hospitality must be reserved for certain people, Cat thought. *Bitch.*

"Yes! *These* shoes are comfortable." Cat pointed at them, too, grabbing at Gloria's eyes with her own.

"Oh, now, stop it," Gloria pshawed. "Let me see—what size are you?"

Oh shit, no, Cat thought. *Here we go.*

Three seconds felt like thirty minutes as Cat's quick mind tried to tackle the situation, pick it apart, and find a chance to take charge herself and turn things in her favor. *Oh, I know what you're doing,* Cat thought. *You appear all smiles, but you are a smiling snake, that's what you are. I see you, Gloria Keene. Butter on the outside. Rot on the inside. I got your scent, woman. I'm on it.*

"Seven and a half."

"Ooo-eeeee, girl, let me have those shoes! I wanna try them out—that's mah size, too!"

Everyone on set and off was watching this very strange interaction, Cat noted. But her body made up her mind before she had a chance to think. Her reflexes said, Fuck it, sistah, this a shit-show. Keep on playin' and see where it leads. Cat took off her shoes, lavender alligator peep toes with four-inch heels and at least an inch of platform. *Takes mad skills to wear these, she thought. Let's see if Madame Butter-fly cannot make a fool of her damn self.*

Cat winced as Gloria stuffed her puffy, pale, flat foot into one of the shoes. *Oh God, they're gonna get stretched out,* she thought, everyone still watching them—watching this strange "show" that was happening, well off-script for the day. Even Reality Amy sat quietly as Cat caught her stewing, pissed at all the attention not going her way.

Gloria popped herself up on Cat's heels as the stage manager quickly stepped to her side with an arm just behind her in case she fell.

"Well, now, lookee here." Cat watched her shoes walk away from her on someone else's fat feet. Gloria teetered like a toddler in a tiara. She headed toward the front of the stage, making sure that all eyes were on her. "I'm gonna salsa! Where's my musi-cah!"

Boundaries played a big part in Cat's life. People who had respect and regard did not have their boundaries breached. They did not have their shoes taken off their feet in public, then mocked. Gloria putting on and prancing around in Cat's shoes was the equivalent of pissing on her territory, like a dog. Those shoes? Gloria's grotesque, side-to-side runway pantomime said, "Mine." This stage. Mine. This show. MINE. And don't you misunderstand, little brown girl. Don't mistake who's in charge here.

Fuck no, you're not in charge. Cabrona.

As Gloria neared the end of stage right and had to turn back, Cat bent down, swallowed her repulsion, and took Gloria's old, sweaty, black orthos and slid them on her well-manicured bare feet. She knew as she did this that she was pretty much fucking herself over in terms of ever landing this show. But she'd already pretty much failed and besides, she didn't want this damn circus anyway. She was tired of being the butt of jokes and being made to feel lesser than. She was tired of feeling powerless, after all she'd accomplished. If she were a different gender, different color, with this brain, this drive . . . She was done being disrespected. Cat had had enough.

"Ooo-eeeee! Lookee me! Lookee me! Where's mah buttah? Where's mah buttah at?" Cat pranced around just as Gloria had, tossing her black hair back and forth, walking as if Jabba the Hutt had legs and feet.

The tone and temperature of the set changed drastically. Everyone had laughed nervously at Gloria's display, which all knew was an over-the-top appeal for attention. But there was a combination of sucking teeth, sincere twittering, no-she-didn'ts, and silent horror at Cat. Her performance crossed over into darkness and drama.

It was amazing what being let go for the first time ever could do to a hardworking, straight-A person. Cat's world had been rocked by losing her show. She was on the road to questioning many, many things she had always taken for granted. This small conquest in this small but rich moment was propelling her in a new direction—but where? She didn't know, necessarily, but she knew that with these damn ugly, squishy shoes on that she felt a twinge of something that she hadn't felt in decades. An old, but familiar, tug. A lure toward something far away, but full of promise. Cat felt that tug, then felt it disappear. She came to amidst the applause of the stage hand, clapping for her.

"Oh, girl, that was good," the sound engineer said to Cat as she adjusted her mic and Gloria huffily traded back her shoes and they all sat back down. Surely Gloria had said something during Cat's pantomime, but all Cat had heard was clapping, whooping, and the roar of blood in her head; all she had seen were the lights on the stage. She had purposefully blocked out Gloria's reaction because she didn't want to feel bad about what she was doing. Plus, Cat had taken over, with force of will. Like a conquistadora, she had stood on that stage, and said, "Move over. This is mine. Because I say so."

Cat was a solid person and she knew what she had done wasn't right or mature, or maybe even sane. She had sunk to this woman's level—but then again, she had beat her at her own game. All the bullying that Cat had been subjected to growing up had finally come in handy. She knew from experience that laughter can expose the truly insecure—can turn a bully into a runt.

Medal for me, Cat thought. *Boom. Mic drop.*

The next ten minutes following the Gloria-Cat shoe

throwdown were like a balloon deflating. Some newsy topic was thrown out for the women to chat about as a group. Exhausted from what she'd just done (and feeling like an oxygen-sucker herself), Cat barely spoke. It was Amy the Mom's turn to take her place on the stage and boy, did she ever. Talking, talking . . . Cat stared at her mouth moving but didn't hear a word. Whatever she said, it was monosyllabic and not too bright. Ugh. *Who's the bully now, Cat?* She told herself to tone it down. *Never turn into one of them, hon. Just turn the tables.*

Before she knew it, Cat was done. Having been told by her agent that she should be ready to tape all day long, she was booted off the stage and out the door before eleven a.m.

Here's to the small victories—or losses, Cat thought.

Normally, she would have started making phone calls the second she had one foot in a car to review what happened with her agent or gossip and whine to Gabi or Luz. This time she didn't say a word aloud. She didn't even pull her phone out of her handbag. She barely said hi to the driver. She rode in silence.

Now what, idiota? *Now what?*

Chapter 10

It was late as Gabi put her ear close to the apartment door after she knocked. It was the entrance to Magda's penthouse apartment, a space of cool grays and chrome. The doorman knew her and let her up. Usually there was staff milling about, either Magda's assistant, her driver, or one of the two nannies. But instead, it was still and quiet. Gabi only heard the muffled sound of a siren from the street, sixty-eight floors down.

The chrome and colors were muted, but Magda's place was happiest when it was loud and full. Magda's children were her joy, but Gabi feared that due to her friend's most recent split with their mother, Magda was on her way down. She'd mentioned something lately about her mother.

"Hey! Stop splashing your brother." Magda's suitpants were about as happy about getting soaked as her little boy. "I see that business again, sister, you're out—understand?" "Ma-Da" leaned forward and pointed at her kids, five and seven years old. Pools in high-rises in Manhattan were rare, and this was a grand one. It had the added benefit of fourteen-foot glass doors that opened onto a terrace for sun-worshippers. Right now the closed doors served to allow Magda's booming, scolding voice more space to echo.

Young Ilsa and Nico settled down a bit while their

afternoon/evening nanny—a petite grad student aiming to get into the FBI—called them to the edge of the pool to reiterate their mother's direction. These were Magda's children, the girl the oldest, with her former partner, a Panamanian-American director of a nonprofit, housed in a downtown office building Magda owned. Magda was "Ma-Da" and the kids called their other mother—their birth mother—"*Mami*." Albita was one of the loves of Magda's life, but their fights were seismic and Magda's drinking and traveling were just too big a burden for Albita to bear. Plus, she'd always suspected that Magda wasn't faithful (and she was correct).

But they both loved these kids. Gorgeous, growing munchkins of joy. Magda needed them and the respite they brought her badly. Thankfully, her ex knew how vital they were to Magda's sanity. Unlike many a partnership that ends in a messy splat of drinking and bitterness, their split became all about parenting their kids—together.

"*Hola, mis ninitos! Listo para galletas?*" As Magda settled back into her pool chair, scrolling through her phone, she smoothed over her blazer and squinted like a misplaced business mogul at summer camp toward a singsong voice that floated through the entry door. As soon as the word *galletas* registered, both children yelled and thrashed in unison toward the stairs of the pool, scrambling to get out. Ilsa left her brother in her wake, but catching the nanny's raised brows, she turned to help pull him out of the pool.

"*Abuelaaaaaa!*" they yelled together. The small, well-put-together woman in her sixties, brunette with highlights, full makeup, gold jewelry clanging together, shopping bags in tow, bent down, stretching her face into the widest smile her enhanced lips would allow to kiss and hug her grandchildren.

"*Ay, yay yay, mi amor . . . beso . . . beso a ti . . .*" She held both in her arms, wet brown skin and all, looking into their hazel eyes with unconditional love. "Ju look so yummy, I gonna eat ju up!" She buried her face in their necks, little Nico first, then his sister. "Mmmummm mmmummm mmmumm . . . Mmmummm mmmummm mmmummm!" she gobbled.

The kids squealed a response.

"*Pero, Abuela, donde están las galletas?*" Nico pleaded for the promised cookies as he tried to stop his grandmother from eating up his shoulders with kisses. *Abuela* finally stopped when he put his little hand on her mouth, trying to push her away.

"*Ay, ay, mi* lipstick . . . Okay, okay! *Aqui están.*" She took out a box and handed it over their little heads to their nanny, who was ready to take it from there. "*Pero!*" Her long, red-nailed finger pointed up for emphasis. "Ju must wash dos' hands before ju eat, okay? Deh pool *es tan sucia.*" Nico huffed and puffed just before his big sister pulled him over to the shower stand in the corner. Ilsa knew that as sweet and loving as their grandmother was, you did not mess with her directions. "Dere go my babies!" She patted down her dress pants and looked across the pool to see her daughter with her face still in her phone, having barely raised her eyes.

"Hi, Ma," Magda said quietly. She heard the *clip-clip* of her mother's heels head her way.

"*Ay, mi'ja,* why with jor face always in dat thing . . . The world goes by ju, and ju wouldn't even know it." Carolina Soto Reveron was a handsome woman. An older and darker version of her daughter. She was petite to Magda's nearly six feet, and as she liked to joke when this fair, lean child came out of her and grew up, "My husband may have gotten the outside, but I got the inside—the most important part!"

She leaned down and cheek-kissed her daughter in greeting. Magda offered a hint of the same, eyes still on-screen.

"Maaaaaa, I gotta work. Two minutes—just let me finish this last one."

"Okay, fine, fine." Magda's mother pulled up another chair and sat down next to her. The room was quiet without the splashing and laughter of the kids. They were across the room wrapped in towels, nibbling cookies happily, while their nanny busied about. Magda's mother sighed.

"So." She smiled at her daughter.

Magda dropped the hand holding her cell, waited a beat, then placed it on the side table behind her.

"Okay, Ma, here I am."

"Now, das better! Well, Nico looks like he's grown three inches, he's just so handsome, like a movie star with those curls and those eyes, and Ilsa, did you get her to try out for the dance school yet because she's a natural, *tu sabes* . . ."

"I know, Ma. The doctor says Nico's on pace to be my height and next week is Ilsa's visit to the dance studio." Magda approached her mother's tendency to rattle off questions and comments like working her way down a memo, addressing bullet point by bullet point, all in order.

"*Que bueno.* An' ju look tired, *m'ija.* Have ju been for a facial this week?"

Magda kept her eyes on her kids while her mother talked to her. Ay, *with the "beauty" stuff.*

"No, Ma. Not this week. Just lots of travel."

"Hydrate, hydrate! *Mas agua, mi amor.*"

"Yeah, I do that, Ma." Magda winked. She may have been fairly masculine in appearance, her mother accepting secretly her life as an openly gay mother and successful businessperson, but damn if Carolina didn't continue her obsession with looking good. *Venezuelans.*

Magda's mother paused for a moment. Her hands both on her lap, she stretched out her fingers and seemed to be admiring her nails, hesitant to ask her next question.

"How's Albita?"

"She's good, Ma. No worries there. She's got the kids after tomorrow. I'm off to the Cali house for a week. Lots going on over there." In addition to her apartment in the Manhattan skyline,

Magda had a modern ranch in Salinas. It wasn't as flashy as this, as she worried about keeping up a big home so far away, but it had to have room for her brood. And it had to impress the women she took home when the kids weren't visiting.

"*Ay,* again? How long?"

"Just a week."

"So, who's with you out dere when da nanny doesn't go with ju? Ju have staff?"

"Yup, just a couple of assistants." *Uh-oh, here it comes,* Magda thought.

"*M'ija.* It must be lonely, no? All alone in dat big house . . ." Carolina had little inkling of her daughter's proclivities. Instead she clung to the traditional idea of Latin families living and traveling in packs. The idea that a woman, even a woman like Magda, would live by herself, so far from her east coast family, was bizarre. There was much buzz in the family and among the wealthy of Miami about Magda's living situation. She had homes on both coasts; an ex-almost-wife who happened to be black (horrors!); mixed children with two mothers! But at least they had good hair.

Magda sighed. She took a breath to take her mother in for a moment. She noticed something.

"Ma. Did you lose weight?"

Her mother waved her off. "Bah, no, *un poco* maybe."

"You're thin already—what happened?"

"No'ting, *m'ija!* I'm good—*todo bien.*" Carolina patted her daughter's hand with her own, her heavy rings knocking on Magda's knuckles. It seemed a stronger pat than necessary. Then she winked, stood up, and called after her grandchildren, clapping her hands. "*Abuelita* time! *Abuelita* time!" *Clap, clap.*

Magda looked at her mother's back. Her jacket draped over her bony shoulders. The cloth of her pants seemingly too empty of their contents.

She wondered.

* * *

As Gabi held her breath, waiting at Magda's door, it was strangely quiet, even for an early evening when the kids were at the west coast house with their mother, Albita. Rather than knocking politely, Gabi rapped sharply this time. The text message that had brought her to Magda's door was one of those text messages that sets a loving friend's heart vibrating with concern. *Someone needs me,* Gabi thought. Her own personal song.

"Yeah," a voice croaked.

It took an extra second, but Gabi recognized that voice. She'd just never heard it jangle like rocks in a bag before. She turned the knob. Unlocked.

"*Holaaa?*"

Gabi didn't need to go far around the corner to see Magda, barefoot, in only her suitpants and a button-down, monogrammed shirt. Her back to Gabi, she was facing the bar and fixing what was most likely not her first tequila of the day.

"Is that my favorite piece of ass?" Magda delivered her slurred query not as playfully as the words sounded, but with a sad and low timbre and tone. Registering grief, Gabi instinctively felt her former feelings of deep love for Magda nudge up against the surface of her heart. The blond woman's back was still turned as she took a swig from her next drink, her shoulders hung low.

"Hey." Gabi dropped her bags onto the slate gray floor by the extensive granite kitchen island. Magda matched her oyster-toned surroundings to a T; the sun-yellow tone of her hair and her rose-flushed cheeks were the only warmth within a thousand square feet. Except now for Gabi's colorful Brooklyn ensemble and messy curls, which clashed with the space like the hippy peacock she was. Gabi, like a walking kaleidoscope, stepped tentatively toward Magda's broad back. "Sweetie . . . what's wrong? What happened?" It had to be serious, Gabi knew, as Magda did not despair over lost loves or lost business deals. Dios, *I hope it's not the kids. Not the kids.*

Gabi heard the gulp of a swallowed sob. This was a bit frightening. Magda didn't cry as far as she knew. At least not that any of them had ever seen. Stoic to the end. Compartmentalizing at all turns. Steeled and hardened when her family pushed her away when she was young and needed them. But as Gabi wrapped her arms around Magda's tall back, the top of Gabi's head reaching just below her shoulders, Magda couldn't keep it together.

Floodgates. Gabi held her and rested her blushed-up cheek on her former lover's crisp, pricy dress shirt. Magda set her drink down with her left hand and put her right over Gabi's, now resting on the middle of her chest. She let the tears flow. They were heavy tears. Not only of sorrow and fear, but of regret and nostalgia and anger. Her father's first phone call in years had been to tell Magda that her mother had stage four pancreatic cancer. There was little or no hope. It was too advanced. She had months, maybe.

"Ya . . . ya . . . Magdalena. I'm here for you. . . ." Gabi rubbed Magda's back and neck. Of the group of girlfriends, she knew the most how Magda had become skilled at sending her emotions to solitary, never to emerge again. Here was an escape from the asylum. Or more like a revolt—it was not going to be contained.

Magda's tears splattered the glass top of the elegant bar. She turned to hold Gabi in a full chest-to-chest embrace. Gabi's hold gave Magda permission to cry and heave.

With her therapy practice and her time working in psychiatric hospitals, Dr. Gomez had become accustomed to managing the tears of others. But although she sympathized with the emotions she encountered professionally, she had a mission in that context: to be useful. Now Gabi wondered: If she let herself feel Magda's despair, what would she find within herself? Her own pain was being held prisoner. Her marriage felt like it was ending. She felt that her life was a fraud, a failure. And her son. How he made her heart ache. Gabi opened the door of her heart a crack and let some of the pain seep in. It was enough to get her own tears flowing. After the previous night of rejection by her husband, after trying so hard just one more time, it didn't take much to turn a brook in her into a river tonight.

Magda abruptly straightened herself up. "Gabi, Ma's dying. Cancer . . . Gabi . . . I can't lose her." Now that words were flowing, the water stopped. Magda sniffed brusquely and wiped her face.

"Oh, Mags . . . Okay, okay," Gabi responded. "*Ven*. Let's sit down. I'll get your drink."

Magda lifted her head and snorted hard. "Actually . . ." She picked up her glass, jiggled it to distribute the melted ice and swung the contents down in one throw. "Can you make me another?" She handed the glass to Gabi.

"Go sit, I'll be a minute." Gabi wiped the remaining tears from one of Magda's eyes with a matronly swipe of her thumb. This was no time to be scolding her for excessive drinking. If ever there was an appropriate time to drink like mad it was when you find out your mother is dying.

Magda dropped herself onto the wraparound couch. She settled back, ignoring the panoramic view of the city to stare at the apartment's loft ceilings. She kept hearing a voice saying, *What? What? What?—What am I going to do to help her? What am I going to do without her? What am I going to do with my father? What are my sisters going to do? What are the kids going to do without their abuela? What? What?*

"Here." Gabi interrupted Magda's despair with the bell-like sound of ice clinking in a new drink. Magda swiftly swigged the tequila and lime. Gabi watched with a tight chest. She knew, not only as a friend and former partner, but as a professional therapist, that Magda's need for drink was formed by the appetite of the abyss in her heart built from a life of rejection from her unaccepting family. She had lost the love of her father simply for being essentially who she was born to be. And if she couldn't win back her father's love, then she'd show him. She'd make more money than him. She'd bed more women than him—she'd always known he was a Don Juan, sleeping with women who were not her mother, not his wife. She'd punish him by not needing him in the slightest and outperforming him completely. And all the while dressed in a man's suit, a better suit. But all this wasn't working right now.

And as grateful as Magda was for her mother sneaking around to see her daughter and grandchildren, she also was reminded each and every time that the visits and phone calls and e-mails were clandestine—just another secret, like her gayness had been a secret for so long. Magda was sick of secrets. And finding out her mother was dying meant the end of the secrets. Or did it?

Gabi handed Magda a tissue. "So, your father called you?"

"I know my sisters put him up to it. The man hasn't called me in years."

Gabi remained silent, allowing Magda to tell what she wanted to tell.

"When he got off the phone—because I couldn't say much, I was just . . ." She jiggled her glass of melting ice. "He tells me which hospital and then says I should probably come down to see her . . . But don't call her. *Don't call her cell,* because she's resting." Magda's sorrow stepped aside as anger took a turn at the wheel. "He had to say that, right? Had to tell me to not call my own mother!" Magda pushed herself up from the couch like a swimmer pushing off from a pool's edge. She strode to the windows and stared at the twinkling cityscape around her, arms crossed.

Gabi spent the next hour finding out more regarding the diagnosis, more about what the family was doing, talking Magda down when she'd get riled up, and making another drink or two for her. Though the sadness remained, Magda was done with tears. She had filled her annual quota. Her heartache now turned into ire at her family, her father, and the universe. Magda got more drunk as she got tired. Her long limbs sprawled across the expanse of the couch, she wound down as Gabi sat upright and alert, needing to stay awake for her own family.

"Hon?" she whispered.

"Yeah?" Magda was officially *borracha*. She could barely lift her head.

"Mama, I gotta head home to the *familia,* okay?"

"Aww . . ." Magda flipped her right side over to face Gabi, eyes still closed.

"You're going to be okay, yes?"

Magda nodded slightly in response.

"Want me to call Andrea to stay the night?" Andrea was Magda's beloved housekeeper. A diminutive Ecuadorian and young grandmother, she was as trusty as they came. And with the bonuses that Magda gave her every year—Andrea had managed to put two girls through a local college, and her first grandchild already had a Magda-financed college fund—she would run through fire for her employer.

"*Ay,* mamaaa . . . Can't you es-stay with meee?" Magda was now holding Gabi's face in her hands, pulling it slowly toward her own. Pleading like the lost lover she was. Looking to assuage her psychic pain with physical pleasure.

"*Ay,* nooo, you know I can't."

Magda had tried several times over the years to rope Gabi into a lovers' reunion, always when she tipped into intoxication. This time, as distraught as Magda was, Gabi knew she couldn't succumb. She disentangled herself from Magda's strong arms and legs, which then went soft and loose with rejection and exhaustion.

"But I looove youuuu . . ." she moaned.

"I love you, too. I'll call Andrea—she'll be here soon, okay?"

Magda didn't answer. She had blacked out already. Head down. Gabi asked her cell to "call Andrea." When Andrea answered, Gabi explained the situation as she picked up her bags.

I've got to help her. But I have to focus on Maximo, my pobrecito. *It's time to bring in the girls for help.*

Chapter 11

"I made it," Luz muttered to herself as she stood outside her brother's apartment door. Having flown in at the crack of dawn and cabbing it to the city as fast as she could, Luz was flustered. *What the hell was going on?* she'd asked herself nearly every minute since her brother had called her the day before. *The bastard.* She knocked.

"Hey, Tomas? It's me."

She heard the muffled shuffle of deck shoes on hardwood.

Her handsome younger brother opened the door with a "Hey" and quick embrace but could barely look Luz in the eye. That wasn't good.

"So, what's up?" Luz demanded.

Tomas remained oddly silent as he led her from the foyer into his minimalist bachelor pad. As her eyes adjusted to the bright lights of his loft-framed living room, all dark wood and angles, Luz was struck dumb with confusion.

Sitting on his leather couch was a young, gorgeous, if obstructively hip-hop-styled, brown teenager. This couldn't be her brother's girlfriend. Too young, barely legal, even for him, and too "street." *Ay Dios,* Luz thought. *He had an affair and got this girl pregnant.* Luz stood across the low glass coffee table from the girl, jaw agape. She knew she should look at her brother for some answers, but she was awestruck by the fact that this long-limbed, lollipop-headed, door-knocker-earring-wearing creature remained seated, quiet, with her face in her phone, typing and scrolling, not acknowledging anyone around her in the slightest.

After thirty seconds of no eye contact, Luz snapped at the teen, "Hey!" Tomas had slipped quietly away, probably to get his sister a glass of water from the kitchen and move far from any potential explosions.

"Yeah?" The girl still didn't look up. Her jeans were too tight, she had too much hair, the ends were dry, her mascara clumpy, her sneakers worn down at the heels. But she was gorgeous. Cocoa skin, just a shade less honey than Luz's. Broad lips and nose balanced by the highest cheekbones Luz had ever seen.

Luz wasn't in the mood to be sassed, and she still didn't know who this girl was, so she stood still, taking it all in and waiting for either Tomas to get back or this *chica* to turn polite. Finally the girl raised her chin, tore her eyes away from her cell, and looked full on into Luz's face.

"Hi." It was a shy voice and even meeker eyes.

Dios mío, Luz thought. Her eyes.

It was rare to see a blue-eyed brown or black girl. Luz remembered a cousin of her mother's with emerald eyes and black skin, young and handsome in a suit, but outside of that, there was no one beside Luz in her family with eyes any color but shades of brown. Her mother chalked it up to recessive genes and a great-great-grandfather who was a German-Jewish plantation owner in the Dominican. But that was nearly one hundred years ago. And here was a girl who looked very much like a taller version of Luz at her age . . . right down to the eyes.

"Hi," Luz responded, her voice catching. Something clicked.

"So you gals have met?" Tomas was back with a water for

his sister. Luz held her hand out for it without moving her eyes from the girl's. Luz breathed in sharply and commenced an investigation.

"Tomas. Who is this?"

Without meeting his sister's drilling gaze, he said plainly, "This is Emeli. Your sister."

Luz took another brisk breath. Your *sister?* she thought. *Not our sister? My sister?* The girl still sat, now biting her nails. Luz had mistaken her lack of manners for sassiness, but she realized instantly, as the girl's eyes started pooling with tough tears, that she was fighting back and losing—that she was scared. Out of her element and scared.

How was this possible?

Luz sat down on a side chair. Emeli's eyes finally dropped.

"My sister? Our sister?" Tomas shrugged and threw his eyes at the young girl. Luz turned to her. "Emeli?"

"Yeah." The girl didn't look up.

Luz turned back to the only person capable of more than a *yeah.* "Tomas. What . . . ?"

"Yeah . . . Um, Em, I'm gonna talk to Luz for a bit in the kitchen—need anything?"

"Nah, I'm good. Thanks." The girl went back to her phone.

"I'll just bring you another ginger ale, okay?" Tomas tapped the table in front of Emeli with assurance and turned to the kitchen.

Luz slowly peeled herself off her chair and then her eyes off this girl—her sister!—to follow her brother in search of some sorely needed answers.

"Tomas, *whaaat the fuuuck!*" Luz hissed, just past the door-jamb so Emeli wouldn't hear.

"Give me a sec." He was strangely focused on getting this girl a soda, Luz noted. *Ay.* He had to have known about this girl for a while. The eldest in the family—*the family I know*—Luz sat and drummed her gelled nails on the small table by the stove.

Her back was to the kitchen door. She heard the glass set down on the living room table, his voice a tone of concern and reassurance to the teen.

"So . . ." Tomas began as he returned to the kitchen. He slid himself into the chair opposite Luz. "Here's the really big news, though."

"There's bigger news than that person sitting out there?!" Luz's eyes bugged. "That girl—teenager!?"

"Yeah. So, Dad is not your real father."

"*What?*"

"Shhh! C'mon! She feels weirded out enough as it is."

She *feels* . . . *Oh Lord*. Luz closed her eyes and shook her head. It throbbed and reeled.

After a beat she opened her eyes and stopped her preacher sway. "What . . . What are you talking about . . . Please, Tomas." She didn't have to work to whisper this time. The wind had been knocked out of her. She was tight with her father. She loved him dearly. She identified with him.

"Ma had an affair." Tomas had the annoying habit of letting words out too slow to Luz's liking. She felt he was cheap with his words, withholding. He wasn't a bad guy. Just a bit controlling.

"More," Luz demanded with her eyes closed.

"Mom and Dad broke up for a while just before they got married. Remember how she was kinda puffy in those wedding pictures?"

Luz nodded.

"So, that was you, she was pregnant."

"I knew that. Everyone knows that she was pregnant with me when they got married." She was trying to be patient.

"Well, so . . . While they were broken up—for, like, I dunno, six months or something—Ma had a fling with Vivian's cousin."

"Vivian? Mom's friend from Claremont?"

Luz held her head in her hands, rubbing her temples.

"Who was this guy?"

"Well, that brings us to the girl—Emeli—sitting on the couch."

"*What* does? *What* does, Tomas? Would you spit it out!"

"Emeli's father is your biological father, Vivian's cousin whom Mom had a fling with before she and Dad got back together and got married."

"And what about Dad? Does he know this? Did he know all along that I wasn't his?"

Tomas nodded.

"He knew this whole time . . . ? My whole life?!"

Luz sifted through her memories. She was particularly close to her mother. She looked little like her darker father. But, Tomas did. He looked very much like their father. His father. *But he raised me,* she thought. *And he knew. Why didn't they tell me? When I used to ask over and over again why I looked different from the rest of the family, why didn't they tell me?*

"And this guy, this . . . Vivian's cousin. Who is he? Why is *she* here?"

"He was . . . well, he's alive. He's just, like, a guy from the 'hood, ya know?"

"From the 'hood?"

"Yeah, Luz, like a gangsta." Tomas leaned down to whisper so Emeli wouldn't hear his politically incorrect phraseology.

Luz's eyebrows went up. This day was getting crazier by the minute.

She shout-whispered back, "My father—my biological father—is a drug-dealin' gangsta from the Heights?"

"Yeah, a Dominican guy."

"Of course."

"He just got locked up."

"Just now? Locked up?"

"Yeah, but not for the first time."

"I'm sure." She paused. "Wait. Why is she here only now if he's been put away before? Where's her mother?"

"Yeah, well. She died four years ago. Aneurism. Hard life." He shrugged.

"I bet it was hard." As soon as she wisecracked, Luz regretted it. "I'm sorry."

"It's okay." Tomas was turning his glass around and around as it sweated further into the small pool beneath it. "It's a lot."

Luz pinched the bridge of her nose. There were so many questions. So many consequences.

"So, where's he staying?"

"Who?"

Luz tutted. "The father."

"Upstate. Long time."

"How long?"

"Dunno. At least twenty."

"Jesus. Did he kill someone?"

"Nah, three strikes. Just dealing."

"Oh, gee, I'm so relieved." They both chuckled slightly.

"Um, can I plug this in somewhere?" Emeli peered shyly around the door frame, her big hair defying gravity. She held out her phone and waved it at Tomas.

"Oh! Sure, sure. Over here . . ." Tomas led her back into the living room. He wasn't gone thirty seconds before he returned, from his sort-of-new sister to his now technically half sister. Luz hadn't moved from her seat.

"So, help me with this," Luz commanded. "She's here now because her mom's dead and her father's in jail?"

"Yes."

"But why is she *here?*"

"Well, her dad ended up sending me a Facebook message through Vivian. I thought he was full of shit, you know, just wanting money, but I knew he was for real because he knew stuff about the family years ago that's not online, ya know?"

"Mmm-hmm."

"So we traded e-mails and then he put me on with his mom, who was just rambling and rambling *en español, sabes?*"

Luz made a *pffft* sound and a cut-it-out sign. They had grown up speaking Spanish, but Tomas had been so sucked into preppy culture that he couldn't even roll his *R*s. His Anglo accent drove Luz nuts.

"So she begged me to take Emeli in. She said she lived in a studio apartment in the projects so she couldn't take her—being so pretty and all—and that Emeli's father didn't want to cause trouble for Mom after so many years, and that I was the son, so I should be the man and take care of family business."

"Well. Wait, because you're the son—the man?" Machismo was rare in Luz's life and she wanted to keep it that way. She thought it was the scourge of their culture. Tomas gave her his tenth shrug of the day. Luz scoffed. "So does Ma know?"

"I wanted to tell you first . . . It's killing me, though!"

Luz had no sympathy for the newly single bachelor and regular withholder. "When did she get here?"

"Yesterday. Right after I called you."

"So she was alone with you last night?"

Tomas nodded.

"Good thing you're divorced."

"Yeah, Jeanne would have hit the roof with this girl."

Luz let out a big breath. They heard the television turn on. Emeli's cell must have run out of juice. Tomas started to get up to help.

"Sit. Leave her be. She's not a baby." Luz didn't know what these feelings were in her. Her thoughts and emotions were kinetic and confused, a swirl. There was a lot of negativity roiling and she made a note to temper it. She knew much of it was selfish. She was a mother and the oldest—she was used to taking care of people. But not a foreign fifteen-year-old who looked like Luz if she had been brought up back in the 'hood—

had never been "saved" by her Vineyard-legacy, black-elite father, the one who plucked her mother up and out of uptown Manhattan. Her mother, a beautiful, brown Dominican woman, younger and "exotic." Her mother used to love that word, "exotic."

"Luz, I can't keep her here." It was Tomas's turn to plead.

"What?" Luz snapped back into the here and now.

"It just doesn't look good. She's a teenager and all, and . . ."

"And, what?" She wanted him to say it.

"And she's your, like, sister, technically as much as I'm your brother."

"Oh, for fuck's sake, Tomas."

He shrugged. Luz understood: the gorgeous, trashy Dominicana hanging out in single brothah's bachelor pad, lookin' suspect. And she was really young. A teenage girl. What would he know about that? But . . .

"You have to keep her," Luz insisted.

"What?!"

Luz waved him down from his panic. "Just until I talk to Mom. And Chris. And the kids. And Dad."

"Luz, I can't wait that long!"

"Well, it'll happen fast, okay? I'm not like you, Mr. Secret Man. I mean, how is this even possible? That we have a sibling and the man who I thought was my father is not my father and my mother doesn't even know about this girl and I'm supposed to just pick up my life and . . . and . . . I don't even know what the fuck!" She was standing now, gesticulating.

Tomas just looked at her.

"Shit, man," Luz said. "Shit." How could her mother have kept this secret all these years? How could her father have done the same? And how could her "real" father be someone she considered a low-life? She knew a lot of black men and the good ones knew what to do, how to act. How to take that target painted on their backs since birth and throw it to the wind, where it belonged. Like her father had done, and had done with Tomas. Sure, her grandparents, her father's parents, were professors and he came from a long line of free, Northern, educated blacks, but still, he was a black man who had lived through times even more dangerous than the present. And he did it, he made it. Shoot, her brother did it. He kept himself straight and didn't knock anyone up, had no baby-mamas—

Oh Lord. Her own mama was a baby-mama. *Carajo!* This was a stereotype Luz had been working all her life to avoid. All these stereotypes. Fatherless, illegitimate, the sneaking around, raising another man's child, the lies, the decades—the horror.

"Tomas. I need you to take care of her."

Her brother rose to protest.

"Nah, nah, it'll be fine. Just give me a day, okay? Just a day. Twenty-four hours."

"We should do it together, right? Talk to them?" Tomas attempted to keep his responsibility alive.

"No! You have a father, okay? Your father has stayed the same! Mom owes *me* answers, not you. And he does, too. Dad." Mom owed everyone answers, as Emeli's introduction into their lives would mean a new sibling, and for Luz's children a new *tía* or auntie, too.

Luz was tearing up now, in a way her brother hadn't seen since their beloved *abuela* passed away more than a decade earlier.

"Okay, okay. Listen, just be by your phone," he said.

"I can do that." Luz pulled several tissues from her purse and blew her nose, wiped her eyes. "Shoot, you don't have no Kleenex in this bachelor pad, or what?"

Her little brother ran to do his big sister's bidding—just like old times. He brought her a new box.

"Does she have clothes, even?"

"Yeah, she came with a bag."

"And feed her, okay? I bet you guys like the same stuff, like pizza." Luz cracked half a smile and felt the dried salt tears on her cheeks crinkle.

Back in the living room, Luz was surprised to find her new sibling snoozing soundly on the couch, sneakers still on, holding the remote. On the obnoxiously big bachelor screen was a reality show about a cake-maker in Jersey—not what Luz would have thought she'd be watching.

"Wow, she must have been tired." For the first time Luz thought of how it must feel to be Emeli. Fifteen years old, suddenly moved five class-rungs up in an apartment downtown, with a new stepbrother and half sister who weren't exactly very nice to her. Her mother was dead, her father in jail, again.

Brother and sister hugged good-bye.

"It'll be fine," Tomas assured Luz, though in part he was assuring himself.

Yeah, she thought. *Just fine.*

Chapter 12

As she slid into her usual pleather restaurant booth, Cat was beginning to feel that her butt and this seat were getting too comfy. For maybe a decade now it was a repeat spot for all her close girlfriends, as well as several other urban tribes, including Long Island moms post-shopping. The upscale diner was easy access via subway, cab, or foot, open twenty-four/seven, solid comfort food—salad, too, for those cleansing days. And without faltering, pics of drag queens on the menus, hinting at the neighborhood's past. Cat visited some memories of much younger visits, usually drunk before even walking through the door.

Maybe it wasn't so comfy after all, she thought, as the memories piled a tad too high. Abruptly, Cat felt old and tired.

Gabi stumbled in, brows furrowed, but smiling. Cat wondered if she was just noticing that Gabi looked particularly harried lately? Burdened. And it wasn't just the bags she was carrying in her hands; those were a constant.

"Hi, Mama." They exchanged warm pecks on the cheek.

"*Ay*, Catalina, the traffic."

"I know. Crazy."

Cat brought up the heavy right away. "Gabs, I am *so* sorry to hear about Magda's mom."

Her friend sucked her teeth and shook her head at the same time, sighing.

"How is she?"

"Well, Magda is Magda," Gabi answered. "She's fine as far as I can tell, but she texted last night that the prognosis is not good. So, as much as she puts up that front, I'm concerned." Gabi knew it wasn't her place or her M.O. to dish further. She was a steel trap both professionally and personally.

"Of course." Cat didn't want to pry too much, but she also couldn't resist some *chisme*—she wanted to gossip a little. Magda and her glamorous but tumultuous life was fascinating to even her closest friends. "And this has gotta be crazy with her family and her father not talking to her, right?"

"I'm sure. But unless I'm there with her, or she's tossed back a few, we're not gonna hear too much about it."

Cat sighed in sympathy. A casualty of being Americanized was the loss of their mothers' tradition of reaching out across every dimension of family and friends for support. It was like playing cat's cradle—the more loops you made, the closer your hands came together and the stronger your network became. The flip side: Their mothers could be equally adept at hiding family secrets, dirty laundry, and everyone seemed to have some.

Cat decided to take a chance and break with her own everything-is-awesome routine.

Rolling her ice water in her hand, feeling the cold wetness of the perspiring glass, Cat began to be truthful for once, her eyes down in shame. "So, Gabs. I'm not doing so well."

"Cat?" Gabi's friendly empathy and therapy skills clicked into motion.

"Yeah. Well. Things just aren't landing." Cat continued to look down. Admitting that she needed help was like clean-jerking barbells. But if she couldn't reveal her disquiet and dilemma with her friend, a best-selling therapist, whom was she going to do it with?

"But, is it just a matter of time in this business?"

"Well, that's just it. It's been a lot of time . . . and in my business, timing is so important. Too much time is dangerous. You fall off the radar, you're screwed."

Gabi let silence hold the floor for a moment. She disagreed with Cat, feeling more so that the real radar is you—you control the radar and you grab that light and beam it right back in your face. But she'd communicate that to Cat in a different, more customized way to her, just not right now. Right now, Gabi felt that there was something else that was eating away at Cat. Something just as big.

Gabi was right. "And my mother . . . she's making me nuts," Cat stammered out at a clip. "Gabi, I think that's why I'm nuts . . . I think that she really just hounds me because she's so upset that she's lost the ability to brag to people about me and that's where I feel her terror coming from—I'm feeling *her* terror!—but I'm not scared so much as she's scared . . . and now she's making me nuts, *more* nuts than I'd be on my own—I can't hear myself!" It was one breathless, lifting-the-lid-of-a-pressure-cooker sentence.

"Okay." Once the mother issue came up, it was all Gabi's hands on deck. "That's a good one—let's hear you: I want to know, Cat, how do *you* feel here, now, about where you're at?" Gabi pointed her finger down at the table.

Cat paused a breath, then her eyes opened wide with panic. "Gabi, I'm too old for this shit!"

Gabi was surprised and confused, which was rare. "Old for what shit?"

"For this! For sitting here and trying to reimagine myself! For not having a husband or kids or . . . just kids!"

The server was on his way to the table to take their orders. Protectively, Gabi waved him off.

"Okay. Now I totally get it, I get it," she said. "It's a sucky time for this to happen and you worked so hard to get where you are. It's been sewn into your identity, deeply, work and succeeding and getting ahead, you straight-A bum."

"You mean where I *was*."

"What?"

"You said . . . so hard to get to where I am. It's *was*."

"No! I mean *are*. Where you are."

"Gabi, I am nowhere right now."

"Bullshit."

"What?"

"I'm calling bullshit on you." A Guru-Gabi specialty, calling out the real, breaking down narratives. "You are the sum of your parts, past and present, plus your potential for the future. No one can take that away from you, Cat. No one can take away what you've done—what you've built, and where you've come from."

Cat's eyes widened. Something sunk in. She was listening. "But, then why does it feel so crappy?"

"Because much of your identity is wrapped up in the sash someone else puts on you—a sash that can be taken away."

Cat was offended at the analogy. "I'm not a beauty queen!"

"No, but you are a Queen. And you are one without anyone else's permission or seal of approval. Your *self* doesn't depend on who hires you."

As if coming up against a wall, rather than a door, Cat deflated. "Yeah, yeah . . . I know. I hear you."

"Don't you dare 'yeah, yeah' me. I'm fucking serious, *carajo*." Gabi suffered no fools as soon as even a hint of whining popped up its putrid head.

Cat's eyes welled. She sniffed tears back as much as she could muster.

Gabi sighed. She didn't want to hurt her friend, but she also knew that this was a crisis point for Cat. If she didn't start infecting her with another way of looking at her lot in life, she could lose her like she'd seen the city eat up others. "Listen, remember that dumb *Blues Brothers* movie?"

Cat nodded.

"Well, I hated that movie—friggin' white dudes with harmonicas—but my brother was obsessed with it, and his favorite line was, 'We're on a mission from God.' These two tubby guys playing music—on a mission from God. Can you imagine?!"

Cat chuckled, remembering a music video where they danced around in black suits, fedoras, and shades, looking lumpy and frumpy, yet they were thought to be cool.

"Think about it: What's your mission from God? Not the mission your mother sent you out on. That was a pretty cool mission, but it was *her* mission, right?"

"Yup." Cat nodded. "But I liked it. I did good."

"Oh, you did more than good! You killed it! But, you also had to pay a price."

Cat nodded. "It was a big price." *An empty home and an empty womb.*

"So. Since you are a Queen and we are all on a mission from God, because why the fuck not, what's your mission? Not yo' mama's, not the network's. *Your* mission."

"Good question." Cat sat up straighter in the booth.

Gabi took a big bite of salad and winked at Cat. "You need to actually read my books, ya know."

Chapter 13

The fluorescent lights of the hospital hallway reached into Magda's scalp and squeezed. This was the side effect of polishing off three-quarters of a tequila bottle the night before combined serendipitously with the dry, metal-tube air of her flight to Miami. As soon as Magda had gotten the call from her father in her office, she rushed to wrap up only vital items at work. Then she drank too much, per usual, sobbed on Gabi's shoulders, passed out—and caught the first flight out in the morning. As one of the few in her family who had escaped the southern peninsula of Florida, including cousins, only a hop-skip-jump away, Magda assumed that most of the immediate family would be there already. She hoped not. She was there to see her mother. Not the whole clan who barely acknowledged that she was alive.

As she approached the room, Magda made out light chatter in Spanish. Her stomach clenched in reflex as she rounded the door frame and gently peeled off her sunglasses. Three of her younger sisters were there: Inez, Veronica, aka Nica, and Diana. Inez and Veronica were sitting on each side of her mother's hospital bed while Diana fiddled with a flower arrangement and an untouched breakfast tray. *All of their kids must be with their fathers,* Magda thought, *they probably don't want to scare them yet.*

On the vinyl recliner, overseeing it all, was Magda's father. She hadn't seen him in more than a decade.

But Magda's eyes gave only a cursory scan of her family, focusing her attention on only one person, her mother. Tubes snaked from the IV pole to Carolina's gaunt, chemo-burned hands, marked with rivers of iodine brown, her charred veins. She seemed pressed far too deep into her pillows than possible for her slight weight. It was as if the gravity of her being was so much heavier than her body. All this was shocking to Magda—the transformation—but curiously, what rose to the top of her mind was that she couldn't remember the last time she had seen her mother without makeup. Not her usual foundation, concealer, eye makeup—though she did have a slight gloss of color on her lips. *Sneaking in colored lip balm. That's my Ma.*

Carolina's gray eyes connected with her eldest daughter's and would not let go. And as Magda, dressed in a pale blue suit and rumpled white button-down shirt, stepped from the doorway toward the bed, everyone followed the patient's line of sight and stopped talking. Magda's sisters dropped their eyes, got up, and slowly carved out room for her as their father sat stone-faced for a beat, staring at Magda. She didn't notice, though. Nor did she notice when he got up from the recliner and joined his other daughters in leaving the room.

The disregard for a sibling or a daughter, the lack of affection for Magda, or even attention to her, was as foreign an occurrence in a Latin family as an *abuela* making brown rice. At any other time, Magda would have made a snarky crack about it, something dour and pointed to turn the pain they caused her to right back at them. Magda's heart had ached on many nights as she lay awake in bed scrolling through social media updates of her sisters and their growing families. Families she barely got to see but who so obviously enjoyed each other, far out of reach of their eldest *tía's* sinful and shameful existence as *un gay*.

Unlike Magda, her sisters feared their father. When he'd

shut Magda out, the whole family played along. Some, out of simple fear of his rage and personal rejection. Magda figured that at least one, probably Diana, was also too afraid of losing her inheritance. And though her father may have felt betrayed by his eldest daughter's choices, the bigger betrayal for Magda was that of her younger sisters, girls whom she'd cared for so well, protecting them often from the furor of the parent they now sided with. Instead of gratitude for Magda, she knew that they resented their sister's defiance and ambition. Precisely the features of Magda's that had freed her from the patriarch—but at the same time distanced her from their love. It all stung.

"Ma," Magda murmured as she reached gently to place her hand under her mother's, feeling her skin barely as thick as crêpe paper. Magda's eyes welled.

"*Ay m'ija . . . Ven,*" Carolina whispered.

Magda's broad frame enveloped her mother's shrunken one, petite already, now, like a fairy. Magda whispered a pained "Ma . . ." as she held her as tightly as she could without crushing her bones made fragile by the concoction that kept her alive this long.

Carolina pushed Magda gently off of her, comforting her eldest, though she was the one very much alive. Magda pulled herself enough away to sit on the recliner pulled as close to her mother as possible, contorting herself to keep both her elbows on the hospital bed, her now tear-slick cheek nestled in her mother's right hand.

They sat in silence, Carolina offering her daughter a sad smile, until Magda stifled her despair enough to speak. She was going to set aside her pain and do what she did best: problem-solve.

"So, tell me, Ma, what happened?"

"*Ay m'ija,* I just got sick, that's all."

Magda's forehead curled up with incredulity. "Ma, you don't just *get sick* with cancer. It takes time."

Carolina shook her head slightly and sighed, as if she

couldn't be bothered with being anywhere but in the moment, managing the present. It didn't matter to her, the why or the how. Just the now.

But Magda continued. "How long did you know you didn't feel well?"

"Oh, I don't know . . . But the doctors are going to see what they can do." Again, it's today, or tomorrow, but no looking back for Carolina. The only way for Magda to get a clear picture of what was happening would be to talk to the hospital staff. And her much-estranged family. Difficult.

Magda pleaded just once more. "Ma, why are you so resigned to this right now? Don't you want to live?"

Her mother just cast her eyes down. Her daughter's gaze was so strong, such a force, just like her father. Her mother chose to win her battles quietly.

"*M'ija,* of course, but we'll just have to see, okay?" She smiled the small, sweet smile she had always used to get her way with her macho, overbearing husband and her headstrong eldest daughter. She'd used it even with one of her other daughter's teenage boyfriends, coaxing him to walk the dog on the weekends in exchange for some of her famous *limonada y pollo asado* to bring home to the family. Magda knew she'd lost this fight. She folded.

"Okay," she sighed. "How'd you get *Papi* to call me?"

"Eh, that was easy. I told him to. He wanted your sisters to do it, but I asked him to. So he did." Carolina paused. "And how are my little *angelitos?*"

Magda brightened at the mention of her children, the next generation, the ones who live once the old ones die. You hope. "They're good. I asked Albita to swing them back here early."

"*Ay, no!* I don't want them to see me like this." Magda's mother ran her hands down her lap, smoothing out the sheets, then attempting to stroke smooth her undone, thinning hair.

"*Mami,* what they care about is you, not how you look. I'll come by with them tomorrow. And Albita would love to see you, too, is that okay? I think it will help the kids if we're here as a unit."

"Magdalena . . . So efficient!" Carolina teased.

Mother and daughter chuckled.

"How long will you need to be here, Ma?"

"Just a couple of days. I told them if I'm going to die soon, then I want to die at home."

"*Como?!*"

"What? It's going to happen anyway and I want to be in my house."

Magda knew there was no convincing her mother otherwise. She also knew that asking her questions about her treatment plan was a waste of time. Even with a physician as a husband, her mother didn't want to know anything when it came to her own health. She was old-fashioned and took orders. They heard muffled sounds near the door.

"Looks like my time's up, Ma." Magda took her mother's hands again and kissed them gently. "But I need to see you, okay? I'm not going to let them keep me away from you."

"No, no, that won't happen." She swatted away the notion. They hadn't kept her away from her daughter in nearly fifteen years. She knew now that her eldest would return the gesture.

"Yeeees, yes, they'll try. But no worries, I'm back later tonight." Magda stood up.

"Okay, *mi amor.* Be well." She leaned to the right to let her daughter kiss her head.

"And I'm bringing you a full bag of makeup," Magda scolded.

"Oh! Yes, yes, *por favor, m'ija.*" Her mother's eyes grew large with anticipation—makeup was a welcome distraction from the maelstrom about to hit Magda outside. They blew each other kisses. Magda turned toward the door, her attitude transforming from love to hard concern.

Carolina's hospital room had been dim. As Magda entered the hallway, her eyes needed to adjust to make out what family members were still there, waiting for her to leave.

It was her father, on his cell, and her sister Nica. The grumpy one. The only other bossy, headstrong one in the family besides Magda. Nica had inherited their father's worst quality, his brash, judgmental demeanor. And she had seemed all too relieved when Magda was forced out of the family, so she could take her place. Nica saw herself as a queen bee—and as everyone knew, there can be only one queen bee.

"How is she?" Nica asked sharply. "You didn't get her too upset, did you?"

"She's fine," Magda responded, ignoring the second part of Nica's question, a trap. Instead her eyes were on her father, anticipating when he'd get off the phone. Magda sniffed at Nica and turned away from her sourness.

Nica glared at her older sister's back and entered their mother's room, leaving Magda and her father alone in the hallway. He looked up at her as he tucked his phone into the pocket of his linen pants.

"So," he said, chin in the air.

"How long did you know she was sick?" Magda's tone was accusatory.

"She hasn't been sick long. This cancer comes on fast."

"Bullshit." Magda was taller than her father by an inch or two and she had no trouble stepping into his personal space, her anger radiating. She hoped her father could feel it searing his skin, burning him as much as it was blistering her.

"Listen, you . . . you . . ." He couldn't say it as he pointed at her face, the nasty slur he was looking for. "Don't you come in here now and cause trouble."

"*I'm* causing trouble? How, Pa, huh? Because my presence offends you so much?"

"It does offend me. It offends the whole family! Your sick lifestyle."

"Sick?!" Magda smirked—she was bemused by his words as they stood in a building filled with people who were actually sick, people so sick they were dying and wouldn't be on this earth anymore, people like her mother. "Well, too fucking bad, *Papi!* Guess what? I exist. And I am her daughter, just as much as those three there." Magda pointed to the hospital room. "I don't have to be *your* daughter, but I am hers. And I have every right to be here for her, no matter what you think of me and my *sick* lifestyle." Magda hissed that word, hissed it for the poison it tasted of. Like it was such an easy choice to make—the real sickness being hiding who she was for so long and being disowned for it.

Her father's face was frozen into a grimace. But he didn't say a word. He glowered and seemed to be calculating where to take this next.

Magda took the moment. "Why did you fucking call me anyway? Why didn't you have one of the girls do it, huh?"

"Only because your mother asked me to . . ."

They both paused. Then, both reminded of why they stood where they were, what circumstances had brought them face-to-face, many wrinkles ago, Magda's father directed his anger at the impotence of them all in that moment, that place, right at his daughter.

"So what?! So I did—I did call you! I didn't have to, but I did it for her! And now you come here and get me upset and get her upset and embarrass this family even further . . ." His arms swung madly as sweat beaded on his tanned forehead. Magda's father's anger was explosive, always had been. There was a calm, then a storm. If the storm took a while to come, you might think you'd gotten away with something. But no, the storm always came. And hard. However, this time Magda was ready to stay on her feet.

"And what the fuck did she have to do to get you to call and tell me what was going on? Because you can*not* tell me that woman hasn't been melting away for months and you didn't notice a thing."

He tried talking over her, but her voice was younger, stronger, her passion and rage too old and deep.

"I bet you *didn't* notice! I bet you didn't notice because you had your head up some *puta's chocha* in your office, right?" Gut punch.

"Like you are no different, eh? Like you can judge me, huh?! Thinking you're a man, having children with women . . ."

"You were too busy taking care of yourself and your needs to know your grandkids or love your own daughter!" Magda drove her index finger into her own chest.

Her father wasn't moved. "Don' you fuckin' talk to me like that, you transsexual!"

"Oh, that's a new one! Good one, coming from a doctor! I'm a fucking tranny now!"

"You are an embarrassment to this family, an embarrassment to me, to your mother, to—"

By now the nurses were calling security and Nica had reemerged from the room. Inside, Magda's mother lay crying quietly at the sound of her family fighting, Inez and Diana holding her hands, trying to soothe Carolina against the rumble of her husband speaking so hatefully to their daughter.

"You know what, *you* killed her! *You* killed her!" Magda was now in her father's face, pointing, nearly chest-bumping him. "You knew she was sick and you didn't do anything! You couldn't give a shit, could you, you selfish fuck!"

She was screaming now, her arms ready to hit something. Her father hollered in return, trying to double his size, raising his arms, shaking his head furiously.

"Stop it! Stop it, both of you!" Nica wedged herself between them. "Get out, Magda! Get out!"

A tense, sad-looking security officer stood nearby with a hand on his baton, ready to step in if needed. A burly nurse had his hands on his hips, scowling at these two adults airing soiled laundry in a building full of people with their own sorrows and pain.

"That's enough!" he said. "You two need to get out *now*."

They both stopped abruptly. Magda's father centered himself, tugged at his dress shirt, and walked out—a prominent local doctor couldn't afford too much drama in a hospital. He left his daughter wound-up and huffing. Magda paced, running her hands through the long top layers of her hair as if stroking her brain, her mind, to soothe it. The bear of a nurse approached Nica.

"Hon, she's got to leave, mm-kay? Like now, or this officer will escort her out."

"I'll take care of it." Nica patted his arm.

He raised an eyebrow skeptically as she walked toward Magda.

"You need to leave, Mags." Her sister was relishing this moment a bit too much, Magda felt.

"Fine. Fine."

But Nica wasn't done. "Did you really think you could just come in here and blow things up like that? That mom didn't hear the whole thing? The both of you are just awful."

Magda paused, her face showing real care as it dawned on her what her mother had just heard. She felt culpable all of a sudden, nauseated. She had so easily let her anger get the best of her. Magda might even have given her father what he wanted, played into his hand. He liked seeing reactions to his actions, enjoyed moving people around like chess pieces, pulling strings. Feeling happy today? Let me remind you of that bad grade you got last week, or that second piece of cake you ate that will go right to your hips. Feeling bad today? Let me help you feel worse.

"I would be around if he let me and you know that," Magda sighed.

"He's never going to accept you and how you live," Nica responded.

"Yeah, and I guess you all go along for the ride, right?"

Nica paused. She didn't have a good answer. At least an answer that made her proud. Her favorite emotion.

"Magda, all Dad has is Mom. Yeah, he has the practice, the other women, but he's just an old-fashioned macho and when she goes, he goes. You should have just kept your cool. You're not the only one hurting here." With that, Nica didn't care to hear a retort, so she turned brusquely and headed back into their mother's room.

Magda wanted to go in and apologize to her mother. And complain. And rage. But she knew that now was not the time. Magda was like a walking ghost of her younger self—she had scales of resentment and layers of bile to rid herself of before she could see her mother again. It wouldn't all be gone in a day, but she could at least try to get a grip on it.

As she squinted to squeeze out the last tears, wiping them roughly away with her hands, she felt relieved to see at the end of the hall her nieces and nephews followed by their parents, all coming to see *Abuelita*. Magda got up off the hallway chair and headed in the other direction so the little ones who had barely, if ever, seen their other *tía* wouldn't see her this way. With broad strides she worked to build distance between their sounds of wonder at being in a hospital and her internal gloom.

As Magda stepped into the elevator, she realized something for the first time: If she hated her father, then she hated parts of herself. Like his temper and his strident tendencies. His way of turning a blind eye to things he didn't like or understand. His philandering. His drinking. When they fought in the hall, Magda realized that they must have looked like mirror images of each other, one just a few inches shorter and older. Mirror images.

There was a bar Magda liked down the road, at a hotel she knew all too well. She jingled her keys in her hand and thought: *Just one drink. And maybe one pretty lady. That's all.*

Chapter 14

"Jesus Christ, I needed this so bad." Luz's curls looked wilted, like thirsty hydrangeas. She reclined almost fully in the restaurant booth, her head tipped back for a few seconds while the lanky server brought her a generously filled wineglass.

Gabi took her in. She loved Luz dearly and deeply admired her chutzpah, not to mention her doting, involved husband. But both married mamas found themselves together tonight for an urgent infusion of sistah *amiga* support.

"Okay. First, *salud* . . ." Gabi began. Luz raised her eyebrows, curious as to what her friend could be toasting to at this moment. ". . . to family: new and old."

"Ha!" Luz brightened. "*Salud* to that."

Both swigged down their wine like water, comfortable enough together to follow their gulps with heads bowed as if in prayer. A "*Gracias a Dios*" for the dulling, soothing effects of this powerfully calming substance.

"I just don't know, Gabs . . ." Luz started off. Following the revelation of Luz's newfound sister and father, one of the first calls she made was to Gabi, the rock-solid therapist friend. Her steel-trap of a mouth helped, too. Luz wasn't ready to share this news of her newly discovered convict father and his rather "urban" teenager, who was now her sister.

Gabi leaned in. "Tell me: What's happened since yesterday?"

She quickly changed her priorities. "But wait . . . first, first, and most importantly, how are you doing?"

"G, I absolutely don't know how to feel. I haven't done much but cry and rage like a banshee to poor Chris . . . and then fend off texts from my desperate brother who's going nuts in this position." Luz paused for another swig. "I'm beating myself up at being so, so angry at my parents, my mother, even my father! I mean, dad, dad-father . . . the man who raised me!" She threw her head into both hands and let out a moan.

"Hon." Gabi put her right hand onto Luz's left forearm. "It's a lot to take in. A lot. Give yourself a bit of time. Anger is a very natural response to all this. Shit, it's a LOT."

"Is it, though? Is it a lot? Does it change anything?!" Luz's azure eyes flared. "I've never been angry like this at my mother or my father, for anything, *annn-yyy-thing*." She drew out the word with her fingertips in a gesture handed down from her mother. Then she leaned back and reined it in. "This completely on-fire, pissed-off feeling is so foreign to me, yet, it's like . . . my life's been a lie—who I am is a lie. My identity! I'm fucking pissed!"

"Hon, I hear you, I hear you. But please remember, you are the sum of a lifetime's worth of experiences, and nothing, no one, can alter that. No one can change who you've been for over thirty years."

"But it's not like I'm starting off being the daughter of a gangster to winning the lotto in life and being the daughter of an Ivy League brother—it's the opposite! It's switched. I'm going backward." Luz's eyes shifted from lit by ire to heavy with hurt.

"Luzita. You are not going anywhere. What you're describing, it's textbook loss aversion. We hate to lose what we already have and you have something truly great in your family and your father—the one who raised you—coming from a very prominent and historic family that you're proud of . . . Nuthin' wrong with that. But they're not lost. You've just added to the . . . uh . . . rainbow of your life's story." Gabi turned playful for a moment, joking about her own hippieness.

Luz rolled her eyes. "Yes, a fucking rainbow! So what am I now? A full-blooded Dominican with no African-American legacy—I mean, you know Dominicans don't want to admit they're black, right?"

"Yeah, we share that one."

As their salads arrived and they oohed and aahed in thanks at the generous amounts of pancetta on their frisée, they continued to talk it through and Luz started to come down off her tight perch, the wine and soothing pork fat taking their effect. Gabi kept her advice to a minimum, instead letting Luz process and release as much as possible before she stepped in.

"Gabs, I don't know who to be mad at first . . . I mean, everyone lied, my mother, my father—dad—but, but, besides the lying, I don't know what I'm really angry about."

"Well, what are you angry about?"

Luz set her fork down. "I'm scared."

"Scared."

"Yeah, really scared." Luz's eyes started to well up.

"Can you tell me more about that?"

"Gabs . . ." Luz was very tentative. "I can tell you this because you won't judge me, right?"

"No, Luz. I don't judge you."

Luz sighed. "I've spent my whole life being able to enjoy a very cushy life. An admittedly lucky life. I haven't been a statistic—the huge numbers of us who have family in jail, fathers incarcerated, brothers—and now I've not only joined those rolls, but I have a surly, hip-hop teen who needs a mom, and a dad, and . . . and she's my sister. When it comes to my life, my family's life, she might as well have been dropped from Mars. . . . Don't judge me."

"Hon, not happening," Gabi assured Luz. "I get it. I get it a lot." Luz mentioning her fear of being a statistic resonated with Gabi. She knew that at some level, she rushed into marriage because she heard her biological clock ticking and didn't want to be another unmarried Latina, another single mother of color. *Shame on me,* she thought. So who was she to judge when it came to being embarrassed about becoming, or being, the so-called underclass of their ethnicity? And here she was, a relationship expert, a professional, possibly heading toward being another stat, a divorced parent. Maybe even a single parent.

"Luz, I don't want you to deny those feelings in the slightest, but . . . but here's a big opportunity. You mention privilege, and luck. Think: For the luck of your birth you are not or were not your sister. You got the big roll of the dice. She didn't."

"It could have been me."

"Yes, girl. It could have been you. And that's for all of us, frankly, but wow, for you, it's a very real and very close alternate universe of sorts."

Luz gulped as her mind's eye imagined it for a moment. "Too close."

"But, so, here's the rub. What if in many ways this isn't so much about you, but about that girl. Your sister."

"Huh?"

"Your 'alternate' universes are meeting and meeting for a reason. Maybe for her reason just as much as yours. Imagine, you're giving her the opposite of loss really. She can have a life now full of gains. Sure, she's lost her mother and even lost her father for a very long time, just as you've lost some ideas of who you are. And you both can mourn that, and you will." Gabi wiped errant salad dressing from her mouth. Luz had barely moved while she spoke and didn't eat another bite.

"But think, Luz, your loss is her gain. And who's to say that that's not the universe's plan for her and for you—for you to change someone's life on such an elemental level, she's won the lotto."

"Yeah, she did . . . but, but . . . ."

"Yeah, I know, your sitch is a bit opposite of lotto, but I think this girl will be the biggest gift to your family."

Luz raised an eyebrow. "Really?"

"You're big on legacy, right?" Luz nodded in response. "Your father has an amazing legacy, especially as a black man."

"True dat."

"Well, as Latinas, particularly Latinas like us, of black descent, we have our own legacy—it's not as rosy or pretty or quote-unquote 'good,' but it is what it is and your children and family will now see how most people of their shade and heritage live. Shoot, you're like a bridge, girl!"

Luz couldn't help but smile. She loved civil rights references. "Okay, I get it."

"See it through her eyes for a second—you're the grown-up!"

"Okay, yes, feeling a bit better now. The anger, falling aside a bit . . . ."

"That's my girl." Gabi winked.

As they talked for another hour, Luz processing and Gabi guiding, Luz began to notice the sag in Gabi's shoulders. Gabi, the brilliant boho, was the sprightly one, bubbly, energetic, a light. But Luz, Cat, and Magda had all felt and noted to each other that Gabi seemed more and more stressed and rankled at her husband lately.

"G? What's going on with Bert?"

"Ya know. I dunno." It was Gabi's turn to put her fork down, licked clean of her favorite panna cotta, and smooth her napkin. She thought and took a last swig of her drink. "I mean, I do know, but . . . ."

"G?"

"Luzita, I'm like a doctor who smokes. I feel like the lawyer who breaks the law, the cardiologist with a fast-food habit."

"Wait—what do you mean?"

"I'm really concerned about Bert. About us. But see, I'm the therapist—I should be able to fix this. To just . . . fix it. But I don't know if I can."

"But you guys seem so happy, right?" Luz was genuinely concerned, yet slightly insecure about what to say. Gabi was a type-A gal who never asked for help. She was the helper, not the helpee. Talking candidly about their husbands, without the armor of neck-rolling and cliché husband-bitching, was a new thing for her.

Gabi didn't look up from her plate as she absent-mindedly rolled, then unrolled her napkin. "He's drinking now every day—every single day—and a lot. Whiskey. And it's getting to be too much for me to run everything and support the household . . . I mean, it's gotten to the point that I don't want to leave Maximo at home alone with him at night because they get into nasty rows, and when he's drunk, he's not good. Just not good."

"Oh, Gab-sters." Luz was deflated and taken aback. "Is he cheating?"

"Probably. I dunno. I'm blocking it all out."

Both women sighed and assessed the weight of what had just been revealed. The packaging of the weight was different, but the mass, strangely the same.

"Have you confronted him about all this, or, how much?"

"We've been in weekly therapy for a year, but seriously, this woman is not doing a thing. She's too soft on him, and I feel like the nagging wife—she's completely transferring something, someone to him of her own. There is not enough digging, too little analysis, and no demanding on her part that anyone take responsibility for what they've done."

Luz was nearly done with her plate. "Well, now, that just won't do." She shook her head. "Is it hard to change therapists because you know so many people in the business?"

"Nah, sort of. But we're all in therapy; it's just a matter of finding one who works and is discreet. I'm giving her another week or two and then I'll look for someone else."

"Hmmm." Luz was somewhat at a loss. When a friend shifts into an unfamiliar place and you're excelling in that place, it can get awkward to be the blessed one. Luz may have her own current problems but thankfully, not in the marital area.

"How's Chris handling all your news?" Gabi shifted her attention back to Luz.

"Ya know, he's just the best. Seriously, I know I hit the jackpot in the husband department, but let's just say it's all gonna balance out as I hit the lotto with fathers." Luz shifted into a game-show voice: "You've just won a *brand . . . new . . . father!* Your father comes with a home in the woods, also known as prisoooon! And if that isn't enough, you've also won yourself a brand . . . new . . . juvenile delinquent sis-TAAAH!"

Gabi laughed. She could always count on Luz to sauce things up just right. "Oh, girl, you too much . . . But yes, you won the jackpot with the hubby."

"Gabs, will you let me know if you and Maximo need a break?"

Gabi smiled and nodded as their glasses were refilled. "Yeah."

"No, really. Just because I have a new daddy don't mean I don't still get use of the old one and all he comes with, including property!" Luz paused, mentioning her father's wonderful nesting and hosting skills, along with the beautiful Massachusetts estate. The thought of space led Luz to ask about the elephant she could sense in the corner of the room. "Would you leave him?"

Gabi exhaled. She gazed out the window, remembering herself in this same spot, the same restaurant a decade ago. Just another postdoc writer stretching her dollars to splurge on the fancy hot spot once in a while. What a different person she had been back then. Or was she just the same and life had changed around her?

"I don't want to be a single mother. I don't want to be a statistic, a stereotype. But I also don't want to be *una cabrona*. I've been nothing but faithful, and I've had my own chances, ya know!"

"Umm, hmmm, I know!" Luz was remembering the night at one of Gabi's book parties where a famous documentary filmmaker sidled right up to Gabi, asking when they could get together, sending her text messages inquiring when they could dine alone. But Gabi was just too good for that. She shut that man down. Now she was thinking that maybe she shouldn't have.

"I just love the idea of family too much—fidelity, loyalty. I hold on to that ideal, really. But at the same time, after all the work I've done to give him, us, a certain kind of life . . . I've given him so many gifts to try to win him back. *Ay, Dios,* I can't even think of the money I've spent. Damn, hon, I really thought this was the one."

"Well, he was the one to give you Maximo! So, okay, now it's my turn to tell you to not be so hard on yourself."

"But, Luz, how would it affect my business to divorce, to have my marriage fail?"

Luz's eyebrows raised as she recognized in Gabi something that all the friends shared: fear of failure, period.

"Listen, don't you think you owe it to yourself to be happy— or even better, to be respected, to show Max as a man how to be respected and be treated with pride?"

"Sure, but . . ."

"Nah, no buts." Luz waved her fork in the air. "You've told me yourself that you can't live your life for other people. It's gotta be about you and that beautiful boy of yours. If it can't be or won't be about loyalty and wanting to keep your family together for the sake of togetherness, then you can make it about you and Max—making sure that you and Max are treated with the respect and love you deserve."

"Yeah, but the business . . ."

"Fuck the business. You know that you'll do great at anything you lay your hands on." Luz found the anger in her against Bert grow, and her desire to protect and love Gabi and her lovely little Maximo took top shelf in her mind. She hated to come down so hard on such a huge decision—which was to be Gabi's and Gabi's alone—but she didn't want her and Max to be exposed to this selfish, entitled "bro" another moment.

"Sweetness, I do not have a safety net." Gabi paused before adding, "Like you do." The net was money.

"I know." Luz acknowledged with her eyes what was hanging in the air. She had a husband who had sold a start-up for millions and a father with a sizable inheritance. Gabi was the first and only in her family to get into six figures, and she had neither an inheritance nor a husband with earning potential.

"Look, I don't want to make you feel bad here, Luz. I love what I do, but if this were to fall apart, I don't know . . . I'm exhausted."

Luz nodded gently. "Will you please bring Max and stay at the Vineyard for the weekend? Please?"

"Ah, thanks, Luzita. That's nice. I've got TV bookings all weekend, though."

"How about two weekends from now?" Luz asked. She wouldn't let Gabi off the hook so easily. Her friend was a workaholic, admittedly both out of necessity and out of drive, and could barely stand to give herself the time for a twenty-minute bubble bath (which may have happened most recently ten years ago).

Gabi knew she needed it. But even more, she knew Maximo needed it.

"Yes? Great. I'll make sure we don't drive you nuts with the kids—and who knows, by then I might even have to bring along my new *hermana*." Luz curled her lip as she said "sister."

Gabi brightened at the mention of her, the opportunity to assist Luz in return. "Maybe I can help with that one."

"Yes, yes! Lord only knows, I have no clue what to do with this girl."

"Just do me a favor?" Gabi asked. "Try to have a forgiving heart with your mom. Families have secrets, and though we may not agree with why they're kept, I'm sure this secret wasn't kept out of a lack of love for you." Gabi placed her hand over Luz's and squeezed gently.

Luz smiled sweetly, her brow furrowed. She took those wise words in as she thought in return, *But, my dear Gabi, someone is keeping a lot of secrets from you, and it's definitely not out of love.*

Chapter 15

The doorbell chimed a second time.

Fine, Luz thought. *I'm fucking coming.* She knew who was on the other side of that door. She'd tried to avoid her brother, Tomas, for a day, but with a sullen teen from the 'hood occupying his living room, and a female one at that, Luz had known that he wouldn't be able to stand it long. It was all too weird.

"Whaaaaat?" she mock-whined as she opened the door.

From the inside it was an aged, ornate wooden *entrada* bolted to the back of the building's own fireproof, condo-approved door, which was seen from the outside. She'd found the door-upon-a-door on her last trip to Mexico—in the town of Xochimilco, a tourist spot where you could board elaborately painted wooden boats to float lazily along the river that surrounded Mexico City. It was the route the ancients had used millennia ago to ferry goods. It had been magical for Luz. Now, the waterway was a colorful way to drink beer on a boat and wave to local children on the riverbanks along the way. Daily the door would transport Luz back in time to imagine those who had ridden the river before her. The door was very unlike her mother's Dominican culture and their African history—Ma had made a face when Luz showed it to her and told her where it came from. *Ay,* such nationalism, Luz had thought at the time.

"Hey, you." Tomas cheek-pecked her and moved in quickly. "Hi. Whassup?"

"I've been cal-ling youuuuu . . ." he singsonged, deflecting her annoyance with his charms. As always, Tomas looked well put-together. Not as preppy as their dad, Luz thought. But definitely reducing his odds, in that button-down, of being pulled over while driving black.

Luz knew she was in the wrong for delaying her brother's needs passive-aggressively, so she had trouble looking him in the eyes. "Listen, I've been on the phone with Chris for, like, hours. He's trying to manage the kids on his own and figure out if they should come back now or wait this out a bit."

In some families you'd expect a younger male sibling to head right for the fridge, pull out a cold one without asking, and plop himself down in a comfortable spot. Not Tomas. He and Luz were playful, but he had been trained to respect her authority and especially her personal space. Luz was big on personal space. When they were children, he remembered how she'd become tense if people were over, particularly if anyone wanted to go into her bedroom or dared to touch anything of hers. When sent by his parents to wake Luz up on lazy weekend mornings when she was a teen, Tomas would practically tremble at her doorway and call out her name in a whisper. She was a golden child to their mother and was also treated with kid gloves by their father. Now he felt he had more insight into the why.

"You want a drink, a *cafecito* or something?" Luz asked.

"Nah, I'm okay." But Tomas's stomach was growling.

Luz raised a brow. "Ya know you can help yourself, okay? I'm not going to bite your head off."

"All right. I'll have a coffee." He sat down at the Saarinen marble table, all art-directed by Luz, in a chair at the end. Controlled.

"How do you take it, again?"

"Uh, light and sweet, like my—"

"Ladies. How could I forget!" She rolled her eyes.

They chuckled. As the chrome espresso machine churned out an overpriced Ethiopian blend and the milk foamed, Luz took in the small pleasure of creating this coffee. But a cloud soon rolled in over the milk foam as she noticed her brother was clearly tense. After her night with Gabi, Luz felt much softer, less judgmental. It was such a surprise to hear all that was going on with Gabi, all that Luz hadn't known about. It made her realize that maybe there was something about her, all perfect and wealthy and put-together that maybe turned people off from being open with her. Cutting her off from what was really happening with those she really loved. *How sad. I'm a jerk,* she thought. Luz remembered yelling at Tomas to get out of her room when they were kids, sometimes smacking him in the back of the head if he didn't move fast enough. *I'm the same as I was then, without the hitting. Is that why I'm terrified of this girl being in my space? I've always not wanted people in my space. Unless I chose them, like Chris, or made them, like my children. But even the kids are afraid to get into my stuff.* Luz set down Tomas's perfect coffee and sat perpendicular to him. She sighed. He slurped.

"So," Luz began, "how's she doing?"

"Fine. Fine." He still couldn't look at her. Withholding again. "Lots of TV-watchin'." Luz assumed she got her overbearingness from her mother and so her brother was much more like their (*his?*) father; he was passive-aggressive. Luz had always thought it was just an annoying personality trait, a black-blue-blood stock feature, the need to saunter around things, to avoid making waves—to get things done, at times, in such a way that you didn't even know he'd done them. But now she realized that it could just as much be the fault of her and her mother. Two in-your-face ladies made of tungsten.

"Okay, so, I talked to Chris." Her neck bent, Luz's head

hung almost to her knees. She was exhausted. "This is going to be a big deal for the kids."

"I know," Tomas responded, looking at Luz directly for the first time.

"But are you sure she's related to us? I really have to ask."

Now her brother raised a brow.

"I mean, related to me, in full?" Luz clarified.

"I talked to Cookie's sister. She corroborates the story." Cookie was Luz's godmother, her own mother's dearest friend and neighbor during their teen years, saddled with her childhood nickname all through adulthood. Cookie had lived down the hall, before she moved back to the Dominican Republic, and was a very Spaniard-looking, book-smart Dominicana, a few years older than Luz's mom. Luz was named after her—her real name, Luz, meaning "light." Cookie had been taking classes at the local Ivy university and that was how Luz's mother had met her father. Though Luz's mother's education had stopped in her teens, when the family moved to the city from Santo Domingo, Cookie made sure to connect her mother with someone who could help her move on up. *To dee top—a dee-luxe apartment in dee sky.*

"You talked to Cookie's sister? How's she doin'?"

Tomas pulled himself forward in the chair to lean in closer. "Good. But yeah, she says that she knew, and Cookie knew, but they were sworn to secrecy."

"Knew what? About me?"

"Who your father was. I mean, is. So, yeah, it seems that this is his only kid besides you and that her mother, Emeli's, had not been doing good health-wise for a while. And ya know, he'd been, like, moving around, like with other women and stuff, but always kinda kept in her life."

"Well, I hope so." A chance at self-righteousness: Luz would take it. "But had Mom been keeping in touch with them, with Cookie and her sister?"

"Gladys is still there, in the same apartment. So I just looked up her number and it was listed."

Luz sat back, nudged by the mounting evidence, and effort. "Wow. Thanks for doing that."

They sat and breathed while Tomas's coffee steamed. So much truth in the air. Huge truths sat in the room with them, big enough to be their own entities. *Pull up a chair!* A family secret. A new father. A new sister. A new kid in the family. Parents withholding. Class lines blurring, overlapping. There sits a big, fat brown mess.

But at this moment, something else aside of all these things was bothering Luz the most. Like the nasty itch of a healing burn, Luz mulled the realization that her brother was only, technically, biologically, her half brother. Sure, Luz was lighter, her eyes not brown, her nose more refined, but all black families were blended families to some extent. Except she'd always thought most of the blending happened generations ago. Not in this generation, in her bloodline. It made her ache with some sort of mourning. As big of a bully she could be with him, she loved her little brother above and beyond anyone except her own children. And now these children had another grandfather. In prison. And another *tía,* an aunt closer to their age than to hers. Her head began spinning again from the implications of one monster of an afternoon, just a few days ago, that began with a pretty teen version of herself, sitting in her brother's living room.

"I just can't help being pissed off, ya know?" Luz stood so she could pace away some of the negative vibrations she felt running through her body, an anger buzz rising. "I mean, who does that? Who lies about who your father is?"

Her brother stared into his cup, recognizing this tone.

"And Dad, too. He knew! Like, what the fuck . . ."

Tomas stated firmly, "I don't think you should talk to Mom and Dad just yet."

"What?" Luz's eyes narrowed.

"Just hear me out, okay?"

Luz sat back down. It was time for her to listen.

"Dad's blood pressure has been an issue, right? And this is really just going to hurt them both—Mom and Dad. So let's just take care of the Emeli situation first ourselves, okay?"

Luz looked up at his pleading eyes.

"I mean, she's too young to be going through this, and there's probably going to be some logistical things with adoption, or maybe legal stuff to get her emancipated—"

"Okay, just stop." Tomas straightened for an onslaught, but this time, it wasn't Luz's anger running the show, it was her realization that they had to manage this lock-step for the best results. "Before we get to that stuff, what's the situation with her father? Damage control here, okay?"

"Uh, what damage?"

"Well, he's in prison, right? This guy?"

"You mean, her, your father . . ."

"Yes, her father." *Don't you dare call him my father again, so help me* Dios, Luz thought.

"I spoke to him after you left yesterday."

Her stomach lurched. She felt disgust. The idea of this . . . convict . . . just made her sick. "You . . . you spoke to him? In prison?" Her eyes went wide. In apprehension but also in awe of her brother's management of what was essentially not his problem. *The divorce toughened him up a bit. Wow.*

"He'd like to meet you."

Luz blanched as much as her cinnamon skin would allow.

"I mean, not right now, of course! Just, eventually," Tomas assured her.

Luz's head hurt. She pinched the bridge of her nose.

"But he did ask if you could please take care of her. She doesn't have a lot of family around—good family—and he knows that she'll do so much better with you."

At the mention of "good family," Luz stood back up again, bristling. "Oh, he knows, huh." She started biting her nails. "He knows shit. That's what he knows."

"Okay, forget about him. Right now, we need to focus on Emeli, okay? We gotta keep her in school and out of trouble. Assuming she is one of us, a sister, we have to take care of her, Luz. With all that we've been given . . . I mean, that could have been us, right?"

Luz sat down for a third time, spreading her arms wider and wider until her hands grasped the sides of the table at either end as far as she could reach. She looked at her wingspan and laid her head, right cheek down, on the table, like a child. As she spoke her voice was muffled as the side of her lips touched the tabletop.

"*Mira*. Look. Just give me until tonight, okay?"

Tomas perked up, his body language shifting, communicating to Luz his relief. She then realized just how much this load was weighing on him—how scared he must be, even as a young, strapping man. *Poor guy*, she thought. *Bad me. Again, I suck.*

"Great. Great." Tomas smiled.

Luz noted his verbal tic of repeating words twice. He'd had it since grade school. When he was a kid it had sounded like a stutter. But as an adult, it sounded charming, an eccentric quirk. Not a bad thing in their family circle. *Family. Huh.* Luz righted herself.

"I just don't think I can manage being alone with her yet—but, and thank you, by the way, for taking the controls there . . ." She trailed off, allowing her appreciation to be heard first. "So, the kids are on their way back with Chris and will be here by like, five—how about you bring her by around six? With her stuff."

"Okay, six. Six is good." Luz saw a hint of a smile on his face. *Poor kid—I mean, kids.* And the stress of his divorce. Which had been a big blow to him. But it wasn't a failure. It was just a mistake. And, Luz noted, he had come out of it a better person. Obviously. So there.

"And, Luz, you're saving me because I swear my doormen are all thinkin' I'm having a post-divorce crisis with some uptown hoochie."

"Ha! Okay, that's funny, but . . . that's no hoochie," Luz teased, "that's my sister! I mean, our sister, *Dios* . . ."

"Yeah, no, your sister first!"

"Shut up, fo' reals, yo." Luz was already starting to accept the situation as just another event in her never-dull life. Just another challenge for her to manage, just another problem to solve. At the same time, she was panicking at the thought that some unrefined "hoochie" was gonna make house at her house—with her own kids. Because Emeli was Luz's sister. From her real father. Who was a drug dealer, in jail.

Coño, she thought. This was some crazy shit.

"Are you sitting down?" Luz answered the phone as Cat called right after Tomas left.

"Yeeeees . . ."

"Girl. Shit. So, my brother just left."

"Wait—what happened to the Vineyard, 'cause I've been texting you and I just called there and Chris said you'd gone home early to take care of some family business, but he wouldn't tell me what it was all about, and then all Gabi would say is 'Talk to Luz.'"

"Good man, good friend. So. Hon, I have another sister."

"*What?*"

"A teenager!"

"Wait. Your mom is, like, in her sixties—"

"No, no, it's not from Mom, silly."

"Your dad has a baby-mama? Oh Lord, Lord . . ."

"Nooo! My dad wears bow ties. He's like chastity on wheels," Luz said, "or maybe not. Okay, not going there . . . So."

"So," Cat urged.

"Speaking of my dad. He's not really my dad." *Oh God,* Luz thought. *I don't like saying that at all.*

"Luz!"

"Seems my mother had an affair or something, well, I guess they broke up—my mom and dad—the dad that . . . Argh!" This was so hard to wrap her head around. What did it mean? Who was she now if not her father's daughter? Did it mean she couldn't claim his legacy bloodlines? Hadn't she inherited her bookishness from him—her sharpness? Who was this new man who supposedly was her father, and what had he given her besides her light eyes and lighter skin? *I can't just stop Dad from being Dad,* Luz thought. *I can't just stop him being my father.*

"Luz?"

"Sorry. Just processing."

Luz did her best to share the backstory with Cat, filling her in on the details.

"So he's in jail now," she said, wrapping up, "and he got in touch with my brother and had someone drop off a teenage girl, like a total, like, ghetto girl." Luz felt bad saying that word "ghetto." She knew it was elitist, even racist, and she hated when she got this way. Some Vineyard snob had really rubbed off on her and now here she was, "ghetto" herself. *Takes one to know one.*

"Ghetto? You mean like a girl from the 'hood?"

"Yeah." Luz paced again, rubbing her head. There were so many places her mind was running and each sentence she spoke seemed to lead her down another route that she was just discovering. The father-route, rife with brambles. The mother-route, messy with loose ends. The sister-route, burdened with the weight of how the other half lived. What seemed to hold all these together in a swirl was Luz's insides asking: *What does this mean about who I am?*

"Well, is she nice? Did you meet her?"

"I did. At my brother's place. That's where she's been staying."

"Girl, you can*not* let your brother take care of a teenage girl!"

"I know. I know. That's why he was just here to ask me to take her in."

"So, are you?"

"Yes." Both women paused. "Yes. And the kids are coming back tonight with Chris—who I haven't even told all this to yet—and then she shows up like an hour later."

"*Carajo.*"

"You said it."

"Want me to come over and help?" Free of the responsibilities of children or spouse and now even a job, Cat welcomed the distraction. "I don't want to be in your way, but I'm here if you need me."

Luz, for once, was grateful for the aid. "I may need you tomorrow, if you don't mind. I just don't think I feel comfortable with her here, just the two of us. I mean, I don't know this girl, and I don't know how to feel. . . ."

"Totally understandable. But . . . how is she feeling about all this?"

"What do you mean?"

"I mean, Luz, is she okay? And what is her name, anyway?" Cat might be short on family, but her heart was huge and her empathy personal.

"Oh. Yes, I mean, yeah. I guess. Yeah. Um, she's Emeli. Like 'Emily' but spelled Dominican, weird, with like three E's or something . . ." Luz was still in staccato mode and slightly taken aback by what felt like a reminder to not be selfish. "Wait, Cat?"

"Mmm?"

"Cat. This girl, I mean, Emeli, and her world are all new to me. I mean, forget for a second about my whole new-dad thing." She growled in frustration. "Just . . . I mean, the kids will probably love her because she's beautiful and young and cool and shit."

"Yup, they will."

"But, what if she disrupts this house? What if she completely throws everything off? What if she gets between me and Chris? What if she brings in drugs! I mean . . ."

"Okay, just stop for a sec. Luz. She's not going to ruin your marriage or your family. She's going to *be* family. So you guys will all adjust and I suspect that just as much as you fear her being an influence on you, you guys can be a great influence on her, right?"

"Right. But will we?"

"I have no doubt that you will. But it's not going to be easy."

"Tell me something." Luz sat and then paused, sucking in a breath. "Don't take this the wrong way, okay? But, you grew up kinda like this girl—"

"Emeli," Cat corrected her friend.

"Yes, Emeli. So, can you help me out with her here? I mean, I just don't know how to deal with someone like that, ya know?"

Cat sighed. She pressed Luz, annoyed. "Like what?"

"Like, from where she's from!"

"Look, she's from the city, right?"

"Yes, but—"

"But nothing, really. Look, she's a kid and we all were kids and you gotta treat her like your kids," Cat said gently.

"Well," Luz harrumphed. "She's far from being like my kids."

Cat was beginning to take offense. "Okay, now. That's just not . . ."

"What?!" Luz didn't get it.

"Luz, pretend she's me. That was me at her age. I mean, single mom, poor, people like you dismissing me . . ."

"I'm not dismissing her."

"No?" Cat waited a beat. "Luz, think of how little control you have over this situation, and how that feels. Well, she has no control over where she came from or her father's failings or being alone and suddenly finding herself with this bougie family!"

"Uh." *She just called me bougie.*

"Hmm. Just sayin'."

Both women waited a bit. Luz admired Cat and felt gratitude that Emeli had an advocate—that both Luz and this teenage ragamuffin had Cat on their side. Because they were going to need advocates, desperately.

"Yup, I got it. You're right. You're right." Luz echoed her brother's tic. "So right."

"I don't wanna be right so much as help, mm-kay?"

Luz smiled and sighed. "Girl. Thank you, hon."

"No problem."

Suddenly Luz shot to attention. "Oh shit, I gotta get a move on here and get a bed ready and make more calls and what the hell am I going to do about my mother and I'm scared to talk to my father and I'm not even thinking about the kids and their father and—"

"Aiight! Go, go and please text if you need me, okay? I'm here."

"Thank you. That helps a lot."

"And if it helps, Luz, every time you look at that girl, think about her as me."

Chapter 16

Cat set her phone down. *Heavy stuff with Luz,* she thought. *That poor young girl, Emeli.* Cat remembered herself at the same age as Luz's "new" sister and imagined how it would feel to be thrown into her world—a sharply different world—so abruptly. And as Cat was now part of that world, she knew how harsh and judgmental it could be, where fewer people looked like you and knew the life you knew. Where everyone's heads are filled with much more than yours (international travel, how to eat edamame, art films), and their expectations of a young woman of color were slim to none: You'll get pregnant by a few different men over your lifetime, sit at a receptionist's desk for decades if you were cute, or maybe just lug dirty towels at a gym until your back gave out. Because it was assumed that there was no brain in that pretty little brown head. No aspirations, no drive, no sense, no entitlement, and no desire for the things they had, their lifestyle. *Yeah, I love sci-fi, too.* Really? *Yes, I'm applying to these colleges.* Really? *No, I've never been pregnant before.* Really? Cat's mouth went sour. That last one she used to be proud of. But now, decades into her diminishing fertility, she wondered: What price had she paid for her success? *Ding-dong! Delivery! Here's your crown, m'ija. Here are your degrees and your celebrity and your paychecks and your free clothes and fancy parties and awards won*

for all your hard work. But, what about babies, husband, family? Lo siento, bella, *you didn't order that.*

I didn't realize I had to.

Shit—what time was it? Cat shook herself out of her thoughts and started moving quickly between her closet, her dresser, and her bathroom. She was still in workout clothes after a halfhearted spin on the bike and she needed to shower and dress up for an early dinner appointment. Now that she'd been laid off, Cat didn't go out much. Sure, she would be getting a paycheck for another several months, but you had to shift your gears down just in case the hunt took longer than expected.

As she turned on the shower as hot as she could take it, Cat wondered: *What am I hunting for again?*

Cat took in the dark, narrow restaurant, an old speakeasy in the East Village full of Mexican wood décor. Like Luz's front door, she thought. But the layout was dark and tight. Sexy, though. And empty at this time of the early evening. *Ugh,* she thought, *I'm getting old.*

Cat was meeting a young woman whose name she knew in passing, a fairly green Latina starting out in TV and online as a host. Sofia Montez was impressive; her father was a well-known politician, a local congressman. Of course, at this point Cat was impressed by anyone actually still working in the business. Plus, she was looking forward to hanging with someone who was neither stuffy nor blustery for a change. There were too many of those at her level. In and out, always in a rush, no lingering. Transactional relationships only. Of course, they tended to have families, and she didn't, so . . .

"Right this way." The wispy hostess, dressed snugly in all black, led Cat upstairs to a balcony level, a flight and a half from the main bar. *It's even quieter up here,* Cat thought. Ten-plus years ago, she had done a lot of eating and drinking in spots like this, but not lately. The word *old* still echoing in her head, she sat down.

"Do you have Herradura?" Cat asked the hostess.

"Sure. We have a library of tequilas." She flipped over one of the plastic-covered menu pages and pointed to the word *Tequilas*. Usually Cat loved spending time with a list like this one, but tonight she didn't want to wait.

"How about just a clean Herradura margarita, on the rocks, no triple sec, with salt?"

As Cat sat, contorting herself to get out of her jacket in the tight booth, she let her eyes wander over the list. How she wished she could taste each and every one. Just a sip. And how she wished that someone else was paying.

"Hellooo, girlfriend!" Sofia was a pretty brunette with green eyes and the olive skin of conquistadors. She came in with a bluster, jacket and bag rustling. She wasn't smiling, but Cat noted her internal smile. One of *those,* she thought—reserved, dry, above it. She liked that. In contrast, Cat was all surface. What you saw was what you got. She was happy, you saw happy. Disgusted, you saw disgust. She had to train herself not to be so transparent on air, but it was why people loved her, right? Nothing phony. Sofia was nearly the opposite. Snarky smile, and maybe, if you were lucky you'd get teeth. But Cat sensed that she was all warmth on the inside.

"*Hola, chiquitita.*" Cat leaned upward for a peck on the cheek.

"*Ay,* woman." Sofia dropped her bags near Cat on her bench, then plopped herself down on her chair with un-self-conscious force. "Whew!"

They smiled at each other.

"Thank you so, so, sooo much for meeting me," Sofia said.

"Of course, hon—"

"Here you go, a clean margarita." The server set down Cat's drink, sweaty already with condensation and possibly from being so near the amazing breasts of the woman serving them. Both women's eyes went wide at the drink, and the twin mountains in their faces.

"Okay, well, I gotta have me one o' dose!" A native of New Jersey, Sofia slipped into urban patois fluidly.

Cat raised her brows. Gracias a Dios *she's drinking with me.*

"Sure, and, ladies, let me know if you want me to bring you any chips, mm-kay?"

"Oh yes, chips *por favor.*" Sofia waited until she was out of earshot to say, "Man, did you see that rack on her? Amazing."

"Ah, to be young."

"I'm not that old, and mine don't look like that."

"True, true," Cat agreed.

"Though my sister's got an awesome set o' *tetas.* Man, they're like gravity-defying boobs, and her waist . . ." Sofia rolled her eyes.

"Oh, girl, *tetas* are overrated. Trust me, when you get older, your sister will be envying you."

"These things?" Sofia pulled her jacket open to reveal maybe B-size breasts held up by a snug tank.

"Hey! I got the same and I'm so glad."

"Right, because otherwise, clothes don't fit."

"*Exactamundo.*"

The server was back. Sofia and Cat made eye contact over her breasts as she leaned down to serve the other margarita and some chips. Both smiled and raised a brow at their shared wonder and appreciation. They ordered some appetizers and refocused.

"So, first of all, thank you so so much for being here," Sofia gushed.

"Oh no, no, you're welcome, of course."

Sofia fawned and Cat self-deprecated. They both ate and drank heartily, particularly for women on television—Cat still getting called in for pilots and tests. Both wore a size six and bonded over being told by producers to lose ten pounds—size two or four was much more preferred in their very *blanco* business. The women ended up swearing allegiance and toasting to their ample asses and the joy of keeping those friendly pounds on. Cultural solidarity—fight the white patriarchy with plump, Latin behinds. After two margaritas each they were toasty.

"Okay, so let me just tell you . . ." Sofia was slurring a bit as she reached out to hold Cat's arm across the table. "Let me just tell you how much it meant to me to see your face on television."

"Aww." Cat was taken by surprise.

"No, really, I gotta tell you."

"Okay." Cat perked up to show Sofia she was paying sincere attention.

"I didn't think there was a place for us out there, in that space, ya know? And just, and just, seeing you and that you were—I mean *are*—a proud and loud Latina and just owning it, ya know?"

"Thanks." Cat meant it. She was flattered, but at the same time she was ambivalent. She was grateful, particularly as she grew up and then came up in the business, that there had been no one who looked like her, only "secret" ones like Linda Carter and Raquel Welch. But she also felt a huge chasm between herself and this maybe-ten-years-younger (or maybe twelve) woman who was of a different generation. She felt beyond her sell-by date. Outdated. Both feelings sat inside her. The margaritas made it a bit better, but also bitter. And then Sofia started crying.

"Cat, I mean it. You are the reason I do what I do. I don't know what I would have done if I hadn't seen you . . . just know that, okay? Just know that."

"*Ay*, hon. Thank you. I mean it. Thanks." Cat now felt honored. And yet, still, beyond her expiration date. She felt her own eyes well up, but it wasn't out of pride or empathy. It was that she felt she had let down this fellow Latina whom she'd inspired by not keeping her show. By getting canceled. By realizing that this wasn't really what she wanted to do. That maybe she had been a fraud, an imposter. Well, she did want to do it—have her own show—but she also dreaded doing it again. How could she stop, though, when she had to be out there helping more women, representing the people who most folks thought only cleaned their houses, answered phones, and handed them their burger and fries.

Sofia and Cat then spent the next twenty minutes playing Did-You-Know-Blank-Is-Latino? From there they moved quickly to which-*macho*-did-your-mother-have-a-crush-on? Then on to the history of their families and why Cousin Tito has so many moles.

Knowing it was late, Cat secretly hoped that Sofia wouldn't want to go yet. It had been forever since Cat had been out this late, and they had great rapport. But Cat also didn't want to seem like a loser with no one to go home to and no job to wake up to in the morning.

"Listen, mama," Sofia said. "I have, like, a late call-in tomorrow, so, wanna do one more drink downstairs, at the bar?"

"Love that." Cat hadn't felt this tingle of possibility in much too long. Maybe she'd actually meet someone, a man to fulfill that last to-do on her list: having a family. That made her nervous. But it was the same good nervous that fluttered in her belly before the control room said "Go!" in her ear for live TV. Cat was jazzed—if buzzed—to her fingertips.

Two hours later, the restaurant was far from the empty, hollow place Cat had walked into. Here was the hustle and noise that she had reveled in years ago. Those nights of hers that ran late into the sun rising in the morning. Nights that Cat danced on tables, smoked hand-rolled substances, and put her tongue in many mouths. But that was when she was right out of college, frustrated at how slowly her life was moving and stunted by work that limited her ability to shine as brightly as she wanted to. Once she turned onto the television track, Cat was waking up at the time she used to come home after a night out. Many times, she'd be in a cab flowing freely up and around the city streets at four in the morning on her way to the studio, and she'd take in the few people they'd pass. They were split between two groups: those who were heading to where they made their living, like Cat, and those stumbling home after a night of adventure. To Cat those nights hadn't always been good, but they were her own adventures. She would gaze at those late-to-bedders with nostalgia. The little beast inside her that was not so tightly wound saw them as familiars, friends in kind. But the hardworking, don't-stop-'til-you-get-to-the-top spirit would whisper, "Oh no, Cat. Those days are gone for a reason. Thank the Lord they are behind you."

"The same, please." Cat signaled for two more drinks, feeling oddly puffed up with the confidence that alcohol gives. Also, Sofia's time with her had made Cat feel appreciated, important, a trailblazer. So unlike how the media world made her feel, especially her former bosses and the producers she'd work with here and there. Their job was to make you feel as small as possible, until they really needed you. Then they crowned you queen of the world. Until the next up took your throne. But those days seemed over. Might as well suck these drinks and this night down while she could.

"Cat—this is Tom." Sofia practically had to yell due to the noise. In the brief time it had taken Cat to get the bartender's attention, Sofia had managed to turn on her bar stool and signal with her body an open invitation to surrounding men. In thirty seconds she'd met two. She pulled a young man toward Cat, parting the crush of bodies now behind their bar stools. Tom was a six-foot, cacao-colored young man, all shoulders and smile. His nubby sweater hinted at brains. Cat gulped. Yum.

"Oh, hi, Tom," she said, and held out her hand formally.

He ignored it, instead gently taking her extended arm to draw her closer and give her a peck on the cheek.

"Oh!"

"Sorry—" Tom politely drew back a bit, showing his palm in supplication.

"No, no, it's okay." Cat blushed and waved her reaction away. Silly her. He was gorgeous. And young, maybe late twenties. When was the last time a man had kissed her cheek who wasn't a cousin saying *hola?*

"So, Cat, Tom is friends with Clark here," said Sofia.

"Hi, Clark." This one was just getting a handshake. Handsome in a hipster Kennedy way, Clark didn't seem as naturally warm to her as did his buddy. Cat had a knack for reading people quickly and accurately.

"My buddy givin' you a hard time?" Clark feigned concern, but to Cat it rang of "Sorry, ma'am." Tom was relaxed but blushing. He'd already moved his body to Cat's right, angling himself sideways into the bar to lean and close the distance between them. She noted this gesture and felt warm. He'd settled in already.

"Nah, not at all. It's how we roll," replied Cat.

"We? What's 'we'?" asked Clark.

"Mexicana."

"Ah! Me too. Dominican," Tom said with authentic pride. An accent wasn't there, so Cat assumed second generation, just like her.

"*No me digas?*" She drew her free hand up to her chest, eyes wide.

"*Si, de veras.*"

They smiled at each other and locked eyes.

Tom followed up quickly with, "But don't go farther than that with me in Spanish *porque mi espanol* stinks!"

Cat chuckled. "Deal!" She raised her hand for an urban-hand-slap-shake. Tom smoothly joined in. They even sealed the deal with an awkward fist pump. It was a nerd meeting. Tom may have been several years younger than Cat, but that only made her more brazen.

Sofia and Clark were tight in conversation while Cat and Tom turned to bonding on their shared experiences of other Latinos finding them not Latin enough. For him, it was his skin color and his mother's side of the family practically disowning her for marrying a darker man. For Cat, it was her talking "white" and the people who still couldn't believe that she could do what she did because, shouldn't she be cleaning floors?

"Wait—what do you do?" he asked.

"Oh, um." He hadn't recognized her, though a couple of folks at the bar had given knowing smiles. She felt the familiar female urge to downplay herself. "I do TV."

"TV? Like what TV? Producing?" The usual assumption of folks who didn't watch television.

"Nope." Cat chewed on an ice cube from her now-empty glass number four. "On air."

"Wait, you're, like, *on* TV?"

"Yup," she said with a pursed-lip smile.

"Wow, okay, that is *so* cool!"

Cat's cheeks warmed. "Well, ya—I mean, I guess," spilled out.

"So, like, where can I see you?"

Her stomach dropped. "I . . . don't have my show anymore."

"Aw. Sorry about that." Tom signaled the bartender for a fresh margarita for them both. Cat noted his pity fixer-upper. Was that nice, or was he just trying to totally get her drunk? But she already was drunk. Very.

"No, no, no . . . It's all good. Ya know. Just doing some pilots now and figuring out what's next."

Tom slowly allowed a smooth grin to cross his face. His eyes twinkled with mischievousness.

"Okay, I just have to see this right now." He started scrolling and typing on his phone.

"Aw, man!" She remained playful as he Googled her.

"Nope! Gotta do this." Two seconds later, he peered intently at his screen, looked at Cat, who was not in full studio makeup and hair, though not bare-faced, then back at his screen and back at the woman next to him. "Wow. That is so cool."

"Okay, okay. Moving on!" Cat waved her hand around as if swatting a mosquito. She turned cool. Tom noticed. He carefully nestled his phone back into his front pocket and seemed to resolve silently not to look at it again.

"Moving on," he agreed. "So, what's next for you?"

"I don't know." Their glasses were set down, sweaty and cold. Cat knew she should have stopped a drink ago, but where did she have to be? "It seems like TV news is dying, and it wasn't the best fit anyway."

"For you or for them?"

"For me, I think. I just need to cover something else . . . or, do something else."

"Well, from what I saw, you seem great at it. Would be a waste to not have you on a screen somehow."

Cat thought he was being aggressively flirtatious, but when she looked at his face, all she saw was a kind smile.

"Yeah, well, do you watch TV?"

"You mean, like news?"

"Sure—or just TV in general."

"I don't own a TV."

Cat groaned and dropped her head in defeat. "That's what I mean! *Caramba*."

"I do have other screens. It's not like I never watch videos, it's just not on a television." Tom drew out the word *television* as if it were a relic.

It was a relic, Cat thought.

"The tele-vi-sion," she mimicked him gently. "Okay. Since you're the future of media consumption, what do you think is happening . . . like, now." The buzz in her head was getting louder and she couldn't necessarily feel her lips or tongue anymore.

"Well, I'm a quant guy—"

"Wait, you're a data dude?"

"A 'data dude'? Well, if you put it that way, yes."

Cat's reporting on high-frequency trading and data engineering had just come in handy.

"But I'm not like a hedge-fund dude. I'm with a start-up incubator."

"Thank God for that." Cat was not fond of the numbers guys she reported on whose work was to just figure out ways to make money off exploiting trading gaps or market fluctuations. They didn't make anything, just took what slipped from folks' fingers or what passed someone by.

"Clark's the Wall Street guy. I'm just tryin' to hang to find out what we can work on together."

Cat nodded. She was starting to hit a wall.

Tom noticed and picked up the pace. "Why not get yourself into one of those new online networks over at the big search guys?"

They talked shop for another half hour, as the bar stayed tight and crowded, bodies started to sweat, and Sofia was ready to call it a night.

"Hon, I love you—looooove you," Sofia drawled as she took Cat's hands in hers and gave her an encompassing embrace and sloppy cheek kiss.

"Love you too, *chica*." Cat noticed over her shoulder that Clark had disappeared. "Wait—where's the dude?"

"Oh, he's out. It's fine, fine." Sofia slung her purse over her shoulder. Cat noticed how young and disheveled she looked in the moment.

"But, you gonna take a cab?"

"Oh yeah, yeah . . . Ciao, Tom," Sofia slurred and hugged him as well.

Cat was concerned, not that her protégée couldn't make it home, but about the situation that she herself was in right now—still in the bar, drunk, with a very attractive, much younger black man. Her mother would drop dead. Hmm.

"Okay, *linda*." Cat smiled sweetly. "Thanks for hanging out."

"No, no, no." Sofia geared herself up with each *no*. "Thank *you*, mama." She came closer again, placing a hand on Cat's thigh to steady herself. "You are the best and you are the reason I do what I do, okay? Don't forget it." Cat was being lectured on self-esteem by a twenty-something. She both loved and hated this girl for it.

"I won't. And, thank you."

"Mmmwah!" Sofia threw Cat a loud hand kiss. She still wasn't smiling—she was the warmest unsmiley person Cat had ever seen—but Cat sensed that Sofia knew she'd given her a gift tonight. She'd let Cat hang loose. Filled her with compliments. Shed tears. Left her with a whole lotta man.

"She's wonderful," Cat mumbled.

Tom smiled. "Wanna continue our chat about your taking over the world at another spot?" He certainly had pizzazz.

"Yes." Cat signaled to close out her tab.

"No, no." Tom handed the bartender his own card.

"You bugger."

"C'mon now . . ." He winked as he signed the receipts.

"In that case, I've got even better tequila at my place." Tonight, Cat felt her inner beast was winning.

Tom raised his strong brow.

Cat doubled down: "Maybe we should go there?"

"Yes." He closed his wallet with gusto. "Let's."

As he let Cat take his thick arm, which he bent like the gent he seemed to be, Cat thought: My mother would just die right now. Die. Actually, everyone would freak out. Anybody seeing me leave? She scanned the room on their way out. Nope. And so what if they did. She needed this.

Cat and Tom had barely made it through the door before his arms, like steel girders, gently encircled her and she responded with pent-up lusty fury. Cat's clothes shed in record time while Tom did his best to be gentlemanly, and happily match his host's desire. It wasn't work on his part so much as their passion surprised him—Cat nearly blinded by her needs, it would take longer for her to feel surprise.

A few hours later, Cat awoke nude and, from the waist down, feeling an accomplishment that she'd waited far too long in her life for. But that fallback feeling dropped away for awe. She was amazed at what she'd just done. What she'd just felt. It tasted like freedom. It tasted real and alive and awake. *Wow.*

Of course, from the neck up, what she was feeling was pain. Six margaritas' worth of pain. Her previous max was maybe two. As she fumbled for her robe to get her to her goal of pain relievers and water in the kitchen, she looked at the mound of man in her bed. Hills and valleys of dark muscle. Undeniably beautiful. *Thank you, Jesus.*

Chapter 17

"Hon, I really miss you." Gabi broke the sound of her and her husband's typing and sniffed. They sat across the room from each other at home as they had for years now, each at their computer, working. Or, at least Gabi was working. "Let's just go out, you and me—" She noticed what looked like a flash of alarm run across her husband's face. They had a sitter lined up that night, which was rare, to cover for an engagement party thrown by new friends. Though Gabi noted to herself that the woman was the kind of friend who would be pissed at her bailing on the engagement party for her future marriage to save her own, current marriage. The situation between her and Bert felt too urgent to Gabi. *For whom the bell tolls. It tolls for me.*

"We just haven't spent any time together . . . out of this apartment." Her face was full of honest pleading and resigned woe. She was tempted to keep talking, to say something therapy-like about "breeding intimacy" or "maintaining connection," but her throat had closed on her. Gabi's silence held Bert's attention like a tether. His eyes widened as something seemed to sink in. She wasn't sure what it was, but the panic was replaced by more wounded—or were they worried?—eyes.

"Oh. Yeah. I mean, are you sure?" He paused, rubbed the top of his thighs with his hands, a nervous tic. "But, but, won't Zuri be mad? I mean . . ." He moved his right hand to run it through his hair. He was looking for a way out—and it hurt Gabi horribly to notice this—but after so many months of being neglected, Gabi knew that whether it was guilt or love, something made him feel inclined to say yes to his wife.

Gabi shook her head. "Yeah. Maybe. But this is much more important." This time the catch in her throat made its way up and cracked her voice. It was rare for Gabi to be vulnerable. She was always in command, a national, well-known cornerstone of fortitude, for Pete's sake. There was little room for weakness from her, or need. Sure, she needed people and things, but she never had to plead.

Bert's face was slack again, still mildly stunned by her request. "Oh, uh, yeah, I mean, I miss you, too." He paused. Gabi was sitting still, her eyes speaking loudly. "Yeah, okay, let's do it."

Two hours later, Gabi and Bert were cleaned up, Gabi particularly making an effort to look lovely. As they entered the restaurant and took in the trendy beauty of the railroad-style, wood-grain, green succulents built flush into the wall, ten feet full up and breathed deeply the scent of char, Bert ambled over to the open kitchen to shake hands and congratulate the new chef in town. The chef that wasn't him. Bert's notoriety from the show gave him props in kitchens all around town, but he was just a smidge too old and too needy to break into the freshest spots. Gabi was left to sit alone at the table for a while, ordering a glass of wine right away. The server was an adorable girl in a cropped tee that looked like it had been used to soak up spilt coffee; proudly grunge. Gabi knew that the exposed inch of her bare, young belly was going to get a long look from her husband. It reminded her what a Sisyphean task she had. And look at where Sisyphus ended up.

Gabi thought back to a particular session with their couples' therapist.

"Are you okay?" the therapist asked as Bert suddenly released a sob in the middle of their session, abruptly startling both women. It was a sound that escaped from him with a jump, followed by a red creep of color on his face and streaming tears, all in a matter of seconds. Gabi was shocked. She stared. She was incredulous and couldn't, or wouldn't, say a word. She couldn't believe not only that her husband was crying, but how he released what seemed like a break in a dam.

All therapists have therapists, and after becoming more and more shunned by her husband, their voices escalating daily in anger and resentment, Gabi knew that another voice and point of view were needed. They'd been seeing Marion every week for nearly a year. She was almost sixty, a round woman with dramatically coiffed blond hair set in Upper East Side waves. Her makeup firmly and colorfully applied, she gave off a sexy grandma feel, like an *abuela* with style. She had been referred to them by a friend of Gabi's, a pioneer in television psychology.

"Bert. What's this about?" Marion asked with genuine concern as Gabi unconsciously shifted her body away from her husband and just stared at him. Finally, she thought, some emotion. Finally, something was breaking through. Was he going to admit it? That he was having an affair, or affairs?

"I'm just . . . It's sad, y'know?" He sniffed and visibly worked at pulling back in all that he'd just let escape.

"What's sad?"

"Just . . . this. All this."

Gabi maintained her silence. She set her jaw as she realized that her husband's moment of honest vulnerability was over as quickly as it had begun. She knew deeply, not only in her trained therapist's mind, but in her soul, that she had married someone with a character disorder. These people were incapable of being anything but lonely. After all, they were alone—all they saw in every human face they encountered was a reflection of themselves. That's where Gabi's pity came from. Right now it was sinking in that soon enough, she'd be alone, too. But only for a while.

Bert shifted quickly from open and emotional to his default setting: slick and closed. Gabi could see his mind working around an explanation. She marveled at how well she could read his face and body language. She could hear him loud and clear without his uttering a word. And yet, she had willingly ignored so much for so long.

Marion seemed intrigued for once. Lately Gabi was questioning the choice and expense of seeing her, as they'd made zero headway and at times Marion's eyes appeared too half-lidded for Gabi not to suspect she was dipping into her own supply of antianxiety medication. But this was a moment in which Marion could redeem herself. Gabi didn't want to be the bad guy here, the nag. She needed Marion to press Bert. Press him until the juice of truth ran out to the floor. That was going to be the only way this marriage could be saved.

"Gabi?" Marion asked, squeezing the wrong fruit.

Gabi turned her head to face her; her eyes until this point had been boring holes into Bert's. Without a blink, she looked at Marion and slightly shrugged. Therapist-speak for "you talk." Marion got the message. Both women turned to Bert. His head was down as he fiddled with tissues, breathing dramatically.

"Y'know, I don't know . . . It must be that, that I miss you, too."

Nah, Gabi thought. *That's not it. That's not it at all. You bastard.*

Gabi's attention came back to her seat in the restaurant as Bert returned.

"Oh, whew, sorry, babe." He scooted between the narrow tables, his growing drinking belly almost knocking over Gabi's water glass. "Yeah, so, he's cool, pretty cool."

"The chef? That's great." Gabi stifled the impulse to encourage him further and coach him into networking with this young "hot" guy, following up, etc., etc. She was always trying to help, but even she had to remind herself that sometimes helping is perceived as a bid for control. Especially when gender was involved.

The meal was four stars and Gabi maintained her confidence as much as she could through the meal, but the pleading and melancholy in her eyes was still clear. Bert reached out for her hand once or twice, but it felt so robotic and automatic that she felt a layer of mutual deception between their skins. She didn't want to think of how many other women he'd touched the same way, and different ways, during the course of their marriage. She knew they had something incredibly unique, a connection that neither of them had ever had before and, she knew, possibly never again. That was her sadness. And that was also why she just kept trying, despite the truth she knew they had both buried down deep over the years.

As the server came by and her slice of naked belly glowed white just at their chin level, Gabi watched her husband's eyes take it in and his smile grow. He held his gaze for two beats too long, then looked up at the server's young, unlined, un-made-up face, took in a sharp breath, puffed out his chest, and leaned back in the chair, like a silverback male gorilla, ready to take her in, or on.

Gabi reached for her wineglass, her ears now only hearing white noise, her eyes glazed over until all in front of her was a hazy blur.

Chapter 18

Luz always brightened when she walked through the small iron gates of her parents' Harlem townhouse, her childhood home. This time, though, as she shut the doors behind her, she heard its metal squeak in another way, another level. It felt like the opening and closing of a door in her life. The rusting iron spoke differently than it had when she was a child. Of course back then, she had barely paid attention, filing the groan away into her subconscious. The noise from the street also competed so loudly for her attention—kids playing on the sidewalk, and in the street, as if it were a schoolyard, water cascading from hydrants, Dominican neighbors yelling for *Anaaa!* Now the neighborhood was clean, quiet, all grown up. Just like her. A daughter with a new father.

Luz had never gone this long without speaking to her parents. She was close to them and her children were so close to them. But she also knew herself. She knew that she could be much too emotional—nasty, even—when prompted and perturbed. And right now they deserved better. She deserved answers, too, but it was hard to get honest answers when you showed up with guns blazing. So, Luz needed time.

As a mother herself, she understood the difficulty of figuring out when a child was old enough to know certain things. But why lie for over thirty years? What had that accomplished, beyond deceiving her into believing she was this proud sistah in a long line of proud sistahs? Had it saved her father—the one who raised her—from embarrassment? It certainly explained how the family had avoided giving her the exact date of her parents' wedding. She had the pictures. Beautiful! But it had been a small shindig at the house. Luz thought it was that way because her mother didn't like ostentation and waste. Not because she had been knocked up and it was a shotgun wedding.

But why would her father raise this other man's child? *Cuckolded,* that was the word for it, yes? It happened often enough that it had its own word. How bizarre. Men.

After warm but guarded greetings at the door, Luz, her father, and her mother sat at the family breakfast nook, where all big talks traditionally happened. The clinking and clanking of tea being made echoed loudly above the silence hovering over them. Luz waited for her proud, stable parents to open this potentially painful conversation. But, they seemed to sit back in apprehension, waiting for their daughter to lay into them. Tomas had called them earlier to give them a heads-up as to why they hadn't heard from his older sister and why she was going to the home today. Luz's parents also seemed ashamed. That made the surly words waiting in her throat taste worse.

"So," Luz said sourly. "Want to tell me what's going on?"

Roger and Altagracia seemed nearly beyond reproach in life. They had raised their children almost entirely without drama, much less trauma. Somehow this made Luz feel even worse. It was as if they'd saved up all their secrets for this one thing, this one day.

"Your mother did the right thing, Luz." Her father's voice was steady and caring.

"What did she do, Dad?" Luz knew right well what she'd done, and what he'd done. But she wanted to hear it from them. Their version.

"Don't be mad at him, *m'ija.* He saved you."

"*Saved* me? Saved me from what, exactly? Life as a drug dealer's kid?"

"He saved you from being aborted."

The air was sucked out of Luz's lungs. She hadn't considered that at all. She had never thought her mother would do such a thing.

Luz was stunned into silence. She sat, humbled.

"*M'ija,*" her mother said gently as she carefully placed her cup onto its saucer—a child of a revolution, the daughter of a married man and his mistress who came to this country with barely an education, barely a suitcase, but so many hopes and dreams, who placed her cup down as if she had stepped off the *Mayflower* itself. "I was young. And, I was es-stupid. But more than that, I was confused."

Luz's father sniffed and straightened in his chair.

"I didn't know where I belonged and I was scared of everything. So, I made a mistake."

Luz, who had been staring at the corner of the table, the crease in the tablecloth, slowly brought her eyes to her mother's.

"Mistake?" she whispered.

"No, no. Ju are not a mistake. But at de time, it wasn' de right t'ing to do." She took a sip of her tea, carefully choosing words in her second language.

"And . . . and you were going to abort me?" Luz's anger was gone, replaced by a desire to understand. To understand her mother at nineteen years old, pregnant by a man she didn't love.

"Jes. An' I am very, very ashamed 'bout dat. I've prayed for years for God to forgive me for even t'inking of it."

"But I wasn't going to let that happen." Luz's father took the baton. "Luz, it wasn't a great situation, but it was what it was. We had broken up for a short while and I didn't want her to go through that."

"And you knew the whole time?"

He couldn't look Luz in the eye.

"You knew that I wasn't yours?"

"Yes," he said hoarsely, picking up his own mug.

Ma brought her napkin up to her tears.

"But how could you not tell me? I mean, at some point, like when I had kids or when I got married. Or how about while I was growing up, when all those kids made fun of how I looked different from you guys, from my brother?"

"It was a different time," Luz's father said after a moment. "We did what we thought was best."

"For whom? You guys?"

Slam!

Luz's mother had brought her hand down on the table, sending a jolt through everyone, rattling the china. Her mother might usually be reserved, but she hadn't made it this far in this country by being anything but a force of nature.

"Enough!" she barked, ensuring that Luz was awoken from her self-righteous stupor.

"Jor father saved jor life! Maybe ees not de story ju want to hear—maybe ees not de story dat sounds good or works wit' jor job or jor friends, but das it! *Dis* ees jor father—dees man! Jor *real* father." Altagracia pointed at her husband with her index finger. The rest of her hand clutched a very wet tissue. That hand would be holding a lot of tissues until this speed bump on the road of life was way off into a rearview mirror.

Tears poured down Luz's cheeks. She looked at her father. As usual, Roger was holding it together. But his shoulders slumped more than usual, his posture now reflecting his true age, the age and weight of his history. His eyes glistened with softness and sadness.

It was her mother's turn to be angry. For Luz's mama, the one mortal sin was ungratefulness. Each and every day of their lives, she had made sure to teach her children gratitude for the bounty they enjoyed. To be grateful for the homes their parents owned, while most of their family lived in rentals. To be grateful they were healthy and educated—self-sufficient, unlike her aunt's family. Luz's cousins had never left the 'hood, at least in terms of their attitudes. At least they had a different last name, Luz often thought. Maybe no one would make the connection.

Releasing a sob, Altagracia got up from the table. She put her cup and saucer on the kitchen counter and made her way up the creaky brownstone stairs to another floor, another room.

Luz and her father sat in silence for a moment.

"I'm sorry," Luz said at last.

"It's okay."

"I'm just . . . trying to figure this out."

He patted her hand. "Just know that you are always my daughter. From the moment you kicked in her belly, I was committed to you and to your mother, no matter how you got in there."

They both chuckled softly through tears.

"Thanks, Dad," Luz said. Then asked, "Does your family know . . . about me?"

"Well . . . I remember once when you were about four years old, Gran'mama came to visit, and she didn't say this to me, but she said to my sister, 'I bet that that's not his chil'. But I'm glad he's doin' the right thing by that woman. She's a good woman.'"

Luz smiled at the warm memory of her grandmother. Luz had always felt so much love from her—it was as if there was nothing else inside of her but love to give.

"That was the last anyone said anything about it."

Typical, Luz thought, for that side of the family. "What about Mom's side?"

"Now, *that* side." Her father's face lit up a bit. "Well, you know how they felt about your mother marrying me—a *moreno*."

For a Dominican to marry someone even darker than herself, and here in the "J'united Es-states?" Sacrilege. This was the land of opportunity, of plenty, of . . . plenty of white people!

Why not up your station and at least marry *un chino?* That was the Altagracia-family take on her father. They didn't care how wealthy and educated his family was. All they cared about was that he was black. Black as night, they'd say. *Como Miles Davis!* Though he was much more Denzel.

Luz had to chuckle at the memories. It was a serious matter, but she and her father historically had a sense of humor about it because it was so absurd. And Roger had the healthiest ego of any black man she'd ever known. It would take a lot more than some racist Dominicans to nick his pride. Plus, he loved his wife much too much.

Roger continued. "Then, when you came out as light as you did, they were so damn relieved, it was even more insulting. But I took it in stride. And no one dared question a thing."

I'm so grateful for this man, Luz thought.

"Plus, when she married me, your mother told everyone to go to hell. She gave up a lot and I gave up some, too. But I never see it that way." He paused and looked at Luz directly and with warmth. "I got the best thing of all. My girl."

"Shit, *Papi* . . ." Luz went into his arms. She wasn't that much closer to figuring things out, but at least one parent was happy. She'd try to reach her mother next. Each character in a story has her own story.

"Ma?" Luz knocked gently on the door of her parents' room, which her mother had left ajar.

Sniff. "Yeah."

As Luz entered tentatively, her mother was dabbing another tissue at her runny nose. She sat on her bed, an aged and frayed cardboard box to one side of her and what looked like handwritten letters that she had seemed to be sifting through. Altagracia patted the bed on the spot next to her for her daughter to sit down. Luz did and then they were quiet for a while.

"So. Dees are letters jor father, dis man downstairs, wrote to me when we were apart and I had gotten pregnant with ju." She handed an envelope to Luz. Her mother's name was written on the front, in what was unquestionably her father's handwriting. It was so rare to see handwriting these days, to know your parents' hand. Luz missed it.

"Oh, how he loved me—well, he's always loved me. But oh, dose days . . ."

Luz smiled at her mother.

She continued. "But it was hard, you know. Mama, *Abuela,* was so worried about me, but at the same time happy I broke up with dat *moreno.*"

They both rolled their eyes.

"Luz, *amor.* Ju know, dose days were hard. Dose times were hard. It was choose him and lose much of my family. But! But .gain *his* family. Great family. An American family who really understood history and education."

"I know." Luz felt her mother needed to be egged on a bit, supported. But she just had to ask: "So, no chance he's really my pop, huh?"

"Pffft." Her mother waved a wet tissue. "*Ay, mi linda,* nooo . . . I wish, but not biologically."

She handed Luz a small sepia photo that looked like it had been taken in the '30s or '40s. It was of a striking, long-faced, very light-skinned man with nearly translucent eyes. Only the waves in his pomaded hair and his full lips hinted at his blackness.

"Dis is your biological father's father, *tu abuelo.* Tito."

Luz took the picture gently. Wow. Looking at members of your family for the first time was like discovering treasure. And not all treasures were equal. But every one had value, as each closed a gap in your knowledge, your legacy.

"He's so handsome," Luz whispered. And he was. His shirt and tie and jacket were impeccable and looked expensive. His skin, glowing, even decades later. *And those are my eyes,* she thought.

"Jes, well, he was a tailor in Santo Domingo. Always dressed so, so perfect." Her mother sighed. "Ju know his son could have been just as amazing, but he chose another path." She straightened herself a bit, preparing herself for the turn this conversation would now take.

"Was he good when you met him?"

"Good? Well, he had promise . . . and passion." She wiped her nose. "But, your father, of course, came with much, much more that was good."

"Did he know about me? I mean, did he always know that I was his?"

"Jes, he knew. De whole time."

Both cast their eyes down. Luz's mother was choosing her words carefully.

"He wanted me to haf an abortion."

"He did?" Luz croaked.

"Jes, he did. But jor father just would no' let dat happen." She pointed to the sky for emphasis. "He said: 'I will take care of her'—or 'it,' because, *m'ija,* at dat time we didn't know—'and I'll raise it, I don't care whose it is.' So he did."

"Did you guys keep in touch? Did his family know?"

"Who?" Her mother's mind was still on Luz's father, the selfless one downstairs.

"The other one."

"Oh. Well, no. But once in a while I'd hear through Carlitos about him. It was too bad how his life turned out." Carlitos was her mother's cousin.

"So, he has a daughter," said Luz.

"Jes. Chris told me. Well, actually my grandchildren told me!" Luz's mother was smiling.

"Yeah, well, they talk a lot."

"Jes like you." She smiled.

"So why am I doing this, Ma? Doesn't she have any other family?"

"Don' ju think she has de best chance wit' you?"

"Well, yes, but . . ."

Luz's mother was mildly indignant now. "Dat is jor sister. No, dis did not turn out da' way I'd like it, but listen . . ." Her mother took Luz's right sleeve between her forefingers and thumb. "Da universe gave ju a gift—jor father gave ju a gift. To live, to be born. I could not haf done it without him. Ju wouldn't be here without him. And now it's jor turn. To give someone a new life." She let go and went for another tissue. "Besides. We are family, and das what we do!"

Luz sighed. *Sure,* she thought. *We're family. And now I have family in jail, and a teenager in my house!*

She kissed her mom on the cheek, gave her a big hug. One day she'd actually read these letters, but not now. She knew her father loved her. Now she had to figure out her relationship to this new "father," this thug baby-daddy to this sullen, door-knocker-wearing teenager in her house. Granted, so far the kids thought she was the coolest thing since junk food.

But what this conversation had made Luz realize was that she was on her own. Her mother saw only the father who raised her. The man she'd left behind was history. It would be up to Luz to deal with the knowledge that not only did she have a new father, she had a father who was a criminal, who contributed to the cultural stereotype that kept men like the man downstairs from being all they could be. Luz knew how the system of this country was set and primed to trap men of color—women, too—into roles that made the majority comfortable. She knew the odds were against people of pigment. But, with such a straight and narrow father, she also had a chip on her shoulder about the negativity of blaming the system. She, at essence, was a bootstrap girl and now she was coming face-to-face with a system that didn't even give you the boots. You had to make them yourself, starting out far behind everyone else's starting line. It would take time for her to see this.

Right now, Luz mulled thoughts that felt selfish but bubbled up in her biased, high-society, privileged mind. If her biological father was in prison and nature/nurture is about 50/50, did that mean Luz was a thug, too? That she had these tendencies? Or was it like a contagion? And to think that she thought she was all that. Maybe she was a fraud now. She wasn't really one of the Vineyard folk, just a Dominican *chica* from the 'hood. Her mother had married well. She'd raised Luz and her brother right. But dammit if Luz didn't feel like decades of her life had been completely rewritten to include passed-over chapters and subplots like a choose-your-own-ending. Except she wasn't the one doing the choosing.

One realization rose to the top of the churning washing machine of her mind as she got up from her mother's bed. "Yes, Ma. You're right. We're family."

Chapter 19

The bathroom lights were dim. Magda was grateful for that. She might not be prissy, but she was still vain. She peered into the mirror, touching the swollen bags under her blue eyes, noting every incoming wrinkle. *I look like shit.* Someone knocked on the door.

"In a minute!" She felt like hell, but she had to get out there.

Magda steadied herself on the sink with both hands. She rolled her head around on her neck slowly, hoping to loosen the tightness radiating upward from her shoulders. Instead, it made her dizzy. She moaned. After two breaths with her eyes closed and head down, she ran the cold tap, wet her right hand and brought it up to her forehead and eyes. Just enough cold water to distract her from the other aches signaling to her from throughout her body. Maybe even the bags under her eyes would take a hike. She loomed close to the mirror again. No such luck.

Mama. I'm so sorry. I miss you too much already.

Walking back to the main aisle of the church, Magda passed several cousins, though none acknowledged her directly, their eyes flicking downward as they realized who she was. They were on her father's side and, like him, they didn't support Magda's life "choices." *It's not a choice,* pendejos.

Her custom-made black suit fit more loosely than usual.

Her mother had passed away just four weeks after her diagnosis, only making it home from the hospital for her last seven days. Magda had been staying in a hotel downtown, not eating, mostly drinking. She had managed to bring her children to see their *Abuela* early on, before she was too wasted away. Remaining in Miami while their mother, Albita, swung them between Los Angeles and New York for her own work, Magda missed her kids dearly. But she insisted that Ilsa and Nico not come to the funeral. They were too young and it was bad enough that she had to deal with her father and his family's freeze-out, not to mention her cold-fish sisters. She didn't want her children to experience it, too—experience the gutting pain of rejection not only from a parent, but from dozens of family members. And in some ways, Magda didn't feel her family deserved to know them much. Maybe it was punishment. Beyond *Abuela,* her children had seen Magda's sisters and their families maybe once a year—and not for want of trying. For their sake, Magda tried to stay in touch with their *tías* but there was little reciprocity. After a while you just got tired of all the stabbing, in the front, in the back. She was just so tired.

Magda genuflected in the aisle, her Catholic school memories making the process of being in church again, after decades of absence, automatic. She sat down toward the back pews, though her true place was at front. Magda counted the heads of her siblings and their families as they settled in. As the priest droned on, waving incense over her mother's coffin, Magda tried to recall all of her cousins' names. She was batting maybe .200. Many of them she hadn't seen since she was a child. Oh wow, she thought, Juan had gotten big. She allowed herself a chuckle as his toddler started bucking in his arms, bored and dressed in a miniature tux with a white flower in the lapel. The little one ripped out the flower and threw it at his mother's head. Juan, a first cousin and a handsome, Euro-looking man, had thrown the family into a tizzy by marrying a dark-skinned Cuban doctor.

She wore her hair natural, in a curly, trimmed 'fro that was now the setting for her son's discarded flower. It looked better on her than it had on him. Lusting after her cousin's wife was probably not a good idea in church, so Magda shook herself from her warm, forbidden feelings and resumed the game of identifying family by the backs of their heads.

Hey, Tio Eduardo—tan viejo. Ha! Rosie made it. Mom loved her. Except for that time her dog left a giant poop on Mami's plants. Dorita. Bruno. Who's that? Looks like Elba. Haven't seen her in a bit—oh snap. She grew a behind.

Magda's view was obstructed briefly. The woman who passed her pew was lean and regal, with blond highlights throughout her thick hair and barely any need for makeup. She must have been fifty years old, but Magda never failed to be stunned by how naturally beautiful her aunt was. Tia Cristina was her mother's younger sister. She was rarely seen, as she'd moved across the country to Texas with her husband, whom many described as a violent control freak. Magda recalled meeting him once and remembered how sour he seemed. Like a bitter lemon candy was always in his mouth.

Eyes turned to Tia Cristina, who was being helped by someone nearly as scandalous: her mother's brother from another mother. Family folklore was that Magda's maternal grandfather had had a mistress for decades who lived not too far from his home, and with whom he had a son and a daughter. Of course, few spoke of these siblings or their mother. But Magda recalled her mother talking years ago about Andres and Camilla, her family from another father. She mentioned it in such a nonchalant way, so matter-of-fact, that Magda didn't dig further. But Tia Cristina maintained contact with them, and here was their half brother, Andres, who carried the same last name but never lived under the same roof. He was older, like Magda's mother, with a stooped posture. But he was broad and held Tia's arm for support.

As gorgeous as it was, Tia Cristina's face was contorted in

despair. All she and Magda's mother ever did was fight—they had barely spoken in years. And here she was. Making a grand display of her pain. *Maybe you should have been around while she was alive,* thought Magda. *Maybe you wouldn't be crying so much now, looking so ugly?*

Seemingly in answer to her thoughts, Tia Cristina looked behind her and caught Magda's eye, her heavy lids communicating something. Magda couldn't figure out if it was sympathy, or an F-you, or what. Whatever it was, she had succeeded in making Magda feel guilty for thinking such bad thoughts about her. Catholic guilt. Worked every time.

"*Ay, chica . . .*" A figure dressed in black embraced Magda, surprising her, her face at chest level.

"Oh, hey, Cat." Magda returned the hug. "You didn't have to—"

"Oh no, no, of course I'm here. Luz and Gabi are on their way. Gabi coincidentally had a speaking gig in the city."

"But I thought Gabi had to get back to Maximo?"

"For you, hon, she delayed her flight."

They both sighed, gratefully.

"Now, scoot." Cat motioned for Magda to move down the pew. They were three rows back from anyone in front of them. Magda thought about a "united front" and all, about moving closer, but she almost couldn't take the rejection. Plus, her mother was the one who truly loved her and accepted her. She was there for her mother, not them.

After Cat performed her rusty genuflection, she moved closer to Magda. They both looked straight ahead.

"Well . . ." Cat said. "Looks beautiful."

"Huh?"

"The coffin and the flowers, I mean."

"Oh, yeah. Looks nice." Magda sniffed. No tears in front of this group.

Still facing front, feigning respect for the service and listening to the dour singing, Cat noted, "They're still not talking to you, huh?"

"Not really."

"Magda. That just sucks. Sucks."

"Eh. Used to it, I guess."

Cat bent to find her hymnal.

"Hey, gals, move over." Luz wore snug pants of black sateen, pointy-toed kitten heels, and a silk sweater with a wide neckline. An ear cuff rounded out her funk. Luz skipped the genuflection. Gabi stood quietly behind her, still in her loud keynote speaking clothes, all bright orange in a sea of black and gray.

"Hey, *chicas*." Cat scootched and smooched her friends, then leaned back while Luz and Gabi each took turns to lean across her and hug Magda tight.

"Thanks for coming, girls. Really," said Magda.

"Listen, I'm here for ya. God only knows how few of these people are. Shit," Luz commented.

Cat winced at her friend's brashness but knew it rang of truth. That was why they were here. They knew that as powerful and rich as Magda was, she was poor in familial love and acceptance. And as much as she tried to hide it, it stung her deeply. Family was everything, not only to her, but to all of her friends. And though each of them had trouble with some family member or other, none had been frozen out so absolutely.

Gabi ended up at the far end of the pew. She locked eyes with Magda, her former lover and dear friend, and mouthed, *I love you.*

Magda returned a *Thank you* as they all attempted to face forward and listen to the service.

"Listen," Magda whispered to Luz, "I hope you don't mind, but Gabi filled me in."

At mention of her own familial worries, Luz raised her dark brows. "Oh! Oh, that's fine."

"Jesus." Magda shook her head. "I lose family, you gain family . . . Fun, right?"

Cat sat in the middle, absorbing it all. When Luz had called to tell each of them about her kids' new "roomie," everyone was incredibly surprised. Each of them had family secrets. The twin cousin with Down syndrome sent away to a home, never to be spoken of again. The other cousin who looked like no one else in the family. The aunt with the female friend she was a bit too close to. How a grandmother had *really* supported the family financially. And how one uncle supported three families.

But Luz's family had seemed such a picture-perfect, high-class model of success and joy that the revelation of a half sister from the 'hood and a con as a real father—well, it threw everyone off, with maybe a pinch of schadenfreude.

After the church service, Magda stood at the cemetery alongside her chosen family: Luz, Gabi, and Cat. Only the closest of family members remained. Magda found it bizarre that, of all the funerals she'd attended, this was her first cemetery visit, but now she realized why mourners avoided the part where someone you knew and loved gets put into the ground. She made a note to herself to call her lawyer and have him draft up a will addendum. Magda needed to be cremated. This was just too awful.

Cat, knowing Magda's mother only slightly, was visibly distraught. Though out of courtesy she made an effort to tamp her emotions down. After all, it wasn't her mother. But Magda remembered when Cat's dog had died. She was a mess. That's what happened when you had no kids. Loneliness.

As soon as she thought it, Magda scolded herself for judging someone who loved her enough to fly from New York to Miami. Then again, Cat *was* currently out of a job, but still getting paid through her contract, so she could be looking for something to fill her time. Or, she now had time.

"How you doin'?" Luz checked in with Magda.

"Good." Magda didn't take her eyes off the casket, now hovering over the pit in the ground. Slowly it began to descend. Magda noted some wailing from off to the right. *Of course,* she thought. *Gotta be loud. Gotta make a show.*

"Oh geez. It's your aunt." Gabi tugged at Magda's jacket sleeve and gestured at the small commotion.

"Oh no," Magda muttered.

Tia Cristina was making her way to the hole in the ground, where the casket now was fully out of sight. Hunched over, bobbing as she sobbed, wailing and lurching, she was still strangely glamorous. But her aim was true and it seemed as if everyone watching reached the same conclusion at the same time—she was going to jump into her sister's grave.

"*Ayyyyy,*" her mother's little sister wailed. "*Ayyyyy!*" It got louder.

Her eyes not believing what they were seeing, Magda was frozen still. She then spotted Abuela Olga, a grandmother-in-law, ambling forward, closing in on her aunt. Abuela Olga was old-school. She was compact, short, wide and burly, her daywear usually a *bata,* the in-house robe-nightgown uniform of *abuelas* worldwide. But today she was dressed in her formal wear, a dark skirt suit with a flower pattern that enveloped her broad frame like gift wrapping on a box. Her brow set, she was as focused on Cristina as everyone else was, but she was the only one moving.

"*Ayyy,* nooooo . . . Take me with you!" Cristina wailed at full volume in both Spanish and English. She stood now in the plot itself, the bare soil moist and soft. Just as it looked like she was going to throw herself into the hole, on top of her sister's casket, Abuela Olga swiftly wrapped one thick arm around Cristina's waist, the other pulling at her shoulder. "*AAAYYYYY! NOOO!*" Cristina screamed and half-collapsed against the old woman's weight. "*NOOOOO!*"

Abuela was pulling her in, away from the edge with the force of only the strongest, surest of women who have seen absolutely everything under the sun, have climbed every mountain and clobbered every obstacle life threw at them.

"*No.* You stop this right now." Olga's voice, in clearly enunciated Spanish, wasn't raised. It ran flat, yet everyone present heard her every word. It projected as only an *abuela's* voice can. "You *stop.*"

"But I NEEEEED to go with herrr . . . !" Cristina's high-lighted blow-out glinted. Magda noticed the long, fake nails on her flailing hands. *Dios,* she thought, it was like one of her kids having a tantrum.

"You are *not* going anywhere." Abuela Olga pulled one last time on Cristina's body, jerking her with a physical *That's enough!* Just as with a child. "This is not about you. This is not your day. *Basta, ya!*"

All the mourners stood in stunned silence. It was as if they were watching a performance—Shakespeare in the Park, tele-novela style. After a moment, crisis averted, the audience snapped out of spectator mode into relief.

Cat had a fist to her mouth, stifling surprise as well as horror of her own. The thought of being buried alive was one of Cat's childhood nightmares. Luz was slack-jawed. She was much too refined ever to have seen anything like this. Black folk are black folk and Latino *es* Latino, she thought, but dammit if there wasn't a gap when it came to what class of ethnic folk you were exposed to. Luz had thought this only happened in Tyler Perry movies. Gabi just tsk-tsked.

Now that crisis was averted, Magda found herself suppressing a chuckle. The graveside theatrics were the very essence of her mother's side of the family. Drama came in daily doses—cousins had been kidnapped back in Venezuela and one returned missing a pinky finger, the family fortune lost. But this took the cake. Magda had to see if anyone else found this as hilarious, in a twisted way, as she did. She scanned the faces present and ended up locking eyes with her father. The father who had disowned her.

For a second he was stone. Then he did what Magda instinctively knew he might do—he shook his head in disbelief and smiled. *Can you believe this* loca? *You see your mother's family? What a mess* . . . Magda let her eyes smile back.

In that split second, she was twelve and her father loved her again. They were ganging up on her mother about the latest gossip-drama she was serving up. Magda and her father had bonded in having both feet on the ground. It's how she identified with him. Magda was pragmatic, not a fan of hysterics. She was type A. Levelheaded. Not prone to tears.

And now here they were. A brief moment of reconnection: Had she imagined it? Nope, it happened. She missed him, Magda realized. Her eyes welled. But she quickly sniffed back the tears that threatened to fall. She was grateful that most of the burial attendees were still reeling from the near-spectacle; they'd missed her private moment. Tia Cristina had been scolded into silence now, not only by Olga, but by another in-law as well—put in her place by the original G's.

"Holy shit." Luz's mouth barely moved and she hadn't even blinked.

"Yup."

"I just . . ." Cat mumbled, ". . . can't believe . . ."

"Typical."

"Typical?" Luz asked in disbelief. "Wow."

Gabi, savvy in the tendencies of their people, commented, "Luzita, it's only just begun."

The priest gave his final blessing over the plot and the muscled ushers from the funeral home—unperturbed, of course, they'd seen it all—began to lead folks back to the parking lot. They followed like quiet lemmings.

Magda turned one last time to her mother's grave. *Ay,* Ma. But she knew her mother wasn't there, really. She was gone. The hollowness in Magda's heart wasn't only for the loss of her mother. In this moment, she mourned two parents. As long as her mother was alive, she had connected Magda to her father in a way that kept their family ties bound. But now that her mother was gone, where was her connection to a father who didn't want her? And why did she care so much? Why did it hurt just now, so bad?

It had been the most bittersweet shared eye-roll of Magda's life.

Chapter 20

Must. Find. Caffeine.

Cat ambled through the terminal at MIA, Miami, toward her gate—the last one, naturally. It stood at the end of what felt like a two-mile walk. Along the way she was assaulted by horrid lighting, clueless travelers, and the Siren call of all things ketchuped, fried, and chocolate.

Fuck it. She swerved right, towing her overnight bag behind her, her right arm leaded down by her carry-on packed with everything, her eyes shielded by glamorous, oversized sunglasses. *Eighty percent off, suckas!*

"Uh, can I have a venti Pike, room for milk, and a chocolate croissant?" Cat knew that sucking down a venti coffee meant several trips to the bathroom on the plane, but she still needed to prep for her speech—paid, hooray!—and plane time was prep time. She shook work thoughts out of her head for a moment. She wasn't ready for them yet.

Balancing with the skill of a former waitress, Cat managed her bags and her coffee and eats. As she plopped it all down with relief at her gate, her phone buzzed. At the risk of losing her call, she struggled to finish taking her coat off. The terminal was sweltering. Cat had been waiting all week for word on the local station's offer. Yes, it was local. Yes, it was a major step down for her professionally. But nothing else was coming through and she was about to hit a wall, of both patience and financial security.

It was her agent.

"Cat. Where are you?"

"In Miami. About to board for a speaking gig in Oakland."

"Yeah, well, you didn't get the local gig."

"Shit."

"Yeah, shit." His tone was sour, contemptuous.

Two seconds of silence. Cat felt his lull as the disappointment of a parent or a teacher—a superior. *Wait,* she thought. *He's not my superior.*

"So, what's next?" she asked, her confidence slightly renewed in reminding herself of their roles.

"Well, we should talk about that."

"Okay. Talk."

"We've been everywhere and you don't want to go to the other networks, so—"

"Because their brands suck, Guy! And that would cost me major in the long run, not to mention my sanity. . . ."

"Yeah, well, that leaves us with little else. And I've really done all I can do for you."

It was Cat's turn to pause. "Wait, what . . . What are you saying?" Cat knew, but she had to hear him say it himself. Just to make sure.

"Just that I think we should both move on."

"Move on?" Why did this feel like being dumped by a boyfriend? Oh, right, because in the past they'd fought hard enough to make her cry and then he'd apologized by sending her fancy cupcakes. To make her fat! What the fuck.

"Yeah."

"Okay. I guess so. Well . . . Thanks. Good-bye."

Cat hung up. Dumped by her agent. Unhireable. No, no, it

was because she didn't want to sell her soul to be the token Hispanic at a conservative, nearly all-white network. He told her of the offer within a few weeks of her show being canceled, but there was just no way she'd take a job in hell simply because it paid. Yup, she wasn't unhireable, but she was still just dumped by her agent.

Cat sat down, moderately stunned. Her sunglasses still on, she looked across from her. In front of her she recognized the daughter of a famous actress. Pretty. There were some tech guys or students. Hard to tell these days. And an extremely large woman, wrapped in too-tight Lycra, wolfing down a Quarter Pounder. In times of stress, Cat would lose herself in the faces and forms of others. As a bored child to a single mother, she'd been taken from job to job with her, from appointment to boring appointment. And in the days before electronics, outside of her library books, all she had to watch were people. She'd try to guess who they were, what their house looked like, and read their lips to see if she could decipher what they were saying. It was a reflex, but now she could only do it for maybe thirty seconds before reality snapped her right back into her own skin.

I'm done.

She didn't know she was crying until a tear fell onto her hand. She dabbed her eyes with one of her napkins from the coffee shop. *Can't let it show on your face, Cat.*

Her phone buzzed again. It was her mother.

She sniffed. "Yeah? Ma?"

"Hello, *querida.*"

Cat tightened up.

"Where are ju? Ees so loud."

"The airport. Headed to a speaking gig."

"Where ees it?"

"Oakland."

"Well, where's dat?"

Cat sighed. She held her head in her right hand, propped up by an elbow on her leg. "In California, Ma."

"Oh! Okay. Das good. California ees good. Ju gonna see any-bah-dee in California while ju'r dere? Like TV people?"

"No, Ma." Cat's insides were winding tighter and tighter.

"Why not?" That was it. She couldn't take it right now. Her mother could not be the priority today. Or maybe, for many days.

"Ma, I gotta go. They're calling to board the plane." She hung up quickly, though she knew she'd hear about hanging up in such a way later.

Oh no. Cat's stomach roiled and moaned.

Leaving her coffee and croissant behind, Cat stood up suddenly, grabbed her bags, and headed to the ladies' room.

"Excuse me . . . Excuse me." She weaved between other women and ran into the handicapped stall. It was big enough not to add to the too-hot, can't-breathe, I'm-about-to-puke feeling overwhelming her.

Cat dropped her bags and locked the door behind her, then quickly took off two layers and her sunglasses. Her hair was matting around her face. *Oh shit, oh shit.* Cat's gut took over. It was not pretty. A full five minutes later, still sweating, her makeup smudged, she emerged from the stall. She could barely look in the mirror as she washed her hands.

What am I going to do? WhatamIgoingtodoWhatamigoingtodo . . .

It had been years since she'd experienced a panic attack like this. Years. The cold water felt good on her hands, but she desperately needed to slow her mind down or there was no way she would be able to get on that plane.

Back outside the ladies' room, in a relatively private corner of the waiting area, she texted Gabi.

Hi Gabs—so sorry—know we just said g'bye but having bit of panic attack.

She thanked God as she quickly got a response.

Panic attack?! Still boarding, call me now.

As she dialed and Gabi picked up, all Cat could muster was a trembling "Hi."

"*Chica,* talk to me."

"Hon, I know I just left you and I so should not be bothering you with this—"

"I can use all the distraction I can get. Talk to me."

Being best friends with a psychotherapist had its privileges.

"Gabs. My agent just dumped me—over the phone!—and my mother called right after and I just . . . freaked out." Trying to keep her voice down, Cat was pacing, hair sticking to her face wet with tap water and sweat.

"Are you sitting down? Find a good spot to sit in and put your head back while you talk to me." Gabi had told Cat about this therapy trick, an oldie but a goodie that she liked to employ when she had a panicked client on the phone. Letting your head drop backward while you talked was usually so uncomfortable that it made it hard to cry or hyperventilate. If you could keep your head this way, you were on your way to fine. It slowed you down first physically, then psychologically.

Cat found a seat at the end of a row—right near the window, so at least she could face away from people near her. "I'm down."

"With your head back, take deep breaths with me."

Together they inhaled deeply, then exhaled, three times.

"You can put your head down now."

Cat's chin dropped to her chest. That had been uncomfortable, but it had snapped her out of the wackadoo whirlwind going on in her head a few minutes earlier.

"Okay. Now I'm just sad, I think."

"Cat, what set this off?"

"Well, Guy called to dump me, in effect."

"But you hadn't been getting along much, right?"

"Yeah."

"Okay, well, he treated you badly and now you're free."

Cat was a bit stunned. Usually Gabi didn't lay this stuff on you until after a couple of drinks. Understandably, though, her patience right now was short. "Yeah, that's true."

"And what about your mom?"

"She just started right in with all her 'Where are juuu going?' and 'Why aren't juuu meeting with any-bah-dee?' . . . I hung up on her."

"Good for you."

"Ha! Except I'll never hear the end of it. She'll make me pay for that."

"Not unless you agree to pay her." Like a hot knife through *manteca,* Gabi was slicing through the bullshit. "Where are you headed again?"

"Oakland. For a speech."

"What's the speech?"

At Gabi's question, Cat felt the panic rise again. *What's the speech? What's the fucking speech? Who am I? I don't have a show, I don't have an agent. Who the fuck am I to be giving a speech right now?*

"Uh . . ."

"Cat. Listen to me. At times of great change, we are forced to face our true selves. We suddenly find ourselves asking, 'Who am I?' Only you can answer that for yourself."

"Gabs, I don't know how to be anyone else—anyone other than who I've been for so long."

"I bet you do. That speech? What would you like to say to those women? Let's say that you're just you—no 'former' this or 'former' that. Just awesome you. What do you really want to say to them?"

Cat thought. She wasn't sure. But she knew it wasn't what she had written down and stashed in her computer case.

"You've got nothing to lose now, Cat. You have no producers on your tail. No agent trying to get you a horrible job. You hung up on your *madre*, for Pete's sake!"

Cat had to laugh at that one.

"You're panicking because you're standing on new ground. It's not soft ground, just new ground. But it's more real than what you were standing on before, okay? New ground is squishy, but damn it if it's not like concrete once it sets."

"Like concrete . . . Okay." Cat wasn't sure what was going on in her head but at least she didn't want to throw up anymore.

"Now focus on that speech. What do you really want to say? Inspire those women to rise up at least half as high as you've risen already."

"Thanks, Gabi. I'm sorry—"

"No sorry. You'll get through this, hon."

"I know . . . I gotta run, I think they're boarding."

"Text me when you get there, okay? And call if you need anything. I'll ring you back if I'm with a client."

Cat's flight had been boarding for some time already. The last passengers were handing over their tickets for scanning. Cat sat still as the final boarding call went out.

"Catalina Rivera, please report to your gate."

She watched the service agent call her name. She stared right at him for several minutes. She was far enough away that as he looked around, he didn't suspect that his missing passenger had her eyes on the gate the whole time.

What was Cat waiting for? She didn't know. She just knew that she was not getting on that plane. Not yet.

Chapter 21

As the family milled about the restaurant in groups of three or five, hugs, tears, and even laughs were exchanged at a rapid clip. Magda stared at her phone. She texted back and forth with Albita, asking how they all were doing, passing along small notes on the services—particularly, of course, the near-casket dive. They chuckled a bit, albeit sadly. Cat and Gabi had cabbed it to the airport straight from the cemetery, both needing to return to commitments at home—Cat, for potential work—while Luz had made a mad dash for the restroom upon arrival at the restaurant, her coffee-filled bladder unrelieved for too long. Magda said good-bye to Albita and her children then, stood alone.

"Señor, what kind of tequila do you have?" she snapped at a passing server who looked no more than eighteen.

"Oh, we're not serving liquor for this event, uh . . . señora." He appeared to shrink an inch as he took in Magda's size, gender, expensive suit, and commanding voice.

"What else ya got?" She held his arm with only her fingers but didn't look him in the eye.

"I think we have some white wine or beer?"

"Bring me the white." She looked about to release him. "But in a regular glass, okay? Not a wineglass."

After a quick look around her, Magda's attention went back to her phone.

"Hey."

Magda looked up. It was Inez, her sister closest to her in age. Inez was strikingly petite next to Magda. Another beautiful golden girl, but this one all woman. Tiny waist, "all tits and ass" as Magda had joked when they were young. Her hair hung in long, tangled blond dreads. She smelled of patchouli and she never wore a bra. *So, this one goes to school in Vermont, becomes a complete granola, almost never comes home, and I'm the one no one talks to?* Inez's reason for not being seen much back home was a controlling, possibly abusive, and much-older husband no one cared for. Magda felt draped by a mutual cold blanket of lost time and sadness. They had been so close once. She missed Inez so much. Two family outcasts. Why didn't Magda make more of an effort to see her?

"Oh, hey, *chica*," Magda said.

They embraced, Inez's dreadlocked head coming just to Magda's shoulders.

"What time did you get in?" Magda asked.

"Just this morning."

"Good. Where's Dave?"

"Oh, he's back home, ya know. Doesn't feel so good."

"Well, that's too bad."

"Señora?" The server had returned with a white mug filled three-quarters of the way with white wine.

"*Gracias!*" Magda said after a beat. She raised her mug, but the server had run away as if he had served contraband. Magda's father was a big drinker. Maybe too big. Magda's mother had initiated a no-alcohol rule just after Magda left for college, as she'd had enough of her husband's drunken behavior, both inside and outside of the house. Magda tried to recall if this was tied to finding out about another mistress, a deal they struck to keep Ma from kicking him out of the house. Whatever.

"Oh, shoot. Where can I get one of those?" Inez breathed in the vapors of the Pinot Grigio. She too enjoyed throwing down a few. She also enjoyed smoking herb. However, any and all drugs at this party would need to be liquid.

"Oh, I'll nab him again for you." Scanning the crowd, Magda spotted Luz, cornered by a fifty-something male cousin. Cheesy playa. Magda couldn't remember if the guy was from the New York end of the family or Miami. But he was bearing down on her friend, spreading as much silky talk as he could. Luz looked stony but amused. She could hold her own.

To the left, where Inez was looking, their father worked to extricate himself from a couple of old-timers.

"*Gracias, sí, sí, gracias . . .*" His head bobbed up and down as he took hands, kissed a couple of cheeks, then turned and ambled toward the front door.

"You should go talk to him," Inez said in her laid-back way.

"Nah." Magda shook her head and took a big glug of wine.

"C'mon. Be the bigger man."

Magda's eyes widened. Inez just smiled her big, sweet, earth-loving smile, radiating warmth and peace like a Buddhist monk. Her beatific face caused Magda to take a breath. And another. Fueled by their reconnection at the cemetery and the resulting memory of how close they had once been, she felt a pull toward her father. At this point, what did she have to lose?

"Right. You're right." Magda handed her nearly empty mug of wine to Inez. "Excuse me."

She turned toward the door and surprised herself by rushing to reach her father before anyone else followed him out. Inez watched, smiled harder, then raised the mug to her lips and finished her sister's drink.

Outside, Magda looked around but didn't see her father. Her blood was pumping now. The anxiety of a child raced through her veins, her nerves.

"*Aquí,*" a husky voice called out.

Her father stood to her right, away from the windows of the restaurant and half-concealed by the small alleyway between it and the building next door. He was smoking a cigarette, something else banned by her mother probably thirty years earlier. He had probably taken it up again in secret once she got sick.

"Hey, *Papi*." She walked toward him, feeling vulnerable. Shoulders hunched.

He offered her a drag.

She shrugged a bit, then took it. It had been a long while since she smoked a cigarette. She drew in too hard, probably out of nervousness, and started coughing. Her father took the cigarette back and chuckled.

"*Cuidate,*" he cautioned.

Magda coughed. "Yeah." She coughed again, choked out, "It's been a while."

They stood in silence for a bit, watching some folks leaving the reception who were helping an older woman amble slowly to the parking lot. Magda saw her extended side of the family for what felt like once a century. No need to say good-bye.

"So," Magda said. "Tia Cristina didn't let us down."

"*Ay,* no. She never does, eh?" Her father took a last drag, threw the butt on the ground, and stubbed it out with his expensive loafer. "Man, but *gracias a Dios* for Olga, though."

"Oh, totally!"

"That woman could take down a linebacker."

"Definitely, definitely."

There was another pause, but it was not so much awkward as the sign of a shift. The gravel under their feet crunched as they both nervously shuffled their stance in a delicate dance of worry. Magda noticed out of the corner of her eye, between her own locks, the glint of sun in her father's hair pomade.

"Your mother told me, you know."

Magda flipped the veil of bangs out of her eyes. "Uh. Told you what?"

Her father stubbed the cigarette butt again and again. "That she'd been seeing you."

"Oh." Magda looked away.

"I know she's got family everywhere, and your sister in Vermont, so I never questioned her trips. And you know, I was too preoccupied . . . with myself. My own things."

Magda read this as code for another woman and lots of golf. She wasn't sure where this was going—his tone was so matter-of-fact. But that changed abruptly. Head down, waiting for the next words from her father, Magda heard sobs. Her father was crying.

"*Papi?*"

He closed the space between them quickly and embraced her in a bear hug. He held on to her so tight that Magda lost her breath.

"Magdalena, *m'ija* . . ." He continued to sob. She'd never heard her father cry like this. It was the cry of the deepest pain. Existential pain. Magda had felt this pain herself the day she found out her mother had passed. It was something she wished on no one. She had stiffened at first, but now she pulled her arms free to hug him back. She rubbed his back, halfway to joining him in crying. She wouldn't allow herself to do so, however, until she knew it was safe.

"*Papi?*"

"*M'ija,*" he said, his face nestled in Magda's shoulder, "your mother tried for years to get me to accept you, to take you back. She told me that it wasn't a choice, what you do and who you are . . . and I didn't believe her." He gathered himself a bit, pulled back but kept both hands on Magda's shoulders after he wiped his face with his sleeve. "I didn't believe her. And now she's gone."

"Yes, she's gone." Magda stared back at him.

"She told me, 'Think of her as your only son.'" He paused. "Your successful only son and his children, your grandchildren."

Magda nodded.

"But you're not my son. You're my daughter."

Magda's eyes instantly teared up, large drops building and falling, a soft river rolling down her tanned skin.

"Pa . . ."

"You're my daughter!" he said loudly, with passion. They fell into an embrace with the energy of an exploding star. Decades fell to the wayside. It was like darkness retreating from a fresh lightbulb that had at last been turned on. Finally.

Inez had been watching them at an angle from the window. She brought her hands up to her face to wipe her own tears, and smiled.

Chapter 22

"Ugh. I dunno if I can." Gabi balanced her cell phone between her cheek and her shoulder. For the to-do list: Buy an earpiece. She shuffled several bags between her hands to get comfortable as she worked to focus on wrapping up her schedule with her blessedly patient assistant.

"You sure, Gabi? Maybe a night out? It's been a while."

"Yeah, I know." She dodged a taxi driving much too fast down a neighborhood street. Her walk home in Brooklyn was a solid ten minutes from the train, but it was such a pretty walk—trees, brownstones, a bit of quiet in the air—that she used it as me-time. Valuable. "But you know *nene*'s been having trouble and I just hate to not spend time with him in the evenings." More like: I don't want to leave him alone with his drinking, chronically depressed, resentful father with a short temper.

"Okay, I'll shoot them a note."

Gabi was one block away from home. She placed all the jangling bags onto her left hand, both palms now red and striped from their weight cutting into her skin, and hung up her phone. It was a weird time to be at home, but Gabi just had to take care of her taxes before Max's school let out. She couldn't forget to file again, like last year. A disaster.

Gabi managed the double locks and bags, then gently kicked a delivery box down the short hall to the main room. Her husband sat at his computer, just past the dining table. He barely gave her a glance.

"Hi, hon," Gabi said warmly.

"Oh, hey." She noted Bert's lack of eye contact.

"How are you?"

He took a deep breath, as if harnessing enough energy to do the big work of paying attention to the wife who essentially supported them all.

"Good. Just workin'."

"'Kay." *Workin' on what? Because it's not like you've been bringing in much money,* she thought.

Gabi dropped the grocery bags in the kitchen and proceeded to put everything in its place in record time so she could get to pulling together paperwork for their accountant before their son had to be picked up. This was the double-edged sword of running your own business: the freedom to make your own hours, against the need for more hours to get everything done.

For a few minutes Gabi considered hugging her husband, maybe sitting on his lap to try and seduce him. But these thoughts remained what they were: fantasies. She had been turned down so often for so long, even after nearly two years of weekly couple's therapy, that today she just couldn't take the rejection. *I'm a good wife,* she told herself. *I'm a good wife.*

"Gotta run down to the mailbox to see if this check came in," her husband hollered from the other room.

Gabi now sat in her small home office around the corner, shuffling papers. She didn't know why, but she felt compelled to see his face before he left. She rounded the corner with just enough time to see his back, on his way out the door.

"Okaaay!" she mock-yelled after him.

She looked over at his computer. Not the sharpest tech-tool in the shed, Bert had to be taught to use the touchpad Mac Gabi had given him for his birthday. He hadn't even owned a cell phone when they met years prior. For the past few months, though, unlike years prior, he had been locking his phone and his computer. Now Gabi realized that the lock was on a timer and she had only seconds.

Her heart pounding in her throat, nearly choking her, Gabi sat down at his chair and did something she'd never done in their eight years together: read his e-mails. It only took ten seconds to find all she had hoped she wouldn't find.

I wish you could be inside me again.

It was from a public relations girl Gabi actually had met once.

Can we still get together on Wed?

This one was a response to a Craigslist escort ad.

Bile rose in Gabi's throat, gagging her further. She scrolled through e-mail after e-mail, down the rabbit hole of her husband's lust. Her gut was a mix of repulsion and satisfaction. How could she not know that this was going on? She knew. She knew for at least a year, if not two. Gabi had done what she'd always advised her clients—and the public—to not do, ignore the signs. Don't confront. Maintain the status quo. *Maybe he'll snap out of it. Maybe he'll love me again. I want my family together. Take a back seat, Self-Respect . . . But I didn't know it was this bad.*

After forwarding the most damaging examples of each transgression to her own e-mail address (*Gracias, Lord, for some sense.*), Gabi put everything back the way she'd found it and bolted from the chair to go to the bathroom to throw up. This was what happened in the movies, wasn't it? Not in real life. Yet here she was, head in the porcelain, heaving. It was brief and she was relieved. Now she needed to make a call before he got back. Her fingers shook as she dialed.

"Cat? If I need you, can you come over tonight?"

After exchanging a few more words with her friend, Gabi hung up. A sob burst forth and the tears began, a deluge. She couldn't even think. Her head was all sharp pain and silent wailing.

She had built a career on relationships, had built a brand devoted to preventing things like this from happening. And here she was, a stooge. Taken, by her own husband—her family. She had tried so hard to head this off. She had known, though. She'd known. She ticked off her own grocery list of signs as she wiped the sweat and tears from her face with a cold washcloth:

- There's no more sex (*Well, two years of maybe once a month, which was serious torture because she was a sex machine.*)
- Locked computer/cell (*You knew it then, girl, you knew it.*)
- Changed habits (*He started back at the gym—you knew it then, too, sucka.*)
- Change in personality (*He's been ungrateful to you and horrible to his own son, whom he thinks of as a mini-Gabi.*)

Shame on you. Shame. Shame. You knew it. You fucking knew it. And you just kept on trying to save it. Kept on believing him. Kept on giving him chances. And you give advice to people about this very thing! Why? WHY?

Gabi, Gabi, it takes two.

Gabi looked out the window—the window in the home she had bought with this man, the father of her child. He wouldn't be looking out this window much longer. It was over. It needed to end.

"Hey, hon?" she heard him call from the foyer. "Woo-hoo! Check came in!" He let the door slam behind him.

It sounded to Gabi like the shatter of a door that would never open again.

Chapter 23

"Hello. We're here to see Eugenio Garces." Luz and Emeli stood under the green-gray prison lights, surrounded by peeling paint, as Luz worked to pull their IDs from her purse.

The female guard was nearly as wide as she seemed tall, even sitting down. Luz looked at the woman's knuckles, thinking, *she could knock a man out with those mitts.*

The guard examined their photos, peered at them, jotted things down, scanned, stamped something and handed their IDs back.

"A'ight now, head down to 2B. Follow da signs."

"2B. Thank you." Luz's politeness got a raised brow from the guard.

Luz's new sibling followed quietly, slightly behind her. Emeli had been nearly dumb with silence on the three-hour ride up to the prison. She had put her earbuds in even before her door was closed and had yet to take them off. Luz wasn't about to scold her, as she'd do to her own children—there was a no electronics in the car rule. After all, she wasn't her mother. Just, her sister.

"Jewelry, headphones, cell phones. If it's not a part of your body or covering your body, put it in here," said another gruff guard. Luz was surprised a bit at the number of female guards.

Then again, most of the visitors in line with them were women. And who would she rather have pat her down if necessary?

Emeli popped her earbuds out with dramatic flair, yet she continued to feign indifference at being there. Luz knew what the false confidence of a teenager looked like, though. She had been one herself. Emeli was still a kid, so Luz wasn't going to call her bluff or embarrass her in any way, but the girl was hers now. Luz surely couldn't replace Emeli's mother, but she could try to love her like family. It wouldn't be easy.

The women went through the metal detector, were patted down, and followed the train of fellow visitors to a large room with tables and chairs set up almost as if in a cafeteria.

"Find a seat on one side of these tables. Your inmate will be on the other side. Do not, I repeat, *do not* attempt to take a table all for yo'self. Tables must be shared and if you do not share, we will make you." They let the visitors file in and kept reciting the rules as if they were a soundtrack to a macabre game of musical chairs. "Contact is regulated and minimal. We will be here with you, keeping an eye on you. We reserve the right to search you if we suspect that unapproved items have been exchanged. When time is up, there will be no lingering."

"This one?" Luz wanted to check with Emeli to give her some autonomy. It was her father, after all, whom they were visiting. Luz wasn't yet ready to call him her own father. Biology was not destiny. She'd have to remember that when it came to Emeli, too.

"Sure."

They both sat. As Luz studied the room, she realized just how out of place she felt, how removed from this world. A world that was mostly brown and black like her. People who looked like her family, her cousins. But people she had always maintained distance from, not out of any effort but simply due to the luck of her birth and now she knew, due to the decisions her parents—all three of them—made. And then, coming up against the low expectations of many of the white folks and world around her growing up, Luz had worked so hard to prove that she wasn't their stereotype. That she was an educated, well-spoken, high-learnin' and high-earnin' sistah. But she was also smart enough to know that she was but one step from all this. Nearing forty, she could be a grandmother by now, a young *abuela* like she'd see on the subway at times. Luz was humble enough to note that although much of what she'd received in life was through good choices and hard work, just as much was the result of opportunities, blessings, luck, and this scene where she found herself now reminded her of this deeply.

Luz had entered the prison feeling herself. Different from all the other people in line around her. Even far, far removed from her own flesh and blood, Emeli, next to her. But now plopped into an ugly orange institutional chair, hedged in by a cacophony of voices in several accents—little ones fussing, *mamis* giving "pow-pows"—she felt humbled, the air knocked out of her.

"Emeli, are you okay?"

This was the first time the girl had come here, too. Luz wondered which of them was more scared and put off.

"I'm fine." Emeli was a tough cookie, Luz would give her that.

They both turned toward the doors as inmates filed in. Luz wasn't sure whom her eyes were searching for—Emeli had shown her some photos on her phone of her father, but she still felt lost.

"*Papi!*" Emeli popped up to embrace her father, tall and olive-brown, his too-big orange jumpsuit wrinkling under her hug. A guard was stationed right by them. He watched them embrace, glancing up and down, watching their hands.

"*Ay, mi linda, dejame verte.*" His voice was rough, that of a smoker. He took his daughter's face in his hands, admired it, and kissed her forehead. She was beaming. Luz had yet to see her so happy. "Ju look beautiful. Beautiful." He dropped his hands to hold hers, and called out to his right, "Rico, *mira! Es m'ija!*" The guard, a dark-skinned Latino with a *cerveza* belly, shook his chin up with a "S'up."

So, Luz thought, *he's a charmer. Dominican all right.*

This was her father, her biological father. He was probably sixty years old. Hair cut into that almost skull-cap wave that was popular uptown, his eyes were Caribbean blue—how fitting— and his smile wide and warm, his chest and arms broad and sturdy like a *beisbol* player. He loved his daughter, it seemed. More importantly, she clearly loved him. Luz needed to know where Emeli's soft spots were so she could be sensitive to them going forward. It would get Luz out of her own head.

"And dis . . ." he said as he swung around to his side of the table. "Dis must be Luz." He didn't hug her or even offer a hand to shake. He just looked at her, nearly through her, with intense curiosity. "Well. Ju are much prettier in person." A backhanded compliment, Luz thought, though his smile was one of relief, not sarcasm.

"Thanks."

All three members of a shared gene pool breathed each other in for a few seconds, the noise of the rest of the room (arguments, crying, laughter) well to the background.

Emeli then gave Luz a side-eye and started speaking Spanish to her father. Their body language helped Luz keep up.

What happened with TT?

Are you eating enough?

Nah, nah, gotta lose weight when you're old—it's a diet!

Milagros sent Belkys away.

Again?

Yeah, but then Belkys ran from the new place so now they don' know where she is.

Coño.

"So, can I ask you some questions?" Luz interjected. They only had ten minutes or so left.

Eugenio moved his eyes slowly over to her. He took her in and leaned back. "Sure."

"Tell me about your time with my mother," she said.

The father raised his brows.

"Do you want me to leave?" Emeli asked deferentially.

"Oh no." Eugenio moved forward, putting both arms on the table. "This is a family conversation and we, we three, are family."

The women looked at each other.

"Luz. I loved your mother," Eugenio said.

Luz breathed in deeply. She knew this was going to get very real, but the reality of his feelings, she was not ready for.

"I loved your mother so much. So so much. But she made de right decision, marrying dat guy."

"My father," Luz said.

"Right. Jor father. Da one who raised you. Roger."

Luz nodded in approval. Gotta give the man respect.

"Why did you let it happen? Let me be raised by someone else."

"Aiii, listen." He ran his hands from the front of his head to the back. "Look at me here. I'm no good. And jor mother was so good. So white. She didn't belong wit me and my family, she belonged with da best people." He leaned back a bit.

Luz's stomach twisted. She couldn't even look at her new younger sibling. So much to process.

"How did you know to contact my brother?"

"Oh, heem? C'mon, I'm a smart guy—stupid in some ways, in my choices—but I am a resourceful man. I've been keeping up on you, just knowing a bit how you were doing."

"How did you do that?" Was he a stalker, spying on her?

"Jor mother would forward me da news on you and sometimes pictures of de kids."

"The kids? *My* kids?"

"Ya ya, nothing too crazy. Don' worry, okay?"

"Okay." *Calm down, girl,* Luz told herself. *He's your father, not some guy off the street. But he is a guy off the street. He feels like a guy . . . who happens to be my father. Shit.* Mami *has been communicating with him this whole time? Oh God, the lies, the deceptions, the double life. I can't take this.*

"I was always so proud of you, Luz. So proud."

Luz tried to swallow the acid of anxiety rising in her throat and instead focus on the agenda at hand, which was to get as much information out of this man as possible before their time ran out. She didn't want to have to come here again. "Did the rest of your family know about me?"

"Oh no." He looked at Emeli. "Did you know about Luz?"

"Nope." She kept her head down.

"No, see?"

Eugenio seemed miffed. Luz had questioned him, and as a fairly senior *abuelo*—one in prison, no less—he obviously wasn't accustomed to that. Interrogation from authority, yes. But from a woman in the family, no.

"Two minutes!" a guard shouted.

"Look. Luz. I know dis is all a big surprise to you. But ju gotta know dat was the past and now I need you to take care of Emeli, okay?"

She looked at her much younger sister, a teen going on thirty. "Right."

"You can be angry at all de secrets, but what jor mother did for you and what I did for you and jor father even, it all helped get ju where you are today. And jor mother was the one who made everything happen. I loved her, but she loved you the most. She gave you the greatest opportunities by doing what she did."

Luz was still looking at him sideways. But she was listening. It was compelling. And there was so much more she wanted to know and understand.

"I'm so proud of you, even if I can't take a lot of credit. But, but!" His finger pointed to the sky. "Now I need you to do the same for your sister." He pointed at Emeli. "She needs the same chances as you, and unfortunately . . . Well, she's also in a very tough circumstance." He gestured around the room. "With no mother now, can you do for her what your mother did for you?"

Bzzzzzt. Time was up.

Startled, Luz moved quickly up and out of her chair as everyone else did the same. Emeli embraced her father. Eugenio kissed her cheeks over and over as if she were four years old. When he turned to Luz, she held out her hand. He looked down at it.

"I'll take care of her. Thank you," she said.

Looking a bit dejected, but moving his chin up, above it, he shook her hand.

"No. *Gracias a ti,*" he said sadly.

As everyone filed out, Luz was slightly embarrassed at the handshake and her palm burned with its memory. Had it been insulting to him? Should she care? Why did it linger and feel so bad? What about Emeli? Had Luz hurt her feelings? Ugh, she could be so snotty sometimes.

After the inmates left and Eugenio had blown a kiss to his girl, the visitors filed out. Luz really didn't want to come up here again. But something told her she'd be back soon.

"So, I thought it better that the kids weren't here after that," Luz said to Emeli as she turned the lock and opened the door. "I'm sure this is pretty overwhelming, and adding a bunch of screaming kids . . . to coming back from where we were . . . well . . ." She gestured for her much-younger half sibling to enter.

The light in the loft-like townhouse was almost as strong as on a beach, and the girl tipped her head back to see where it was coming from. Luz saw her jaw go slack and her grip on her bags loosen a bit. She stood very still, clearly very intimidated.

"It's nice," she said in the flat affect of a teenager, wrapped in the accent of an American-born Dominican who almost never left her neighborhood.

Until that moment, Luz hadn't realized just how much she wanted this girl to accept her. She had thought of acceptance as a one-way street: I'd better like this kid or she's out. But that was her tough side talkin', the side that did the deals, that did the work. Luz's other side, the loving den mother and family advocate, was there, too, and she needed approval.

"Let me take those for you."

Emeli hesitated, seemingly unable to believe she was awake right now, and alive.

"Okay," she said finally, though her face showed concern for where her few belongings would go.

"I'll just put them down right here in the kitchen, okay? We can set you up in your room after I give you a tour, *sí?*"

"*Sí,* okay." As her bags were set down within her sight, she relaxed.

"So, this is the kitchen—the epicenter of our family madness."

Emeli's face was flat, unchanged. Luz told herself, *Tone down the thesaurus words there, sister. You're gonna freak her out even more.*

"The kids are running around here all the time."

"Oh, right." Emeli's eyes were darting between the fancy chef's stove, the stainless-steel fridge, and the kitchen island that was probably as big as her bed.

"Please be at home here. Want something to drink?"

"That's okay."

"Well, please help yourself while you're here or just ask one of us, okay? Now, this is the living room-slash-big room filled with toys and screens." Luz turned them around to face a space that was likely larger than Emeli's entire apartment. They had two more floors to go. The girl didn't speak, just nodded. Stunned.

"We have parental blocks on the cable so the kids don't accidentally turn on anything they shouldn't see. But if there's something you want to watch, just ask. Are there shows you like to watch?"

"Not really."

Jesus, Maria, Jose, *caramba*. Such a tough nut to crack, this girl.

Luz clapped her hands together. "Okay, then. Let's head upstairs." As Emeli followed her, Luz had to remind herself: *She's a kid. She's scared. She's not being a sullen, disrespectful brat. She probably has no idea what to do, how to feel. Be nice, Luz!*

As they climbed the stairs, Luz felt the urge to fill the silence, even if it just made her feel better. Though she couldn't imagine how it could make Emeli feel worse, unless it was just annoying. And in that case, too bad. *Get used to it, sister! We're a chatty, noisy, loving bunch.*

"So I moved some things around in my old office to give you privacy. I still have my bookcases in there, so you'll never run out of things to read."

Nope, she didn't lighten up at that.

"It's small, but it has a door." Luz welcomed her into a room about twelve by fourteen feet. Not small for this teenager. She was used to living in a room about half this size.

"This is where I am?" Emeli's voice was tentative.

"Yes!" Luz was so happy to detect emotion, any emotion. "This is your room." She didn't add out loud "for now." It still hadn't sunk in fully that she had another child to take care of— although they were siblings, Luz thought of Emeli as a child and was, for now, inclined to treat her as such. Luz would much rather be her mother—it seemed she needed one. *I'll figure it out,* Luz told herself.

Emeli walked in slowly. She felt the carpet under her feet.

"Sorry about that carpet. I hate carpet. We just haven't gotten to yanking it out yet."

"Uh-huh," Emeli mumbled. Unbothered, instead, comfortable.

Luz leaned against the doorway as the girl fingered the bookcases. "I got those at ABC warehouse in the Bronx. I'd been eyeing them for years."

At the mention of the Bronx Emeli cracked a smile. "I know that place. My cousin lives up there."

Luz lit up at the mention of family. "Really? On your mom's side or your dad's?"

"I'm not sure."

"Oh." She led the girl around the stairwell. "This will be the bathroom you can use."

They walked in. It was fairly narrow but long, and nearly all cream-colored: cream marble backsplash, cream mirrored tiles, ecru tub with a rich teak wraparound frame. Emeli took it in but was stuck staring at one item.

"Um, what's dis?"

"Oh! That's a bidet." As if naming it helped. "It's one of those things that, see, you turn it on like this." Luz bent down to turn on the spout.

The girl looked at her quizzically.

"It's for, uh, cleaning yourself after you use the toilet."

The girl raised her brows. "Oh!"

"I mean, it can take some getting used to, but I'm sure the girls will be more than happy to show you how to use it!" Luz pictured her twins taking turns on the bidet, showing their new sister—cousin?—wait, *auntie? Tía?*—how to use the appliance. She chuckled at the thought. But thinking of them suddenly snapped her into Mama-play.

"Actually, let's rip through the girls' room and I can show you the master bedroom later—not like you'll need to go up there. I thought maybe we could make some cookies for the kids before they get home. Ya know, the smell of fresh-baked cookies and all . . . ?"

The teen shook her head, not understanding the reference.

"They say it lowers stress levels."

The girl nodded, chin up. Okay. Whatever you say.

Luz was tired already. And she hadn't even been through one night with this new girl. Sister. Auntie. *And who am I?*

Chapter 24

Waiting backstage, Cat popped another mint into her mouth. Her stomach was roiling and she was sweating. *C'mon, girl,* she told herself. *Breathe.*

She deliberately pulled air into her lungs, concentrating on the sensation, in and out. Her fight-or-flight programming was on full alert. There might as well have been a hungry grizzly bear in front of her, Cat felt so terrified.

"A water, please? I'm so dehydrated," Cat stage-whispered to a producer.

There were two reasons for the smidge of confidence Cat retained: First, she had managed to board the next flight following her scheduled departure, though it meant arriving with very little time to spare before her presentation, so she was running on adrenaline. And second, what Gabi had said to her about having nothing to lose. With her new speech, produced in a frenzy on the plane, Cat could tank completely, thereby losing all future speaking gigs and getting skewered on social media—maybe they'd say she had lost her mind and she could ride that to a comeback? Or she could be crazy-like-a-fox enough to start a whole new line of work.

The idea of this speech as an opportunity to focus-group was keeping Cat upright. That, and the potential for happiness. For launching herself into a new space, one that didn't depend on whether she was "Latin enough," one that didn't make her eyes glaze over in boredom and abject ennui. One with room to grow, one that she loved. There was no question in her mind that she was going to step through the door before her, even though it wouldn't be possible to go back. Step into the light . . .

"Here you go." The producer proffered a bottle of water, chilly to the touch. "So, we should start."

"Yes, thank you. Start." *You'll have to be more eloquent than that,* chica, Cat told herself.

Cat's host strode onto the stage and into the lights. From behind the two-story-high curtain, she could barely hear but she could see. A packed house of women looking for business inspiration were waiting for her, this brown woman, to tell them they could do it. Okay. But did it have to be so cut and dried? Did it have to be about business exclusively? No. More than half of success was psychological. *Get the business stuff from books,* Cat said silently to herself. *I'm here, goddammit, to get you off your ass. And me as well.*

". . . Let's welcome, Cat!"

Here you go, girl. Just feel it.

As Cat walked onstage, her Spanx did its usual mild roll down her middle. She paid it no mind. She just focused. She felt as if she were about to bungee jump down a cliff. But this cliff dive—well, this cliff dive led somewhere. It would have to. Cat had no choice.

"Hello! Hello, everyone! Thank you so much for having me here. It's a real honor."

Cat paused, but it wasn't for effect. She was gathering her internal forces. Some members of the audience shifted. Some peered closer. Some, she felt, were already impatient. But she had their attention. Now or never.

Leaving the podium and putting her notes aside, Cat leaped into the abyss.

"So, I missed my plane. I missed my plane here. On purpose."

There were murmurs from the audience.

"Yup, on purpose! And you're going: Uh, whyyy? Why would someone like me miss a flight on purpose? How could I be so irresponsible . . . ?

Because I was afraid. And I was afraid because I had just been dumped by my agent. At the airport.

Yup, dumped.

Now I'm sure you all remember how it feels to be dumped. And if you have never been dumped, well, odds are you may not be the dumpER forever."

Some light chuckles.

"Being dumped is hard—it sucks! He dumped me, he said, because . . ."

She mimicked his voice and tone.

" 'I've done everything I can for you, Cat. I think we've come to the end of the line, Cat.'

And you know what? He was right. He had done all he could for me. I've done maybe six pilots. More meetings with more studios than I can count. Web sites, radio, everything—but there were also things that I couldn't do for him. I couldn't take another TV job out of desperation. I couldn't take another TV job at a place I knew was sincerely toxic. And I couldn't take another TV job where I would be a puppet. Saying and doing what my producers wanted, regardless of my feelings on what I was talking about—regardless of the facts!

Now, I loved my time in television. I love the frantic nature of the business. My mind works a hundred miles a minute, so I need to do things that can keep up with it. I'd never had another job that used all my skills—used me on all cylinders. Not one. TV was it. But, there's TV and then there's TV.

So here I am.

No show. No show on the horizon. I speak, I write. But now that swinging into the next gig is not so easy, I'm asking: "Who am I?" Who am I.

Well, I'm the daughter of a 'leetle' Mexican woman who came to this country at the age of fifteen. She had me on her own and raised me to rule the world. She put every single ounce of her hopes and dreams about the opportunities this country had to offer into me. She packed them all in like a tin of sardines, like a clown car.

Cat pantomimed as she spoke, garnering some chortles along the way.

But we didn't have a lot of money. She was uneducated. We were alone. My mother worked two full-time jobs while I hopped from caretaker to caretaker, sometimes a tía here, sometimes a cousin there. Sometimes a very freaky white lady down the street who wore makeup like Cruella de Vil!

And as soon as I could work—while going to school and getting straight As, mind you—I was put to work. I started baby-sitting at ten years old, even became a full-time nanny over the summer when I was twelve. Imagine hiring a preteen to care for two kids while you're gone for eight hours a day. Disaster!

But nope, nope, I didn't let it show, all the stress. I didn't let disaster happen. Even though I was so exhausted and so sleep-deprived at times that I'd chew my cuticles to bleeding nubs—though my nails always looked fabulous . . .

Once I was old enough, I started waiting tables alongside my mother at a chain restaurant. The horror!

More chuckles.

Can you imagine being sixteen years old, when your parents are, like, 'totally pains in the butt,' and there I was, having to work next to my mother sometimes for thirty hours a week or more. Again! All while going to school and getting straight As!

So, but, who am I, besides a person who just got dumped?

I'm the product of that hardworking woman, an immigrant. Of course, while I was growing up, people had many different words to describe my mother and me. I won't repeat them, but I bet you can imagine what they were. We just kept our heads down and kept at it. Then college came and I'm in the Ivy League and we just keep going at it, keep working, keep moving forward. Like a steam engine. Like one giant steam engine—nothing could stand in our way!

So there I was two years ago, suddenly with my own television show. My own national television show. My brown butt had a show! And I was the first in my family to graduate from high school, let alone college, then a master's degree—and from an Ivy League school. There I was, singing the theme song from The Jeffersons *as I moved into my doorman-building apartment.* "Movin' on up! To a dee-luxe apartment in the skyyyyy!"

I finally had a piece of the pie.

But guess what? All these things I wanted to accomplish, these items I could check off my list, the things I wanted to do my whole professional life have been done. Now what?

You'd think that I'd feel super-accomplished, right? That bio that was read just before I came onstage was impressive, right? I'm asking because, honestly? I'm not impressed. Now, I'm not going to stand here and give you some feel-sorry-for-me-and-my-fame-and-riches story. But I am going to ask you: Why am I not impressed?

Are you impressed with everything you've done with yourself? When was the last time you were most proud of yourself, in a good way? In a 'Hey, that was kinda awesome' way? I take it that if you're here you're looking for improvement. For tools to get ahead in life. You want me to impress you. Well, how's this . . . ?

I figured it all out just now.

The reason that everything my mother and I worked so hard for doesn't impress me or make me particularly happy may be that we got it backward. Could the American Dream that we tried so hard to make true be a little bit backward?

Some disgruntled mumbles came from the audience.

Wait! Wait! Stay with me here. This country is miraculous.

My girlfriends and I have a saying: "By the luck of our birth." If we had been born in the native countries of our mothers, as little as one decade earlier . . . my goodness, I'd be so far from standing here, I might as well be on the moon. And I am ever grateful to the universe for the good fortune to be who I am, where I'm from, today.

But! And you knew that "but" was coming . . .

But, once we have that house and that car, that dream, are we completely happy? Once we reach our goals, do we stop and just . . . be happy? Or do many of us keep searching for happiness?

See, I think I'm not impressed with myself because I was chasing the wrong thing. I thought that if I got those degrees and got that show, got those accolades and that mantel filled with awards and fan art, I'd be happy. Here's the truth: I was miserable. There's a part of me that enjoyed the day-to-day. I enjoyed being recognized, I enjoyed some free clothes—who wouldn't? But like my agent, when it comes to this race, I think I've done all I can do.

See, my dream is to be fulfilled. My American Dream does not live in that house in my dee-luxe apartment in the sky. I think I was chasing fulfillment through accomplishment. But what if accomplishment, true accomplishment, was a result of fulfillment—happiness—instead of the other way around?

"Life, Liberty and the pursuit of Happiness."

What if we were to do things that made us feel fulfilled, which would make us better at what we do—which then brings about raises, promotions, recognition, even that house!

Many of us who were the hope of our parents grow older and come face-to-face with a scary question: Whom did I do this for? Was this really for me? Is it okay that it wasn't? When do I get to drive this freight train?

Is what you're working on currently, or what you'd like to do instead of the career you have now, a source of happiness? Can you truly say that, once you hit a certain net income, or once you have money left over to put into savings every month, then you'll be happy?

I don't know.

I dunno.

For me, what I do know is that today, I've jumped off a cliff. I'm taking a leap.

Where am I going?

What's my next chapter going to be?

As a dear friend said to me right before I missed my flight, on purpose: What have you got to lose?

And maybe that's the answer. Not asking, "What do I have to gain?" but "What have I got to lose?"

What have you got to lose? What have you lost already? What are you ready to gain?

I don't have it all figured out right now. And you probably don't either.

Whaddaya say we figure it out together?

Write that next chapter?

And I promise I won't go missing any more planes!

Thank you.

Even as the last words left Cat's mouth, she saw people standing up. As she bent her head down in gratitude, the roar of

800 women nearly knocked her off her feet. She looked up and witnessed her first standing ovation.

Cat smiled so hard her cheeks burned. Her eyes welled.

"Oh, Cat, before you go?" The young producer poked her head into Cat's tiny dressing room. Cat was beyond exhausted, from straight-up stress response for nearly twelve hours, a funeral, to performing with all new material, not bombing totally, being mobbed by dozens of women afterward, each of whom just wanted to tell Cat how inspiring she was and how moved they were and how they, too, could now ask: "Who am I?" Cat's makeup was running, her hair frizzing, yet she didn't think she'd ever felt so alive.

"There's just one more person who really needs to see you . . ."

A handsome, lean-faced, forty-something woman peered in. Not cocky but strong and deliberate, she exuded astonishing confidence.

"Cat, I'm Audrey Grey. Executive producer over at Alta Productions for Gala."

Gala? The largest online content creator in the country.

"Oh! How are you?" Cat got up to shake her hand.

Audrey smiled. "Listen, I was just out there . . ."

"Oh, yeah, well . . ." Cat fell into her usual self-deprecating mode.

"It was fabulous. It was great." Audrey pronounced every word with such clarity that it mesmerized Cat. "I really needed some new talent to host our tentpole show. I want you to do it."

"Me?"

"I know, people think Web and we don't pay, but that's bullshit. Okay, we pay a bit less, but something tells me that if I gave you this show to not only host but produce, you might be interested."

"To produce?"

"Executive produce."

"That's big."

"Your voice, your outlook. I want the show to be through your eyes."

Cat raised her brows and held on to Audrey's card, feeling it between her fingers.

"Let's talk tomorrow." Audrey took Cat's hand, shook it firmly. "After you have a drink and get some sleep." She winked.

Cat smiled broadly. *Tonight may be the best sleep of my life.*

Chapter 25

Ay.

Magda unfolded herself out of her drop-top Audi, feeling for the first time in a long time the complaints of her body parts as they acclimated to a new environment: one with much less alcohol. (Well, it had only been two days.) Compensating for the aches, the sun warmed her fair skin. As she let her attention move to gratitude for the feeling, she smiled.

Magda needed that smile. This was to be her first visit to a psychotherapist, a specialist referred to her by her dearest Gabi, and Magda was anxious. There was only so much Gabi could handle; she couldn't be Magda's sole support system. It was a heavy load. And now Gabi had a load of her own.

Damn loser husband, Magda thought. *The fuck. I should pay someone to knock him out.*

She shook her head in hopes of shaking off the negativity. After all, revenge took care of itself. Give bad people enough rope—rope being time, usually—and they'll hang themselves, with no loss of energy from you. Happiness is the best revenge, Gabi always liked to say. It was a jolly saying and Magda believed it enough, but she couldn't resist imagining knocking Gabi's husband out herself. *Just one punch.*

Sighing, she put her car keys in her pocket and raised her head to see where she was going. It wasn't necessarily a fancy location. Fairly plain and dry. Magda usually preferred well-curated places and people, but this appointment wasn't about suits, vacations, pretty people and high-end tequila. This was about getting her head on straight. About having a relationship with her father. Though he'd had a breakthrough, Magda wanted to make sure that her bitterness toward him for rejecting her coming out didn't sabotage their future. It surprised her how happy she was to be receiving her father's love again. It angered her as well. Ambivalence was a tough thing to live with. And life was too short, as they'd both just experienced with Magda's beloved mother.

"Goddamnit!"

Magda turned her attention toward the sound of a frustrated female.

"Shit, shit, shit . . ." A woman, ten feet away, was trying to pull items back together into a now-busted box. It appeared that the bottom had fallen out; tacks rolled on the ground, and pens joined them. Notebooks dropped open.

"Oh geez. Here . . ." Magda instinctively bent down to help.

The woman wore snug cargo pants of olive green, a pair of black and white Vans, and a fitted gray T-shirt. The shirt had pulled up her back, allowing Magda a long look at her smooth brown skin, defined waist, and the hint of a tattoo. On her head was a pile of dreads rolled into a large bun, some dreads blond, some dark brown. Funky.

"Oh, thanks," the woman muttered. "Thanks."

As Magda focused on helping with the mess, she put off looking the woman in the face. She was rewarded for her focus as she helped lift the newly secure box into the arms of its owner.

"There . . . Hi."

Lord, she was beautiful.

"Thank you." The woman smiled a big-toothed, full-lipped

smile. Her top lip folded right into the bottom of her nose. Her eyes were round and dark, makeup free. The box was heavy and she faltered for a second, attempting to shift it with her left knee, like a flamingo taking a nap.

"How about I take that and you grab the door?" Magda offered.

"You sure?"

Magda didn't wait to answer. She just took the box, easier with her broad, strong frame. This woman had Michelle Obama arms, but they were a bit too short to wrap around the box like Magda's.

"What floor?"

"Just to two, actually," the woman said as she opened the door for Magda. Once inside the lobby, she pushed the elevator button and it arrived quickly. They stuffed themselves in. She asked Magda, "What floor are you going to?"

Magda felt a quick rush of embarrassment. Not only for her own sake but for her family's, she knew that going to therapy was the best thing to do. Still, she was a therapy newbie clinging to her macho tendencies, afraid to admit where she was headed. Sense prevailed.

"Uh, four actually." The woman pressed "4."

Had Magda been at a bar, drinking, she would practically have been down this woman's pants by now. At least she would have gotten a name and phone number. *I'm nervous,* she thought. *Shit.*

The elevator dinged on "2." The door opened.

"Well, this is me." The small lady with the pretty dreads stood in the doorway of the elevator and leaned in to take the box from Magda.

Magda handed it over carefully.

"Thanks—really a big help. Bye!"

At the last second, Magda held back the elevator door. "Oh, wait!"

The woman placed the box on the ground in front of an office door. "Yes?"

"I'm Magda."

"Oh, I'm Cherokee." She leaned forward to shake Magda's hand. "Good to meet you."

Magda let the elevator close. That was a warm smile. Was the woman just being nice or . . . ? She might not even like girls. Like that had stopped Magda before. But this was different. *Dios,* she was so warm. So, normal.

Magda got off on the fourth floor and followed the signs to a Dr. Amalfi's office. She hoped no one was in the waiting room, no other clients—patients.

When she was buzzed in, the only one there was a nicely rounded Mediterranean-skinned woman with long hair and a warm smile.

"Hello, Magda!" She reached out for a handshake. "I'm Dr. Amalfi, Emma. So glad Gabi referred you."

"Yes. Yeah. Well. Thanks."

"Gabi mentioned that you're a newbie, so I'll be gentle." Magda chuckled. The therapist continued. "Though if you know Gabi, you probably know all too well how this works, yes? Water?"

"Water? Yes, water, thanks." Magda was rattled, though not necessarily in a bad way. "Question," she called out a bit as Dr. Amalfi went behind a wall to grab some water.

"Yes?"

"Have you been in this building long?"

"At least five years."

"Oh." Magda expected a "Why'd you ask?" but the doctor did that frustrating thing that therapists do—she let the air hang empty, forcing Magda to follow up. "What's that company on the second floor?"

Dr. Amalfi reappeared and handed Magda a cup of water.

"That's a tech start-up of some kind. I've met a couple of the kids from there. They seem nice." She beckoned Magda to follow her to her office. Again she let the silence linger.

"Oh. 'Kay."

Emma's eyes narrowed, knowingly. "I did once get to chat a bit with a woman there—beautiful, with dreads."

Magda warmed up. "Yeah, I just met her."

The doctor watched Magda's cheeks flush and her eyes wander to the right. She smiled. "Well, let's focus on the fourth floor before we head to the second."

One Year Later

Chapter 26

"Wait, are you saying that being able to choose the hair color or eye color of your unborn child is a good thing?"

Cat was again in the host seat. But her new show was as far away from her previous show as purposefully as possible. The set was compact, modern but eclectic, mirroring the tastes and style of its host and creator. Mid-century modern furniture with a Peruvian throw here, an indigenous clay sculpture there, and of course, flowers—big, color-saturated flowers. It was upscale-tequila-bar-chic, and every member of the panel was a woman.

"That's *exactly* what I'm saying!" responded one of Cat's guests.

Two guests were agreeing enthusiastically that genetic sorting and selection during test-tube fertilization was not just a good thing for women but inevitable. Both were Anglo, one woman in her fifties, with the spiky red hair of a successful marketer and entrepreneur who didn't have to toe a company line, the other, more plain and QVC-host, but just as feisty, in her early forties. Cat's third guest, a round, witty blond blogger, shook her head in disappointment at her "sisters," while a petite, long-lashed Indian-American doctor looked stunned.

"Have you gals lost your minds?" They tried talking over Cat, until she issued the inevitable—but friendly-fired—word slap: "Does *eugenics* mean anything to you? Eugenics? Nazis?"

She delivered the kicker with the charm and wit of a scripted line in a dramedy; it did the job. They were stunned into silence. "What happens when you give people the right to select who gets to live and how?" Cat gestured to the camera. "And when we get back, tell us where you would draw the line between hair color and skin color." She gestured toward herself and the other guests. "We'll be right back."

At "cut," the production team sprang into action. It was half as big as the team on Cat's previous show but multicolored, young, vibrant, and relaxed. Cat popped out of her chair for a quick makeup check.

"Hey, hey." She headed over to her girl Patty. "Did you catch that one, gurl? Skin color—snap!"

"It's like they don't even know what they're saying." Patty was a gravel-voiced Italian Jersey-girl, so fiercely loyal to Cat that she'd followed her from their previous network. Both were making less money but getting something much more valuable in exchange: their sanity. The hours weren't as crazy and there was flexibility in taping. Cat was the executive producer as well as the host, so she called the shots. And she had brought along with her a couple of other producers who were all too happy to leave the madness that was network and cable television for a start-up online channel. Risky? Sure. But freedom and diversity and getting something new on the résumé as heads rolled left and right on the old-fashioned telly? Priceless.

"You gotta stop touchin' yo hair, girlfriend!" Patty admonished.

"I know, I know! I hear your voice in my head all the time—'Don't touch it!'"

Patty rolled her eyes, covered Cat's, and sprayed. "Go. Done. Don't touch it!"

"*Sí, sí, señora!*"

Cat's hair was a different form of TV hair for her, and in general. It was grown out, loose—purposefully disheveled and touchable. Patty loved it, though she was a bit nervous at first to go against the old-school TV grain of perfectly shellacked hair. But she listened to Cat, took the leap, and surprised the host with exactly what she wanted. A kind of crown that reflected who she really was. Wardrobe helped, too. On a tight budget, Cat got one cram session with her favorite stylist, Kitty, a Lower East Side rocker chick in her forties. Cat now dressed much more downtown artsy than her previous employer had allowed. Kitty zoomed in on dressing Cat in not only what reflected who she was as a person, but also, she pushed the boundaries of who she'd been before. A new slate. A new look. For the first time in her life and for longer than she'd like to remember, Cat felt like she lived in her own skin.

"Cat, here's what's up." Cat's senior producer, Eve, followed her toward the set. "We've got twenty to twenty-one minutes on the new study of kids and screen time—"

"Ooh! That one's gonna be good." Cat reflexively placed her palm on her belly. Four months and counting.

"And did you want to follow up on the eugenics thing, or does that hit too close to home?"

"Ha! That's a good thing!"

"You sure?" Eve was Jewish, forty, a serious investigative TV journalist who, as the mother of two elementary-school-aged boys, had been thrilled to jump ship for a bit less money and a lot more flexibility. Plus, she and Cat had a shorthand, combined with the respect and ability to argue but love each other 'til the end. "You haven't officially announced it, really." Eve drew her eyes to Cat's belly.

"Right. Well, no better time than the now!"

"Aw, c'mon! What about a press release and shit?" Eve loved a bit of press. "Could be great for the show!"

"Tell ya what, *amiga:* How about we tape this, I present my little bit o' news, and then we use the clip with the press release . . . ya?"

Eve's eyes lit up. "Let's do it." She hustled back to the control room, jazzed.

The floor director hollered out a "Five to start!" The two pro-eugenics ladies chatted emphatically with each other, bonding over their shared fantasies of creating a future filled with model babies. Patty had popped up on set to powder them a bit. She said a prayer aloud as she did it—or maybe it was a curse—she could be such a *bruja*.

Cat confidently made it back to her seat, jiggled her earpiece back in, and looked at her notes.

"Pssst, Cat, your phone." It was the floor director, Andy. She had left her phone on a stool by his camera.

"Oh, shoot—who is it?"

He looked quickly and mouthed: *Your mom!*

The show had been on the air only a month but the on-demand viewing numbers were encouraging. Cat hadn't spoken as much to her mother since hanging up on her at the airport a year ago. Cat was a family gal and it still made her feel guilty, but she also knew that at the time she was having a crisis. A big one. And anyone close to her who was not able to help her stay standing, who made it all the harder, would have to be set aside for a while. Or she would have lost everything.

But once she finally found someone—younger, but so successful—to have a life with, a family, she had to allow her mother back into her circle. Pregnant and fulfilled, Cat finally realized that though her mother's methods may not have been the most conducive to allowing Cat to breathe, she truly did what she thought was best. After all, the odds had been against her. A Latina, Mexicana, single mother living at the poverty line, trying to give her daughter the best the world had to offer her. Cat knew she had been hard on her and the solace that this realization gave to Cat was like a tether releasing her from pain. When Dolores called or scolded or passive-aggressively hinted that Cat could do something different or better, Cat didn't let it own her anymore, it didn't reach her insides. She was her own person now. Getting fired and hitting rock bottom can do that. And after Dolores fell off her chair, raised the roof in rage, and drowned her sorrows in *dulces* at the news that Cat was going to have a baby out of wedlock, she learned that her daughter had boundaries. Cat made clear: *If you're going to know your grand-child—and I want you to—you've got to accept me as I am.* It wasn't easy, it took months of being firm but as loving as she could be, but she did it. *Abuela* was now onboard.

And here Cat was. On the set of her new show. Truly *her* show, a show she had created and one she ran. Strangely enough, it drew more viewers than her network show ever had. An all-female, all-the-time show that focused on issues big and small, with guests split among ages, races, and cultures. It was smart, just like her and her guests. Full support from the top brass on both coasts made it all so much easier. It was dreamy, actually.

Add to this Cat's move from a dull, overpriced apartment near midtown to a two-bedroom place in Harlem with enough space and schools nearby for what was soon to be her growing family. Dammit if she'd never been happier in her life, and had never wanted something—someone—so badly, as this baby. When she'd felt the first flutter of something alive inside her, she thought she'd fall apart with joy.

Here she was. About to reveal why she'd been wearing loose tops and chewing ginger gum first thing every morning. And her mother was on the line.

"One minute to start!"

"Andy, I'll call her right back, okay?"

I will, Cat thought. *I'll call her right after we wrap.*

It's time for her to meet the father.

Chapter 27

Luz chopped leeks while her husband put some finishing touches on his "gourmet" pizza for the kids. Low-volume old-school R & B played on the mini-speakers in the kitchen. Just husband and wife making dinner together in the quiet of their kitchen after a day's work.

The quiet was short-lived. Luz felt the floor vibrate even before she heard the roar of her incoming children. All three yelled with fake terror and tore between and around their mom and dad at the kitchen island, bumping both parents on their way to evading what must be some monstrous creature.

"*Ay!* What's going on here?" Luz called out.

"Maaaaa, she's going to tickle us until we peeeeeee!" one of the twins tried to explain while running, bobbing, hiding, and screaming with joy.

"I'm coming for you and I'm huuuuungry!" Emeli poked her head around the doorframe, hands like claws, eyes crazy big, mouth smiling.

The gaggle of siblings screeched in anticipation.

Luz smiled. Her husband had just put their pizza in the oven and turned around to help his wife finish up the grown-ups' dinner—"The kids will never eat leeks, *amor*"—wrapping his arm around her waist as Chris saw her face light up at the sight of Emeli.

It hadn't been an easy year. For anyone. Emeli joined the family abruptly and her father was going to be in jail for a long time. This meant a new school. New home. New family. New way of life. Ever grateful to her husband for his personal and financial support, Luz was able to build her own business, already nearly as lucrative as her previous position, and work from home on her own schedule, so she could focus on the homefront.

At first, Emeli was resentful beyond belief—resentful of her new family's affluence, their multicultural ways, her nieces and nephew's noise and curiosity. But Luz's daughters and son had won Emeli over and then some. They made her feel needed. Special, despite her surliness. It was as if they just "got" it. Understood where her pain was coming from—fear and insecurity—and rarely took it personally. As for how she felt about Luz, well, the relationship was much more like a stepmother and daughter than two sisters. But Luz was okay with that for now, and so was Emeli. She had needed a strong, older female to hang on to, to believe in her. And Luz knew that things would continue to evolve between them and the family as a whole. And boy did her husband, Chris, know how to crack Emeli up—God bless him.

Luz protected Emeli a bit from the rest of the family— *protected* wasn't necessarily the word. Luz shielded her, maybe even kept her to herself. Luz wanted to strengthen their own ties before building ones between Emeli and the rest of the family, even her mother and father—the ones who raised her. As for managing the initial mess in her head after learning that her parents had been all too good at keeping secrets—and that a branch of her bloodline led to a prison upstate—she was getting there. It helped that she was inclined to focus on her children and husband instead of herself. She needed to make sure they were happy first. And now they were. So, now it was time.

Seeing Emeli now, running around with her kids, Luz had

never felt so fulfilled. There was, however, one more item on her to-do list.

Dun-dun-duuuuunnn!

The ominous-sounding doorbell was her husband's sense of humor. The kids screamed even louder. "Aaaaaiiiii!" They ran back into the hallway. "Hide! Hide! Quick! C'mon!" came their various little voices.

Emeli froze.

"Hon," Luz asked her, "can you take the kids to wash their hands?"

"Okay," she answered, looking slightly green with nerves.

"Here we go, *chica*. Hammer time," quipped Chris.

"Seriously, brothah. 'Hammer time?'" Luz dried her hands as she made her way to the door. Luz's husband playfully patted her ass as she made her way by him.

"Oh, hi, baby," Luz's mother greeted her at the door, with a kiss on the cheek and a half hug, her right arm cradling a big, fashionable purse.

"Hey, Ma, Dad."

Her father couldn't hug her, his arms full of bags.

"Dad! What's with all the *bolsas*?"

"Well, you know your mother. Had to shop for this event."

Luz's mother rolled her eyes. "*Donde están mis niños?*" she asked.

"Oh, they're running out back with Emeli. They'll be here in a minute."

Luz's mother was dressed in nearly her Sunday best. More like Saturday at a Broadway show. Luz made a note of her mother's need to both impress someone important she was meeting for the first time and her need to primp as a way to prepare herself for something that might be difficult psychologically.

"We're here." Emeli appeared in the kitchen entryway, standing tall and brave. She was a very different girl than she had been a year ago—and yet much more herself, paradoxically. She was the same Emeli, but without all the armor. Her hair still big and flopped to the side like a cool teenager, but her clothes just a bit looser, less skin showing, and the skin on her face clear of the stacks of makeup she'd had when Luz and she first met. Emeli looked refreshed and at ease, her face newly open.

"*Abuelaaaa!*" the younger children yipped as they ran to their grandmother.

"*Ayyyyy!* My babies! Mmmwah mmmwah, come here, more *besos, mas besos!*" She took each one's face in her hands and offered each a "You're so beautiful," a "You're so strong" in Spanish. It was like a beam of strength transferred from one generation to the next. Luz's kids would internalize these moments and turn to them during hard times as talismans, sustenance.

"What am I, chopped liver?" asked Roger.

"Grandpaaaaa!" Nina, 'Fina and Nico made his legs disappear in a cloak of loving little arms and torsos.

Emeli still stood. Smiling and quietly watching, not knowing her place.

Luz took her mother by the arm and led her to Emeli.

"Mom. This is Emeli."

Altagracia locked eyes with the teen. Emeli seemed vulnerable. But, she need not have worried. *Abuela* took the girl's hands in hers, and said in Spanish, "Emeli. So nice to meet you."

Emeli tried to respond in kind. She managed, "*Sí . . . gracias . . .*"

In that awkwardness, there was a shift under their feet. Decades of lives lived and hearts broken flew past and between them. The older woman lowered her shoulders, smiled sweetly, and took Emeli's beautiful, light coffee-skinned, blue-eyed face in her hands.

"*Que bella,*" she said, as her eyes welled and a tear broke free.

Emeli's eyes welled up, too, for the first time in months. The two women embraced, two generations far apart yet held together by history and by a man who made some bad choices but also, one truly good. Altagracia and Emeli held each other with equal intensity.

Luz wiped away a tear. *My mother. My sister. My life.*

The sniffles and silence were broken by a friendly, "Group hug!" Roger wailed as they all made their way to the women, piling into a scrum.

"Yes! Group hug!" Chris and the kids joined in, all making squishing noises of joy. Luz watched it for a beat, taking it all in. Then, she, too, joined, her arms spread as wide as they could go, encompassing her beautiful, expanded, family.

Emeli and *Abuela* laughed at the wiggling kids, angling to get a piece of them. Luz cried, happily.

For years Luz had wondered about herself. Who she really was. Where she fit in. Who she wanted to be.

Right here, she thought now.

This is it.

This is me. This is we.

Chapter 28

The host pulled a bang behind her ear. "So, this book really came out of a hard time for you. Tell us about that."

Gabi was on the set of the number-one network morning show on television, kicking off a round of interviews to promote her new book, *Super (Single) Mom.* She looked different from how she had a year ago. She sat up straight, still in her boho-chic gear, but looking much less frazzled than before. She radiated positivity and was markedly more magnetic than she'd ever been before.

She smiled at the host, who seemed genuinely intrigued.

"Well, Natalia, yes. My whole practice, my whole career, has been about healing in relationships and bringing joy and fulfillment to our lives as spouses, couples, parents." Gabi paused before continuing on commandingly. "But as I was taking care of so many others, I discovered that I had disappointed a tremendously important person: me."

"And that's a big deal, right, to help others so much only to realize that you're not doing the same for yourself?"

Gabi had known Natalia for years and had been a guest on her show, giving advice, dozens of times. To sit in the same spot and admit that she had fucked up was a big deal. Well, her husband—ex-husband—fucked up, too, hurting her in some of the worst ways you can hurt someone. But Gabi had done something truly wrong. She had ignored the wise voices in her head and she had tried too hard to fix things, to the point of not letting Bert breathe. Or herself, for that matter.

She had known when he started working out again after years of lying on the couch. She had known when he said he was taking a walk and returned hours later, smelling of booze. She knew when he stopped wanting to go to bed with her. Yet, she kept hammering at it, at their household, trying to fix things by simultaneously appeasing him as much as possible (home-cooked meals and doting) and haranguing as much as possible. But she couldn't face the truth, couldn't confront him. Instead she chose to maintain the façade, maintain the semblance of family no matter how false. No one is blameless even in a betrayal so dire. She now knew that.

And Gabi didn't even realize how bad and wrong and hard it all had been on her (*sublimate!*) until she, now on her own with her son, started her first session with a personal trainer, a gorgeous, Irish twenty-something with livid blue eyes, and a mess of black curls. All he had to do was touch her legs to guide them in a stretch after their first workout. It set off electricity of such force that she was sure she was shaking. It was the first time she'd been touched by a man in nearly two years. After she got home from training, Gabi collapsed onto the floor of her shower, crying. She cried painfully. Now she was fully, physically awake. The realization of how she'd put herself, in effect, to sleep, her body and her needs, threw her into a new kind of mourning that day.

But Gabi's mourning quickly turned into awakening. And she began doing one of the things she'd always told others to do: She took her own advice. She worked on getting herself physically into shape. (And yes, continuing to see her trainer, though never crossing that boundary. She'd get there, physically, with several others soon enough.) And even more importantly, Gabi understood that the unhappiness at home and the now-clear depression in her ex had made her son anxious and fearful.

So Gabi dropped all her corporate consulting work for months, instead seeing just a few clients at a time and writing her new book, to focus as much energy as possible on the true, lasting love of her life, her child. Gabi lived in daily fear of her drop in income and the possibility that she'd end up worse off after the legal battle of divorce, but she stuck to her guns with her time and making Max her priority. And now, here she was again. Back in the saddle, so to speak. Back on the high chair, on people's television screens. Another book. And this one was her most personal yet. She'd soon find that her authenticity was contagious and it was to be her most successful book yet.

"I was like a doctor who smokes!" Gabi blurted out to Natalia.

The host sat back in surprise.

"It can be hard to direct that same helpfulness inward, toward ourselves. But it's such a powerful thing to be able to help yourself, to look at yourself, and ask, 'What do you deserve? Where is your joy and truth?' and then make the changes that get you there, to your answer."

"Those changes included a divorce in your life, right?" Natalia flinched a bit at this question—not an easy one to ask publicly of a regular guest.

"Yes." Gabi set up a boundary. She was classy like that. She'd acknowledge her divorce and her situation—after all, it was in the book title—but, she would not speak badly about her son's father or drag either of them into the spotlight.

"And now you're a single mom and that's who you wrote this book for, all the single moms out there."

Gabi smiled at the jolly swing of morning anchors. "There are few things like being a single parent—a mom or dad—and I frankly wouldn't wish it on anyone. But! Life happens, and there are times when it's actually much better to go it alone."

"But we do hear a lot about kids in broken homes and the spate of single mothers and how awful it is, bad for the kids—

and some folks may say that you're celebrating what they think is a negative situation."

"Here's what I know. I know that a happy parent is a better parent. And a happy home is a better home for a child. And if you find yourself, like me, doing it alone, the time to beat yourself up over it is over!"

"But what do you say to these folks—I mean, it's a big deal now, so many children in single-parent homes, and mostly women, right?"

Ooh, Natalia was pressing.

"Yes, it is mostly moms, like me." Gabi paused. "As I said, a happy and fulfilled mother is the best mother of all. Sometimes that means making changes and all the time it means listening to yourself, knowing yourself, and putting yourself up as just as important as your kids' needs or your partner's needs. As I've said for years, put the oxygen mask on you first, then on those who depend on you. 'Cause, hon, if you ain't breathin', you can't be there for anyone else."

Chapter 29

"Maaaaaa! He won't stop touching the flowers in my hair!"

"No flowers! Go to your *tía* right now and fix your bow tie, *m'ijo!*" Magda was always good at being firm with her kids, but today she may have raised her voice, but it was done with a smile. Her kids were racing through her bedroom and in and out of the walk-in closet, Nico suited up in gray and Ilsa in a cream dress with a scalloped hem, her head covered in curls of cocoa and those beautiful mini-orchids her big brother was currently after.

Magda looked at herself in the wall-sized bathroom mirror. She looked better than she had in years. She looked beautiful, handsome. Fitted suit, starched white shirt with black pearl cuff links given to her by her father just days ago. Cuff links, she thought. He gave me cuff links. The symbolism struck her. She rubbed one between her fingers.

Reconnecting with her father had been more powerful than she'd imagined possible—mostly because she hadn't imagined it possible at all. He'd even persuaded her siblings and their families to come around. A mother's death could definitely alter a family's dynamics. For Magda's family, it had been seismic but ultimately positive.

"Mags? Let's do it in ten!" a female voice yelled from her bedroom door.

"Okay! Ten."

Magda looked into the mirror, leaning on the countertop. *Ma, I wish you were here. I wish. I love you. I hope you're with me. Thank you. Thank you for loving me in spite of . . . or, because of who I am . . .*

When she realized she was tearing up, she dropped her head back—the stop-crying-trick she had learned from Gabi—and sniffed them back in. She smirked and swiped a hand through her blond cut, giving herself an Elvis smile. She still had it. Better than ever, baby.

"Hey, caught you." Gabi rounded the edge of the door.

"Hey, girl." Magda smiled.

"You ready?"

"Yeah. Yeah, I am."

"You look fantastic."

"So do you." Magda admired Gabi's curls atop her head, the beautiful roses positioned in an ode to Frida Kahlo, her lips a tropical red. "Thanks for being here."

"I wouldn't miss it for the world."

They both paused to savor the moment.

"Listen, your cousin is insisting that I bring you some of the tequila he brought over but . . ." Gabi demurred.

"That's okay, I'm good with seltzer. Actually, can you bring me some? With lime?"

"Tell ya what, I'll prep it for you now if you meet me at the door so we can get this train moving on American time, okay? Not Latin time. Too many of your corporate buddies showed up." Gabi winked.

"See you in two." Magda was about to get married, legally, for the first time. She had been with the mother of her children for a decade, but the marriage laws at the time hadn't allowed them to tie the knot officially. Now she had the same right to mess up as everyone else. At least that's the way Gabi joked about it. Magda was surprised at how happy she was—surprised and nervous. It wasn't a very familiar feeling for her. And she was lucid. She had stopped drinking almost completely the day of her mother's funeral, and stuck to her weekly, sometimes twice-weekly, therapy. She wanted to be fully present and awake and alive for this new phase of her life. She owed her mother that. And most of all, her kids.

"Oy, where is our girl?" Luz whispered to Cat from their seats.

It wasn't a big wedding. Magda's apartment could fit nearly one hundred guests, but there were closer to fifty or sixty in attendance, one-third of them business clients, the rest, all family and only her closest friends. Magda would have preferred that it be even smaller, but her immediate family alone added up to twenty heads and now that they were all talking, everyone who got an invitation made sure to show up.

Cat responded to Luz, "Gabi went back to try and pry her out. Are we on Latin time or not?"

"Girl, we'd better not be," Luz sassed. "The Anglos are gonna be pissed."

"Pssst, sup, lovelies!"

"Get your fine ass down, husband." Luz ushered Chris in, past their legs. Tomas, Luz's brother, sat down between his sister and Cat. He cheek-smooched his sister, then gave a full-lipped kiss to Cat, the soon-to-be mother of his child.

Ooo, girl, we're next! Cat mouthed to Luz, pointing at herself and Luz's young, handsome brother, her other hand already in his, a beautiful, simple engagement ring glistened on her finger. Tom glowed with pride.

Luz rolled her eyes at the two of them. "Lawd." She turned to Chris. "What are the chances that those two would have ended up at the same bar, the same night, and not know who the heck they each were?!"

Chris shrugged. "Mama, sometimes that's the way the universe crumbles. It's fate, you sexy thang, fate . . . Hmmmm, you look so good right now!"

Luz harrumphed at the honest admiration that was her husband's attempt at changing the subject. "But what happens if they break up? What if he dumps her or cheats on her—I mean, he's so much younger!" She was starting to rile herself up a bit at the sight of her little brother now engaged to and a father-to-be of a child of one of her best friends, at the wedding of another dear friend, no less.

"Luzita, we're in a good place and they're in a good place. Don't worry." He patted his wife's hand. "Plus, we've already managed to fold in your new sister—what's another one?" He winked. Luz smiled. Her temporarily quelled worries were interrupted.

"Luz, *nena*'s gotta go to the bathroom." Emeli looked like she'd stepped out of the pages of *Teen Vogue* as she leaned forward in her seat to whisper to her big sister seated in front of her. One of the twins was squirming.

"Hon, can you guys just wait—oh! Here they come!"

Music started and first down the aisle came Magda's son and daughter, Nico and Ilsa, soliciting irrepressible *ooh's* and *aah's* from the attendees. Walking casually down the aisle behind them was Cherokee, the start-up gal Magda had met in the lobby of her therapist's building, resplendent in a simple white gown that showcased her gorgeous deep brown skin and a slight belly bump. Her dreads were pulled off her face and set with antique comb and pins. Her locks fell down her back in a cascade. In honor of her new spouse's heritage, she wore a mantilla. It was all antique lace, draped in such a way that reminded Gabi of the Spanish ladies illustrated in her daughter's favorite book, *Ferdinand*. Oh, that glow of love was real, Gabi couldn't help thinking.

Following soon after down the aisle was Magda, as fine as a tanned, blond knight, her gray suit nearly silver in the metallic light of the apartment. Her friends and family beamed and she clasped hands with Gabi, Luz, and Cat as she passed them.

Magda's father sat front and center, the groom's side. She took his hand as she passed.

"Hi, *Papi*." She squeezed.

Hola, m'ija. Te amo, he mouthed as he held her hand, placing his free one on top in an embrace. *Te amo.* This was only the second time she'd ever seen him cry, the first being when they talked at her mother's funeral reception.

She held his hands in return. "Thanks, *Papi*. I love you, too." She leaned down for an embrace.

Everyone present watched. They were all moved by this public reunion and show of support from a father who once wrote his daughter off because of how she chose to live her life. This daughter who had sought solace for years in the compulsive pursuit of women and booze and money. But now what everyone bore witness to was the supreme power of love. Family love and the love of friends.

It was all so real.

NEVER TOO REAL

Carmen Rita

About This Guide

The suggested questions are included
to enhance your group's reading of
Carmen Rita's *Never Too Real*.

Discussion Questions

1. The first chapter reveals a lot of how Cat feels about being stereotyped. Do you think she handled each encounter (with her guest on the show and her boss) in the best way possible? How would you have managed these situations?

2. Was it a surprise to find out that Magda and Gabi had been lovers, and if so, why? What do you think of Gabi's role in Magda's life and their enduring friendship?

3. What do you make of the reactions of Magda's parents to her coming out of the closet, communicating it by drastically changing her appearance? What about the housekeeper's reaction? What do their differences say about Magda's family life and everyone's roles?

4. What do you think about Cat's "lucky penny" confrontation with her mother? Do you agree with Cat's assessment of why her mother was so adamant about her stance? If not, why? And what does that, and their lunch, reveal about their relationship?

5. As Luz is older than her brother, Tomas, were you surprised at the roles they each took once the family secret was revealed? What do you think it is about Tomas that made him more likely to take on his role? What about Luz?

6. The vitriol between Magda and her father explodes at the hospital—did their dynamic, and her father's insults, surprise you in any way? If so, how? What about Magda's sisters?

7. We hear from Luz's mother about her reasons for keeping secret the identity of Luz's father. What do you think about her reasoning? What role did history have in her hiding the truth?

8. Though Bert betrays Gabi, she plays her own role in the end of her marriage—what do you think that role is and was there anything she could have done differently? Or, is the blame all Bert's?

9. Magda's mother's funeral reveals deep family dynamics. Which character's reaction at the burial and funeral reception surprised you? Do you have family members of whom these scenes remind you?

10. Are there potential conflicts that may arise from Luz's sister moving in with her and her family? How do you see those conflicts playing out in the future?

11. In her final speech, do you agree with Cat's assessment of her life choices so far? Have you ever felt that way? If so, what did you do about it?

12. How do you feel about the friendships among these women? What do you think brings them together for so many years and through so much? Which character would most likely be your friend?